Endangered

Books by Ann Littlewood

Night Kill
Did Not Survive
Endangered

Endangered

A Zoo Mystery

Ann Littlewood

Poisoned Pen Press

Poisoned Pen Press
6962 E. First Ave., Ste. 103
Scottsdale, AZ 85251
www.poisonedpenpress.com
info@poisonedpenpress.com

Printed in the United States of America

To Lee, my wingman. Always.

Acknowledgements

A tale that encompasses drug and wildlife crimes necessarily touches on a great many law enforcement agencies as well as other public entities. My heartfelt thanks to these individuals who did their best to set me straight on how all this works.

- A US Fish and Wildlife Inspector who prefers to remain anonymous
- Lt. Randy Drake of Washington State Patrol
- Deputy Paul Prather, Clark County Sheriff's Office
- Officer Aaron Schmautz, Portland Police Bureau
- Chris Shea, Clark Regional Emergency Services Agency
- Clark County Animal Control Manager Paul Scarpelli
- Mike Keele, Director of Elephant Habitats, Jan Mothershed, Animal Registrar, and Tracy Mott, Veterinary Technician/ Hospital Keeper, all of the Oregon Zoo, for information and insights about caring for confiscated animals.
- Cindy Bishop for information on how animal shelter staff manage meth-contaminated reptiles
- Lisa Feder, Director of Shelter Operations, and Erin Griffin, Public Relations/Marketing Manager, of the Humane Society for Southwest Washington

I hereby officially apologize for any and all errors I've managed to make anyway.

I am also indebted to a number of other animal experts, among them:

- Amanda Kamradt, zoo keeper and Conservation Committee Chair of the American Association of Zoo Keepers, Inc., generously reviewed a draft and corrected errors.

- Jennie Erin Smith, author of *Stolen World*, not only wrote a fine book, but also Skyped with me from Europe to answer my questions.

- Christy Hensrude at Zazu's House macaw shelter showed me her facility and the abandoned pet birds she cares for.

- Bill McDowell of Woodland Park Zoo, Seattle, Washington, told me which tortoises are most valuable and reminded me that sometimes private enthusiasts are more skilled than zoo staff with specific species.

- Eric Kowalczyk also of Woodland Park Zoo, advised me on mixed-species bird exhibits.

- Jerry Novak, Pacific Northwest Turtleworks, provided information about turtles and tortoises

I would also like to thank the staff person at Southwest Medical Center who gave me a pleasant and useful tour when I showed up unannounced, but who preferred not to be named.

My writing group offers endless support and excellent critiques, so a big "thank you!" to authors Christine Finlayson, Evan Lewis, Marilyn McFarlane, Angela Sanders, and Doug Levin, as well as Holly Franko and Cindy Brown, who read early versions for me.

Cynthia Cheney has offered her canny and experienced perspective on every one of the Iris Oakley mysteries.

Both of my sisters provided excellent assistance in proofreading, which is greatly appreciated.

And last, but hardly least, I thank Drew Fillipo for choosing a fine name for the baby mandrill.

Chapter One

"Lost satellite reception." DellaStreet spoke in crisp, unapologetic tones. I made the only possible response, a muttered but intense, "You useless piece of—"

DellaStreet, named after Perry Mason's secretary, had gotten us into this wilderness before abandoning her GPS duties. The paper map of Washington State was equally useless. We were deep into secretive back roads, dipping in and out of forested canyons—Sasquatch territory with no long-range visibility, no road signs, and no other traffic. I pictured hikers discovering our skeletons in the zebra-striped zoo van years from now, picked clean by insects and rodents, me still at the wheel and Denny Stellar seat-belted next to me. The Vancouver *Columbian* headlines: "Remains of animal keepers found at last!" My parents would be raising my son. And DellaStreet would still be stuck to the windshield with a question mark on her worthless little screen.

The van smelled of mud, animals, and frustration. The Finley Memorial Zoo education staff always cleaned it after they brought animals back from a school class or park demonstration, but a vague essence of red-tailed hawk, king snake, and opossum lingered. Windshield wipers beat against a fitful rain, the heater throbbed, and something loose in the back rolled and clanked annoyingly.

We were on a rescue mission and, so far, we couldn't find our ass with both hands.

This trip was supposed to be a break from my routine of cleaning and feeding the bird collection, or, in Denny's case, the reptiles. "I haven't had this much fun," I said, "since I last got poison oak."

"You were just trying to suck up to Neal," Denny said. "Unpure energy, negative results—guaranteed."

"Unpure? That's not a real word." Denny invented the word, but not my motives. The plan was to showcase my flexibility and cooperative attitude, thereby earning points with our boss.

Not that he had offered me a choice. This morning, I'd found a note from Neal Humboldt, the zoo's curator, on my timecard asking me to come to his office first thing. He'd spun his chair to face me when I stood before his desk, his compact body dense with energy, intense blue eyes already looking past me to the next item on his list. "Oakley, need you to go pick up some exotic pets from a farm somewhere north of Battle Ground. The owners got themselves busted for drugs and hauled off to the slammer. Animal Control wants us to park the animals. We'll keep them in quarantine until the trial. Won't hurt us to do the agencies a favor. Take Denny and the Education van." He twisted back to his computer.

"Um, where? Exactly…"

His hands froze over the keyboard. "Oh, right. Here's the address." He shoved a piece of paper toward me.

"What kind of animals? We'll need carriers."

"They said parrots and reptiles. That's all I got." Back to the keyboard.

"Just a day trip?" I asked and kicked myself. The subtext was, "because I have a kid and can't go kiting off on unplanned overnight trips." Not good to remind him of my limitations. Iris Oakley, able to leap tall exhibits in a single bound.

"Yeah, yeah. Get back by four. Shouldn't be any overtime."

So I'd found Denny and the van and plugged the address into the GPS and here we were, with the morning ticking away. I stretched my shoulders and neck, aching from the tension of peering through a rain-pelted windshield looking for a mailbox or driveway. Also from the tension of not talking to Denny about breaking my best friend's heart. I couldn't face that conversation when we were cooped up together with no escape.

"We've been sucked into a parallel universe with a road shaped like a torus," Denny said. "It's a continuous loop until the end of time."

I was tempted to agree, but I caught movement in the rearview mirror and flinched as a patrol car closed in swiftly on our bumper. It swept past us on a blind curve.

We were saved.

◇◇◇

I pulled through a wide-open metal gate and parked between the patrol car and a Clark County Animal Control truck, hoping that our van could extricate itself from the mud when necessary. Other trucks and cars advertised the Clark County Sheriff's Office, Washington State Patrol, and the electric company. One had a little satellite dish on top and TV station call letters on the side.

We climbed out of the van into chilly air and stretched. Two big dogs barked and paced behind us with more anxiety than aggression, a black dog with some Boxer in him and a Chow mix. Directly to our right was a muddy vegetable garden punctuated with stumps and fenced with hog wire. Tall trees, mostly young Douglas firs, surrounded the house and barns and crowded in along the driveway. How did the garden get enough sun to survive? Lichen-frosted trees stood evenly spaced down the fence line, a few apples clinging to their crooked branches. All the open spaces were churned-up mud, mud everywhere. Currier and Ives it wasn't.

"A stump farm," Denny said, his dark blond hair bare to the weather. "Log the trees and starve trying to farm it, then give up and let the trees come back. Must be animal hoarders hiding out here so they can have all the dogs they want. Might have rabbits in that barn. Maybe a donkey somewhere around or pygmy goats. Not real farm animals. Pets."

I'd known Denny a long time and had no trouble tuning out his stream-of-consciousness guesswork. He took off toward a barn fifty yards in front of us with long strides, tall and hunched forward. "Wait up," I called. "We need to talk to the cops first."

Denny stopped and jittered in place, then swung toward the single-story gray house to our left. Three homemade plywood dog houses near the front of the house had no door flaps, no bedding. All they provided was a partial windbreak. Next to the front porch, the traditional frayed blue tarp sheltered a heap of firewood, chunks spilling out at the edges.

A Clark County deputy sheriff on the porch looked perturbed by our arrival. His uniform was way sharper than our dark brown shirts and pants. He wore a khaki shirt, olive-green pants, and thick-soled black shoes that had picked up a lot of mud. He got to wear a star on his chest and an ear bud with a coiled tube down to a pocket, plus a belt with a gun. I felt underdressed.

"I'm Iris Oakley from Finley Zoo," I said. "This is Denny Stellar. We're here to remove the exotic animals. The zoo agreed to hold them."

The crew-cut deputy relaxed, nodded, and led us through the rain toward the closer of the two barns. I scanned the place as I dodged mud puddles in his wake. Both barns were roofed in rusted metal and sheathed in weathered wood siding. Feral blackberry canes arched along their sides. A green Vanagon camper with moss-edged windows sat composting alongside the closer barn. A man in a black wool jacket and knit cap pointed a camera at us.

We stepped out of cold, wind-driven rain through a sliding wood door into the barn. I paused, startled by heat and busyness. Nothing in the weathered exterior hinted of this warm, bright space. The moist air smelled of marijuana sap. People stood on ladders removing grow lights; they snipped off bushy plants and hauled them out of the barn; they photographed everything. Thick batts of insulation bulged along the walls and ceiling, their shiny aluminum surfaces reflecting the peculiar orange glow from the fixtures still hanging. A boxy heater roared. Thin black water tubes dangled everywhere, their ends in white dirt-filled buckets.

Bird keeping could be surprisingly educational.

"The Tiptons kept most of their birds back here," our guide said.

"Tiptons?" I said.

"The people who lived here and presumably set all this up."

Denny, often oblivious to expectations, veered off. The deputy led me to the rear of the barn and opened a door. I heard wings beating, shrill cries, and soft thuds. He flicked on a switch. I stepped into the narrow, harshly lit room and stopped short.

At least two dozen parrots fluttered and cried out from a chicken-wire cage stretching to our right. The birds flew to the far end where they clung to the wire or other birds' backs, wings beating frantically. Three of them weren't frantic—they were dead on the floor. An aisle ran along the interior wall. The deputy walked unheeding down this toward the massed birds.

"Hey!" I said. "Don't go down there. They're already scared to death."

He stopped, looking surprised and then offended.

I moderated my voice. "We'll take it from here."

"Fine by me. Get them out of here so we can shut off the electricity. And try to stay out of our way." He took his hurt feelings and left.

I backed out of the little room and closed the door so the birds would calm down. Staring unseeing at the crime scene technicians bustling around, I tried to reorganize my thinking. What on earth was this mass of ill-kept birds all about?

Denny swung back from a far corner of the barn. "Are the reptiles back there? I don't see any."

I shook my head. "Parrots. Lots of them. We don't have enough carriers. They look terrible."

Denny bounced on the balls of his feet. "I need to check the other barn."

"Go take a look. I'll be there in a minute."

I slipped into the back room again as unobtrusively as I could and took a second look. The birds didn't thrash around as wildly this time. Most stayed where they were, hanging from the wire sides or clinging to the few perches. Their bodies and wings were green, with yellow, red, and blue markings on faces and shoulders. Amazon parrots. A couple different species—lilac-crowned, red-crowned, and one or two others. I'd have to look them up.

Two of them flew toward me and veered back, clumsy in the tight space. They settled on a dowel in mid-cage, hyper alert. Both had broken wing and tail feathers, probably from bashing into the walls.

Focus on the basics: fill the empty food and water bowls. I found a plastic bucket and carried it out into the grow operation, looking for a water tap.

Denny came charging back and nearly slammed into me. "Ire, they won't let me into the other barn. They say it's got turtles, but the meth lab is in that barn and they won't let me in. Come talk to them. Please." He wheeled and headed out the way he'd come.

Meth lab? "In a minute." I found the tap and carried the bucket back, moving slowly and avoiding eye contact with the birds. They stirred, but didn't flush. I spotted a bag of parrot food behind the door, a brand I didn't recognize. The guano thick on the floor said the birds were eating it when they had the chance.

After filling the water bowls and setting out the crummy food, I gathered dead birds off the floor and put them into the bucket. Bright wings spilled over the edge. This cage was filthy, too small, and badly designed. No natural light, no decent food, not even good perches. No wonder birds were dying.

Who were these people who didn't give a rip, who couldn't be bothered to find out what parrots needed to stay alive? A small, hot fire of anger ignited. I left so the birds could relax enough to drink and eat and stepped outside the barn, back into the weather. I turned away from the house, rain peppering my face and hair. Outside the smaller barn, Denny paced in front of a woman deputy leaning against the exterior with her arms crossed. He was saying, "No, no, not tomorrow. The parrots are in bad shape and this might be worse. They could be *dying* in there."

"Like I told you, this is a *meth lab*," the deputy said. "A serious hazard to your health, which is why I'm standing here in the rain to keep people out. You'll have to wait until it's cleaned up." She was about my age and seemed too slight for law enforcement. Then again, she carried a gun.

I elbowed Denny to shut up. "Fish and Wildlife asked us to get these animals into safe situations. We wouldn't want any trouble between Clark County Sheriff's office and another agency."

The deputy looked me over and apparently decided a zoo uniform and the name label over my pocket were all the information she needed. She shook her head slowly and firmly. "Just so you know, you make meth wrong and you get nerve gas. Think about it."

I did think about it. The people we'd seen entering the barn weren't wearing respirators. No nerve gas. "People in there now are wearing protective gear. You could ask whether they have extras on-site. Then we could make a quick assessment of the situation." I thought that last bit was a nice turn of phrase, and apparently it did the trick.

She sighed, straightened up, and walked inside. She returned in a few minutes and resumed her post. The barn door opened, revealing a white jumpsuit and hood. The figure pulled off a paper dust mask and became a woman. I made my pitch and learned that she was with the health department. Negotiations led to a determination in our favor, at least for a brief inspection. The price was jumpsuits, face masks, vinyl gloves, and disposable booties. "No one told me we'd have two more people to outfit," the health department woman said. "We're going to run out."

She sent the deputy off to the parking lot rather than ruin her booties in the mud. We waited in the drizzle until the deputy returned with an armload of packages and an even less hospitable attitude. I hoped the gear was top quality and we wouldn't be poisoned for some theoretical reptiles. We suited up and walked in like astronauts exploring a new planet.

Inside seemed at first to be a typical farm barn. It was cold and smelled like motor oil. The inadequate light from a dirty window and a single bulb hanging from the ceiling revealed a room crowded with an aging tractor, shovels hung on pairs of nails, coils of hoses. That was the front room, maybe a third of the barn. We walked through an interior door into the main room. A few fluorescent fixtures, nothing like the banks of them in the first barn, threw a cold blue light. Another box heater kept it warm. Sharp chemical smells penetrated my face mask. I quelled the urge to hold my breath.

"Make it quick. Still dust and vapors in here," said a muffled male voice from another astronaut outfit.

On the left was a kitchen—sink and stove, pale laminate counter top. Plastic litter overflowed a shiny galvanized garbage can. The counters looked like a classy high school chemistry lab. Tubing, an assortment of glass flasks and plastic bottles. Bunson burners, a digital scale that would be ideal for weighing baby birds, a box of Red Devil lye. A new fridge, nicer than mine. The perimeter was barricaded with red tape strung around the barn's support posts. White figures worked inside the tape, photographing and fingerprinting and stuffing items into bags.

I stopped gawking and pivoted to follow Denny. On the other side of the barn, a few heat lamps hung over a low plywood corral. Twenty or so tortoises of several shapes and sizes moved sluggishly over dusty straw bedding. Again, far more animals than anticipated and in equally primitive housing.

Denny stood with his hands resting on the plywood barrier. I could see only his eyes, but he looked to be wearing the blank expression he put on when he encountered something marvelous and desirable. "A grab-bag of expensive torts. No sulcatas. Radiated. Pancake? Damn—is that a spider?" he muttered into his face mask. "What the hell is that one?"

I gathered he was pawing through his mental catalog of tortoise species.

He leaned over the wall and picked up one the size of a baseball. The tortoise waved its stumpy legs in the air, then cried out shrilly and peed a surprising little flood. I jumped.

Denny put it back. "They urinate in self-defense, and they look dehydrated already." He walked around inspecting the corral. "Water bowls are dry because they're set under those cheap heat lamps, and the little ones couldn't reach into them anyway. I'm seeing scraps of iceberg lettuce and that's all, so crappy nutrition." He waved an arm, encompassing the corral. "This is an amazing collection in lousy conditions. It makes no sense."

The implications clicked. "These aren't pets," I said. "This is a wildlife smuggling operation."

Chapter Two

The drugs that led to this bust weren't our business. The animals were. I fumed while Denny studied the tortoises. The parrots were terrified because they had no experience with people, at least not until they were trapped in a Mexican forest, jammed into containers of some sort, and smuggled into the US. A similar fate must have befallen the tortoises. This wasn't a food market in China or a pet market in Bangkok or any of the other places that regularly hit the news with confiscated wildlife. These were smuggled animals in our very own Washington State. They were to be sold over the Internet and shipped to people who didn't know or didn't care that they were getting frightened, sick animals with poor prospects for survival.

Staying in this barn wasn't going to help the survival of anything. I could feel vile molecules soaking into my lungs and swimming up to my brain. "Let's load these tortoises and get out of here before we're all tweakers."

"You can't just throw turtles in your van," said the health department woman. "They're contaminated with meth."

"We'll rinse them," I said.

The man in the haz-mat suit nodded. "That should work. Clean the turtles and seal them off from the air circulating in your van so you won't breathe in any dust."

Denny and I looked at each other. No way were we going to put animals in air-tight boxes.

I swiveled to look at the kitchen area. "We'll use that sink."

The woman shook her head. "Not today. The Narcotics team isn't done with this area yet. Red tape means hot area."

Denny's arms flew wide. "They need to be out of here. They get poisoned like anything else that breathes."

The haz-mat man said, "Nobody coordinated with us. The site should be cleared tomorrow. Time's up."

We were ushered back outside, Denny sputtering. I stripped off the face mask and, for once, appreciated the cold damp air. I led him away from the woman guarding the barn. Our protective gear cut the wind and blocked the rain. "Denny, stop ranting. We're not rolling over without a fight. I'm going to find out who rules this scene. Try not to piss anybody off."

Leading the way from barn to barn to house porch, I talked with several uniformed officers of the peace as well as Health Department staff and a woman from the Department of Ecology. We ended up on the porch away from the steady drip from leaking gutters, me and Denny, a Washington State patrol officer, a deputy from the narcotics team, and the Department of Ecology woman. I did my best to sound professional. It didn't help that my jumpsuit had a lot in common with the fleece sleeper I zipped my two-year-old, Robby, into every night. Our position was simple: We needed to move the tortoises today because they were exposed to toxins.

The replies were variations on "come back tomorrow, or maybe the next day."

Denny, mouth tight and grey eyes stormy, rocked on his heels and crossed and uncrossed his arms. For the most part, he kept quiet.

A sheriff's department car pulled up in the parking area, setting off the same big dogs that had barked when we arrived. A white pit bull crawled out from underneath the VW camper and joined the chorus. A man with a catch pole in his hand and "Animal Control" on his jacket emerged from a white truck and approached her. The hubbub interrupted the deputy who was employing a great many words to say "no" to me.

Our group on the porch was further distracted by two deputy sheriffs escorting the photographer in the black jacket off the property. He limped a little, but managed to retain his dignity despite the hand of the law on each elbow. A man leaned against the TV station van and watched with a video camera on his shoulder.

"The Tiptons are going to be famous," I said.

Denny erupted. "Do you want the media to hear you let these animals die?" he demanded of no one in particular. "You got the dog catcher here to look after a bunch of mutts, but you're going to let endangered reptiles die because you can't bother to fingerprint a kitchen counter?" The trooper scowled and Denny stopped, but the point was made.

We were abandoned on the porch as the officials regrouped in the kitchen.

The trooper emerged and said, "Go ahead and move the birds first, and we'll see if we can clear the kitchen in the meth barn." Denny left it to me to announce we couldn't do the parrots today. We didn't have enough carriers and the birds needed to settle down and eat. This was not a welcome message since it meant the electricity couldn't be turned off in the marijuana barn. It was raining too hard for the barn to burn down, but my heart sank when I realized we had to come back a second day.

More official consultation. Next offer: take the tortoises out of the meth barn as fast as possible. We could have half an hour.

I took a deep breath. "You said we need to rinse them to remove toxic dust, and you're right. We can't rinse them outside in icy cold water. You won't want us to bring them into the house and contaminate it. Is there a water heater in the marijuana barn?"

A reluctant head-shake.

"Then we have to rinse them at the kitchen in the meth barn."

We were ordered, rather than invited, to strip off the protective gear on the porch and drop anchor in the house, Command Central, and wait. The implication was that the technicians would hustle through their work at the meth lab, but no one promised anything.

We'd barely settled ourselves on rickety wooden chairs around the kitchen table when a shattering scream erupted. Three men in various uniforms sitting in the dining room smirked when we jumped. The blast came again, raucous and piercing.

Another animal health disaster? I followed my ears. In a back corner of the living room stood a seven-foot-high wire cage, about four feet by three feet, holding two huge macaws. The corner was dim, but their blue wings and gold bellies were vivid. These birds didn't act frightened. They seemed aroused and irritated. Side by side, they shifted their feet on the single perch running across the middle of the cage and let out the occasional unnerving shriek. The upright cage was large for a living room, but not big enough for them to fully spread their wings, much less fly. Their food bowl still held a little seed mix and scraps of orange peel. Another bowl had an inch of water. The cage held no toys, mirrors, or other entertainment options. The concept of environmental enrichment hadn't made it to the Tipton farm.

One bird was bare-bellied, half naked from neurotic feather plucking. These looked like the pet birds I was expecting. When I reached in to top up the birds' water and seed bowls, the less-plucked one side-stepped toward me and implied that he or she would bite me good with an enormous curving beak if I didn't get my hand out of there pronto.

I chatted with them, explaining that I was on their team in all this chaos. I promised a much better life in a much bigger space. The one closest to me seemed to listen with declining hostility. The other shrieked and clambered around the cage, maneuvering with beak and feet. I'd worked with smaller parrots, but these big macaws were new to me.

It was almost noon. We fetched our lunches from the van and returned to waiting in the kitchen. I hand-fed my carrot sticks to the macaws, who each grasped one with a foot and nibbled on it, biting off chunks and letting most of it fall to the floor, wasteful feeders like other parrots. The friendlier one rewarded me by allowing a fingertip to scratch his emerald forehead through the bars.

Each bird wore a closed band on one leg, near-proof they were hatched in captivity since that kind of band must be put on when the bird is only a few weeks old. Each also bore a blue band, probably from their breeder. The blue ones were "open" bands, C-shaped strips of aluminum that were closed around the leg with special pliers at any age. The blue bands were dented and scratched where the birds had chewed on them.

I washed up and sat down to eat. My sandwich was soon gone, and no one came to tell us to move the tortoises. The sense of victory over officialdom oozed out, replaced by a suspicion that we'd been conned into docility. I half-expected a health officer to come back and say, "So sorry, didn't work out, come back tomorrow." Denny fidgeted and brought up treatments for reptile lung problems, biker gangs as meth customers, and the stupidity of shipping raw logs overseas instead of milling them in the US. I opted to ignore all of this.

He got up and paced. "Every minute they breathe that crap is a minute closer to pneumonia." He finally took himself outside. Through the kitchen window, I could see him juggling four apples. He was pretty good at it.

I couldn't think of a single thing to do that would pass the time. It didn't help that the house was threadbare and sad. The vinyl kitchen floor was faded, the pattern worn off in front of the sink and stove. Linoleum counter tops in an old-fashioned pattern of speckles were also worn colorless. The walls and hand-made plywood cabinets wore the same dull beige paint. But it wasn't dirty, not even the chipped enamel sink. The kitchen spoke of poverty, hard work, and limited lives.

The cops in the dining room griped with each other about budget limitations on the gear they wanted and issues with leave time and holiday pay. It sounded remarkably similar to zoo keeper griping.

All these agencies were focused on the drug bust. I had to wonder how much they cared about trafficking protected species.

Would they go the extra mile to bust the criminals who whole-saled these animals to the Tiptons?

Nobody paid any attention when I walked through the dining room and living room and found the bathroom. After I flushed, I took a peek into the vanity drawers. Knowing more about the Tiptons couldn't hurt. The drawers revealed a big assortment of over-the-counter stomach remedies on the left side, kelp pills and primrose oil on the right side. Herbal remedies such as "women's rejuvenation" and "whole-body tonic" in the medicine cabinet. Some of the Tiptons hadn't been feeling well. An opened box of tampons below the sink. No makeup. A can of Bag Balm. Cheap toilet paper. The mirror showed mud on my chin, cause unknown.

The hallway to the three bedrooms was lined with posters and framed prints of the US flag, the Declaration of Independence, and political slogans, among them "The tree of liberty must be refreshed from time to time with the blood of tyrants." Another: "Extremism in defense of liberty is no vice." The doors were open and I peeked into each bedroom. No animals. One room held two twin beds, the other a double bed. Both were messy—clothes on the floor, beds unmade. The third room was tidy, with one twin bed and an old dresser. A picture of Paul Revere on a galloping horse was taped to the wall.

The living room was faded, but also surprisingly clean, given all the mud outside. No file cabinet. Disconnected gray cords dangled from a small desk in a corner—the Tiptons had a computer, nowhere to be seen. I yearned to get my hands on it and explore their email for information on animal suppliers and collectors. No family pictures in the living room or dining room or on the fridge.

The three men in the dining room were drinking coffee and sharing a bag of tortilla chips. Either they were on break or they had soaked up their quota of rain for the day. The crew-cut Clark County deputy sheriff texted on his cell phone. An older Washington State Patrol officer thumbed through a gun catalog. The third was an electrician who had objected when we said we couldn't move the birds today and therefore he couldn't shut off the electricity—the parrots needed the heater. I scanned the living room one more time and walked back through the dining room toward the kitchen.

"Patriotism and crime, quite the combo, eh?" Boredom had overcome any grudge the electrician held for the inconvenience we'd caused. He was over-fed, straining the buttons on a standard blue work shirt. He leaned his chair back to a dangerous angle.

"Part of some extremist group?" I asked.

"Can't say. It looks to me like a homemade mix of Bible-thumping and survivalism. The back porch is stacked with boxes of canned food. I saw a metal box full of seed packets, from one of those apocalypse outfits." He put the chair and his life in jeopardy by rocking back and forth. "You've got your anti-government super-patriot thing going. Lived way out here so they didn't have to deal with the real world. But that's only my opinion. Not like I've worked a lot of crime scenes." He seemed to savor the words "crime scenes."

Had he been here for the bust? More likely he was good at eavesdropping. The cops looked as if they were about to tell him to put a sock in it, but they didn't. Mr. Hefty set his chair down with a thump. "They didn't hold with doctors, either. That wife could hardly walk. They've got her in the hospital."

"Where did they get the parrots and tortoises?" I asked. "They don't know anything about how to take care of them."

Three sets of shrugs.

"Have you found any international connections? Do you know yet who wholesaled the animals to the Tiptons?"

Three puzzled head shakes.

The electrician said, "Now I understand, and I could be wrong, that meth labs are kinda rare these days, what with the controls on cough medicine."

"Controls" seemed to be another tasty word and this topic was more interesting to his companions. The state patrol officer said, "Harder to get big quantities of pseudoephedrine now. They could have found another source—another state or Mexico—and brought it here to process. Lord knows the demand is still in place."

The deputy sheriff stood up, stretched, and left. I caught his name tag as he passed. Gil Gettler. The state patrol officer walked toward the bedrooms and made a phone call in a quiet voice.

So much for my pitch about wildlife crimes.

I wandered back to the living room and pulled out a drawer in the computer desk. It held only pens, pencils, and rubber bands. "Don't touch that," said the patrol officer, phone still in hand. "Why don't you stay in the kitchen, please."

What were the hazmat people *doing*? I could have stuffed the entire lab into garbage bags six times over in the time we'd waited. Clocking out by four o'clock was a lost cause, and being late to pick up Robby at day care was a strong possibility. I settled disconsolately into a kitchen chair. Denny came back inside, shook water off his head, and began a monologue about tortoise nutrition with analyses of fresh greens and hay.

The Animal Control guy arrived and saved me. He sat down in one of the two empty kitchen chairs with a sigh and poured coffee out of a steel thermos.

"I'm Iris Oakley."

Denny nodded at him.

"From the zoo, right? Ken Meyers." Medium height, about level with me. About my age, twenty-seven, or a little older. Calm dark eyes, brown hair. Denny and I watched him as if we'd never seen a man drink coffee before.

The electrician pulled on a jacket and left.

"Did you catch that pit bull?" I asked.

"Lord, it's damp out there." He wiped his face with a handkerchief. "She was happy to find a friend. She's loaded up. I struck out with the other two." A little pause separated each sentence. After Denny's motor-mouthing, Ken sounded thoughtful and a little sluggish. "Lucky mutts. Cops shoot dogs if they have to. These ran off when Old Man Tipton fired a few rounds. I'll try the live traps tomorrow."

So there was actual gunfire. "We heard that the wife was taken to the hospital. Was it just the two of them?"

"No. They've got a couple of sons. Grown ones. They went to jail, too."

This was way more interesting than Denny's ramble. "Every agency in the state seems to be here."

"Meth brings everyone together." A chipped front tooth showed when he smiled.

"What do you do with the dogs?" I asked.

"Humane society. They'll be out of the rain and fed. How's it going with the parrots and turtles?"

"Turtles live in water. These are tortoises." Denny was fed up with many things, among them bad taxonomy. "And we wouldn't be sitting here if they'd let us load them."

"I had a box turtle when I was a kid," Ken said, unperturbed. "I guess the Tiptons liked having a lot of animals around."

"Not pets," Denny said. "That's what I was expecting. A Burmese python, maybe. Green iguanas, monitor lizards. Those get too big, and people get rid of them."

I said, "We think this was commercial. I spotted a stack of new cardboard boxes, just what you'd need for shipping tortoises. I suppose they made the sales by email. " I turned to the remaining officer in the dining room. "You have the Tipton's computer, right? You've got wildlife crimes here, not just drugs. Maybe you can find the source—whoever the Tiptons got the animals from."

He looked up from his catalog. "Department of Agriculture was informed about the birds, and US Fish and Wildlife is involved. Also Washington State Fish and Wildlife."

"You'll share information with them, right?"

That earned me a tolerant nod.

Ken and I agreed that the Tiptons hadn't spent much money on caring for their dogs. Ken said one had a skin condition that was common with dogs left outside. He was pleasant company, another animal person. But he finished his coffee all too soon and stood up. He washed his cup and left it in the dish drainer.

On his way out, he said in my direction, "Watch out for rattlers. Drug dealers like their hot snakes."

"That's Denny's job. The things that bite me aren't venomous."

When the cop started pushing buttons on his fancy cell phone, I inspected the kitchen cabinets and the back porch and learned nothing of any use. I sat down again. Denny went outside and juggled apples.

A long half an hour later, we were told to get our turtles out, the faster the better. We charged off to the meth barn. Two new sets of protective gear were waiting for us. The red tape in the barn's kitchen area had been replaced with yellow tape. The garbage can, flasks, and tubing were gone. The air was a little better.

Denny rinsed tortoises in the sink and set them in a dish pan with a running commentary about each animal's condition and species. I assembled cardboard boxes, taped the bottoms, and poked holes in the tops with a ball point pen. I found paper towels to dry off wet, struggling beasts and packed them up. Most of them had a high, rounded carapace on top—some with fancy yellow and brown markings—and a flat plastron on the bottom, four scaly legs, a beady-eyed head, and a neck with wrinkled skin. They ranged in size from tennis ball to volleyball. Two of them seemed flattened, not rounded. Denny said those were pancake tortoises. The littlest tortoise blew bubbles from its nose, and Denny was stricken with worry.

I moved the zoo van to the meth barn and left the engine running and the heater on. As Denny finished rinsing, I loaded tortoises in a drizzle. The deputy guarding the barn had disappeared. Pausing for a moment, I pulled off the claustrophobic mask and shoved the hood back, grateful for easy breathing. It wasn't four o'clock yet, but the light was already dimming, clouds and twilight closing down the day. January in the great Pacific Northwest—cold and dark and wet. I wanted to go home, away from this sorry place with its ugly commerce. I wanted to hold my kid.

A half-grown Doberman emerged from the blackberries between the barns. Black and tan, uncropped floppy ears and a whippy tail. It looked skinny and scared. I made kissy noises toward it, but it crept back into the brambles. Ken had left bowls of dog food in the dog houses. I hoped the Dobe got to it before the bigger dogs ate it all. I suited up again and went back for another load.

I emerged from the barn for the third or fourth time balancing two boxes of clean tortoises when a woman materialized at my elbow. A wild cloud of gray hair was half-hidden under a dark green plastic parka. She was short and a bit plump, but that grandmotherly impression was countered by the rifle slung under her arm. No, it had two barrels. A shotgun?

Her voice was soft, but urgent. "Can you tell me what happened? Where are the Tiptons? Was anybody hurt?"

She was a decade or two older than my mother and definitely not an agency person. She seemed nervous, which made me like the shotgun even less. And she'd waited until the farm yard was empty, everyone inside the house or in one of the barns. I put the boxes in the van, uncovered my face, and aimed for a soothing tone. "The family was arrested for drug trafficking. No one was hurt."

"The boys are in jail? Both of them?"

"Yes, and the father."

The woman nodded and the shotgun muzzle dipped. Her forehead wrinkled with a fresh thought. "They arrested Wanda? Is she with Liana? She won't do well without Liana."

I relaxed a little. This was just a concerned neighbor. "Is Wanda the mother? We heard she's in the hospital. Who's Liana?"

The woman turned away. "Their girl. I hope she's with Wanda."

"We didn't hear anything about a girl."

The woman considered, looking over her shoulder at me. "Maybe she escaped. Yes, that's possible."

I couldn't tell whether she was relieved or worried about that. I addressed what *I* was worried about. "Um, why the gun?"

"Perhaps you haven't met the Tipton men." She glanced around the farmyard. A formal nod. "I appreciate your assistance." Before I could organize the questions I wanted to ask, she ducked under the crime scene tape and walked with an erect back into the woods and was gone.

I *so* did not want to come back here.

When the tortoises were all loaded, I took a peek at the parrots in the marijuana barn. They had eaten most of the food. I topped up the bowl again. "Listen, you guys," I told them, "One more day in here and we're all out of this place *forever*."

Chapter Three

"Iris, you don't know that these animals are smuggled." Dr. Reynolds, the zoo's veterinarian, spoke in a reasonable voice similar to the one I used with Robby, my toddler son. "It's rare, but it's legal to import wild birds with the proper permits, and then it's legal to sell them. We don't know for sure that they *are* wild caught. They could be captive-bred. Every one of those birds could be legitimate. We don't have enough evidence."

I was shut down in mid-rant about wildlife profiteers and how the zoo ought to move heaven and earth to see them arrested. It was eight in the morning, way too early for moral indignation. The vet—a slim, serious woman in a lab coat—outranked me, and I had no choice but to simmer in silence. We were at the zoo's hospital building, where Denny had taken over one of the three quarantine rooms for the tortoises. He and Dr. Reynolds had stayed late the night before to set up housing for them, while I'd defected to pick up my son. The tortoises were now sorted by species and housed in Denny's best efforts at the right conditions for each, with particular attention to their humidity and food requirements.

He held the littlest one, which was still bubbling from its nose and looked to be on its last legs. I stifled another diatribe about the people who snatched it out of its native habitat where it could thrive for decades and sent it instead to an early death in Washington State.

"Can't speak for the birds," Denny said, "but some of these guys aren't legal in trade."

Yes.

"And that's the curator's job," the vet said. "Neal will follow up."

Denny thrust out the ailing animal, which was about four inches long and beautifully patterned with yellow lines radiating from each dark shell plate. Dr. Reynolds flipped her long brown hair over her shoulder, pried one leg out from its shell, and stuck the tortoise with a needle full of antibiotic. "Our job is to keep these healthy and let the justice system sort out the rest." She put the tortoise back into its own little habitat. "Marian will set up the middle quarantine room for the Amazon parrots. The third one I have to reserve for zoo animals, so we're maxed out. Where does Neal want to put the macaws?"

Good question. "He hasn't said. Would you mind asking him?"

"I will. And, Iris, be sure that all your clothing is washed with disinfectant after you handle those birds. The Amazons are likely to be carrying viruses. Wipe out the van and the carriers with disinfectant. We need to protect the macaws from exposure to the Amazons and the zoo's bird collection from exposure to either of them. I can test for herpesviruses and vaccinate over the next few days, but that isn't any guarantee. Hygiene is essential."

She was treating the Amazons as wild birds despite the quibbling.

"Also," she added, "wear a face mask when you're handling them."

Right. I didn't need any bird-borne diseases either.

"Let's go," I said to Denny.

He shook his head. "You don't need me for parrots."

"Neal says you're going. He wouldn't let me have anyone else." I had tried for my friend Linda, the feline keeper, or Hap, the commissary manager. No luck. Neal had tagged me and Denny for this job, and me and Denny it would be. I herded him away from the torts to the employee parking lot, ignoring the reasons why he couldn't possibly go.

I took the driver's side of the van again. Denny driving and talking at the same time could be life-threatening. I stuck in a Shakira CD, one of the Spanish ones so I didn't have to strain to understand her words over the heater. The only Spanish I knew was "mojito."

DellaStreet woke up and, according to her little screen, began searching the airwaves for her mother ship, no doubt so she could learn once again that she wasn't in Chicago. She had failed to find the Tipton farm yesterday, despite her advanced satellite communications, and wasn't needed today. I sent her back into hibernation.

The rain was at it again, this time with wind tossing the tree tops around. There's not enough coffee in the world for January in the Northwest.

Exit signs slipped past on the freeway. Denny was soon bored. "Why is Neal hot for a new aviary when the reptile building is just as decrepit?"

"The reptile building isn't falling over. The aviary is. He'll get around to Reptiles."

"In my lifetime?"

I didn't answer. After a few miles, he said, "Calvin will retire, and you'll get to design it."

Calvin Lorenz was senior keeper of Birds and my immediate supervisor. "He hasn't resigned yet, and there's no guarantee I'll get his job when he does." Calvin had been talking about retiring for years. If he did, then he wouldn't be with his birds anymore. Arthritis battled with his love for everything in feathers.

"If you go for it, you'll get it." Denny stuck a foot on the dashboard, searching for a comfortable position.

"Maybe. More stressful." Single parenting and a full-time job provided plenty enough stress. I didn't feel like sharing my shaky decision that I would try for senior keeper.

A mile or two rolled by with Denny shifting on the seat, tapping a foot, adjusting the heater. He said, "Pete and Cheyenne have lasted a long time."

I glanced at him. They were animal keepers hired two years ago who shared my house. "Why wouldn't they? Cheyenne's happy with the new elephant yard, and she's on the design team for the new barn. Pete seems fine with being a floater. They've got a good deal living with me." Why was this coming up? "Did you hear something?"

"No, just thinking about the future. Possible changes."

"How adult." Was this an opening to talk about how he had broken the heart of Marcie Altman, my best friend? I couldn't find the strength.

Denny launched into lighting equipment for tortoises, all the ways to emulate sunshine. Since daylight mattered to birds as well, I listened with half my attention.

I pulled off the freeway onto increasingly narrow side roads. We found the farm with no trouble this time. The gate was open and the Animal Control van was back in yesterday's slot, along with most of the vehicles we'd seen before. Ken was there, setting up live traps for the loose dogs in the pouring rain. He directed a chipped-tooth grin and a wave toward our van. The rogue photographer was also back, still in the black jacket and wool cap, a camera bag hanging from one shoulder. He backed up from the house, shooting it from various angles, unconcerned about the camera getting wet. His limp seemed to be a permanent feature rather than a recent injury. He turned his attention to the roving Boxer mix and snapped it as well. The dog backed away.

"Ire, check out the gate," Denny said. He hopped out and pulled it partly shut to expose its greeting. I peered at it through the van window.

Bare plywood and red acrylic paint, the lettering possibly done with a child's water color brush. The boards varied in age and decrepitude, no doubt created and wired to the gate as inspiration struck. The message was unambiguous, if incorrect: PRIVAT PROPERTY KEEP OUT. That was the most weathered. Others announced:

Trespassers will be shot!!!

Attack Dogs Lose on Property!!!

If you are Government, We Shoot to Kill. No Sellers, No Politicans, No Phonebooks Delivery, No Census, No Nothin.

Denny pushed the gate back open, got into the van, and shook his head like a wet dog. I held up a hand to block the spray. "Charming welcome. They didn't figure out that red is the first color to fade." My sign-painter father would be pleased with my analysis.

I drove us through the gate and across the muddy yard and parked close to the house. Aside from Ken and the photographer, no one was wandering around the property today. Too wet and windy. We went inside to check in. Before we'd left the night before, I had reported my visitor and what she said—that the raid had missed a Tipton, a girl. The sole deputy remaining had raised an eyebrow and turned away to make a cell phone call.

This morning I asked the deputy who seemed to be in charge, a solidly built woman with blond hair, whether they had learned anything about the missing Liana. She thought about it and apparently decided we couldn't cause too much damage. "The mother's been asking for her. She says she has a teenage daughter, but there's no birth or school record of a girl associated with the Tiptons or with this address."

"Which fits," said Gil Gettler, the crew-cut one who'd been in the house with us the day before. "These people probably kept getting more and more isolated until that last kid was totally off the grid. Home birth out here and nobody'd ever know."

I couldn't imagine how big a paper trail my son Robby had already. Hospital birth, social security number, health insurance. Not yet three years old, my boy was totally documented.

"I wonder if she's wherever the other Tiptons are staying," said Gettler. "They're not likely to have all that many options."

"What?" I said. "They're not in jail?"

The woman said, "You didn't hear? We've got a judge who'd probably let Ted Kaczynski out on bail. The Tiptons were released yesterday."

"It was a lot of bail," Gettler said. "Nobody thought they'd make it."

"Well, they did. And now nobody knows where the hell they are." She turned to us. "Don't worry. They've been warned not to show up here until we're done with the place. So they must be camped out somewhere else."

Denny and I exchanged a look. This did not sound good, but what choice did we have? We got on with the job. I moved the van close to the marijuana barn and quick-stepped inside before I was soaked. I was relieved to find that the heater was going and no more parrots had died. I unloaded pet carriers, stacking them inside by the buckets holding marijuana stumps. "Why'd you take all those down?" I asked the chubby electrician, pointing to the row of long fixtures leaned against the wall.

"Good for fingerprints," he said. "You'll get the birds out today? I need to shut this barn down."

"I'm going to try." I turned to Denny. "Get the nets, will you?" I pulled on a face mask and light-weight leather gloves. The gloves wouldn't provide much protection against a bite, but thicker gloves made it hard to hold a bird gently. I went with the largest of the three nets I'd brought. The trick was to nab the bird flying, straight into the depths of the net where it would be surrounded by soft cloth, and not whack it with the rim. I stepped into the cage, hoping that the avian panic attack would send one into my clutches, but they all crowded away from me. I moved closer, and one finally lost his wits and flew past me. Bingo. I grabbed the back of its neck to control the beak, squeezed the wings together where they joined the body, and eased the bird out of the net.

I'd read endless news reports about the trade in wild animals. It was a different matter to hold a quivering bird in my hands and feel the too-thin breast muscle. This one had a toe missing, a raw stump. Strangers crowded together had fought to space themselves out and the weak couldn't escape. I released it into an animal carrier.

I caught birds and Denny stacked carriers in the van, where the heater was running. I was grateful they weren't in the barn with meth—at least we didn't have to rinse them. By lunch time, I had most of them caught up and we were low on carriers. I hadn't added any injuries except a broken feather or two.

Ready for food and a break, I pulled off my gloves, shut the back-room door behind me, and looked around the marijuana part of the barn. The activity level was diminished, with only two technicians working. Denny wandered around uselessly. "This is old shit," he announced. "The water tubes are starting to crack and so are the buckets. They've been growing for years." He poked a finger into a bucket.

"Denny, these cops are focused on the drugs. They might not have looked for evidence about the wildlife violations. Don't mess anything up."

"Right. Maybe they missed something. I'll look around."

Not what I meant, but I was okay with it.

I spent a few minutes sorting through a garbage can in the corner of the grow room until a technician noticed and told me to leave it alone. I didn't find anything useful.

The rain had let up, so we gathered our lunches and trotted to the house under a thick dark sky that promised more deluge any minute.

"I want to take a look at that VW," I told Denny.

"The tires look good," he said. "This might be their only wheels. Every other vehicle here has a logo on it."

"Not if they had something to leave the jail. Unless you can rent a car from the slammer."

I peered through its road-grimed windows. "There's room inside for boxes of animals. You could drive this to LAX, pick up a load, and come back here to market them. No one would expect to find illegal wildlife out here in the boonies."

"Let's take a look."

That had been my inclination, too. I itched to pull the door open and search the van for gas receipts, feathers, whatever. But that might mess up crucial fingerprints. Reluctantly I stepped back without touching it. "No, better not. We can make sure the cops go over it."

Movement caught my eye—the skinny Doberman. She slipped into the brambles along the barn. I looked around for Ken. He wasn't in sight, and his white truck was gone. If I caught her, she could stay warm in the house while I tracked him down, instead of spending the night outside in the blackberries or in a wire trap. "You go ahead. I want to see about that dog."

I broke off a bite of meatloaf sandwich. Moving slowly through the mud in the dog's direction, I flipped the morsel toward the place she had disappeared. She emerged to snap it up and half-crouched at the edge of the weeds, looking wet and miserable. Ken could charm a pit bull. I ought to be able to woo this one. I squatted and chatted softly, flicking another bite toward her. She gulped it. The next bite landed closer to me. She whined, took a step forward, and changed her mind, backing into the berries.

When the chill had crept up my calves and knees to my butt, I stood up stiffly and meandered closer. A spattering of rain warned me to give up soon. I squatted again and duck-waddled toward the gap where she'd disappeared. She couldn't be so scared of people that she had to pass on a meatloaf sandwich. I make a great meatloaf.

The heavens opened and dumped water on me. In seconds, my hair was plastered to my skull and rivulets ran down my neck, under my collar, and between my shoulder blades. I heard her whine again and the sound helped my eyes and brain sort through the vegetative chaos. Through the soggy tangled brambles, I made out the dog watching me, lying down with her nose pressed flat on...a person. On the chest of a girl. A dead girl. I teetered and struggled with my balance, then scrambled up and pushed a sharp-spiked blackberry cane aside.

I'd found Liana.

Chapter Four

The afternoon was a herky-jerky blur of uniforms, questions, and prohibitions. A whole new law enforcement bunch showed up, the homicide team. I hadn't much to contribute, but I delivered the scanty details several times. Most of the afternoon Denny and I spent, once again, cooling our heels at the kitchen table, forbidden to finish loading the parrots, forbidden to depart. We gleaned from the cautious communications of people coming and going for coffee and the bathroom that the girl I'd found had been shot in the chest, that it was not clear how long she had been dead, and that crucial information would be available only after lab results came back. We overheard comments both bewildered and snarky about how she could have lain there undiscovered since the original bust. "Hid in the bushes and caught a stray shot" seemed to be the consensus.

I topped up the macaws' food and water. They were a task for the next day—one more visit to this miserable place. I worried about the birds already in the van and I worried about transporting the macaws, but mostly I kept seeing Liana in the cold.

No matter how strange and felonious her upbringing with this outlaw family, she should have had her chance at a decent life. So young, maybe seventeen. A small, sturdy body. Strawberry blond hair in long wisps, the white skin and freckles that came with it. A broad face with features too small for beauty but right for strength and determination.

I was reading too much into a glimpse and a clean-scrubbed kitchen.

I phoned my mother and arranged for her to pick up Robby at day care. I left Cheyenne, one of my housemates, a message on her cell phone that I'd be late. Then there was nothing to do but wait for some official's permission to finish our task.

Denny was as rattled as I was and wouldn't stop talking. He processed and reprocessed scenarios for her death. The first ones were reasonable: Her own father accidentally shot her during the bust or the cops accidentally shot her. After he'd sucked the juice out of those, he tried on another: she killed herself rather than be captured.

He seemed to be working out a screenplay for this last one when I noticed that, after two hours of waiting on hard wooden chairs, we were alone in the house. "Let's blow this scene," I said. "Load the rest those parrots and get gone." We pulled on our jackets and walked out as if we had permission. It was late afternoon and almost full dark. Spotlights on the corners of the house and barns illuminated the yard unevenly. Our van still idled, keeping the heater on, although a glance inside showed that the tank was on its last gasp. Exhaust fumes lingered, held in place by the still air. I opened the rear and checked the birds. They seemed to be alive.

The temperature had dropped; sparse snowflakes floated down. The girl's body was gone. The blackberry brambles were cut and piled to one side to clear the area. I paused at the tape barrier and looked at the cold ground where she'd lain. The harsh light seemed as unkind as the icy mud.

The parking area still held two vehicles, but we'd been forgotten. No one interfered or questioned us. The remaining officials must have been in the meth barn. Lugging out the last animal carrier, we startled the overweight electrician. He said, "I thought you were long gone. I'm shutting down the electricity. Another minute, and you two woulda been padlocked in."

"Go ahead," I said. "We got all of these birds out. But don't shut down the house. The macaws need some heat." He helped us find the Tipton gas can and empty it into our tank. I pointed the van toward home, eager to put this day behind us.

We didn't get far.

Halfway between the gate and the highway, out of sight of the house, the headlights revealed a log across the driveway. It wasn't a big log, but enough to stop us. "Blow-down?" Denny said.

I automatically shut the van off. We got out and headed for opposite ends to toss it aside. Three men emerged from the woods. They weren't wearing uniforms, and they didn't look like good Samaritans. "Uh-oh," Denny said.

"*Get them*," one of the men bellowed.

Their timing was off. We scrambled back inside the van, but one of them grabbed my arm and pulled before I got the door shut. Half out of the van, I wrapped my elbow around the steering wheel and held on. He was stronger by far. I let go before he dislocated my shoulder somehow slammed the door, and hurled myself toward him. He staggered back, but didn't fall.

"Jeff, get the other one," came a roar from the front of the van, and my attacker hesitated. The man giving orders stood in the headlights, big-bellied and bearded. "You are trespassing and you're stealing my property. *Get the hell out of this van.*"

The man who had yanked me out shoved my chest and sent me hard into the mud on my rear, and, bizarrely, winked at me before going back to the van. Whatever Denny did, it resulted in a yelp of pain. I'd barely gotten to my feet when he was standing beside me breathing hard. I turned away and dug my cell phone out of my pants pocket, only to have it slapped into the mud. Denny threw an awkward punch, and the guy shoved him against a tree. I reached into my jacket pocket and clicked the lock switch on the key. The van chirped, a bird sound lost in the fray.

The old guy stayed in front, in the headlights with snow flickering around him, and yelled at the other two to open up the van. "*Get my birds out of there.*" He sounded like an Old Testament despot on a bad day, rasping and furious.

I sucked in a breath. Another. The fear-fog cleared a little. I strained to think, to pay attention. Two men confronted us, fists ready. Both wore jackets, jeans, and muddy lace-up leather boots. The one that attacked me had thick dark hair and a dark beard. The other was a little smaller and clean shaven with a green ball cap. The third, the old guy, had a shaggy gray beard and a brown jacket. Father Tipton and his sons, without a doubt.

Tipton Senior closed in on us, and I stopped memorizing details.

"We don't mind hurtin' you if we have to. That's my property and you're not getting away with stealing it," he said in a voice that could carry half a mile. His chest heaved and even in the headlight glare his face looked flushed. *"Get my birds."* The two younger ones stepped away from us and started yanking on the van's rear door. He was a grizzly bear and he had two grown cubs obeying him.

He came toward me, huge in the front beams, triggering predation-survival strategies. Don't run, don't cower, pray it's a bluff charge. I stepped forward, holding my arms out to look bigger. "*Stealing?* You buy smuggled wildlife and let them die because you can't be bothered to take care of them, and you say *we're* stealing? We're trying to save their lives, and you can rot in hell." I hated that my voice shook.

He frowned and his head jerked back a little. Denny grabbed my arm, and I shook him off.

"You *poison* people with meth," I ranted. "You are guilty of crime after crime. So don't talk to me about stealing, you greedy, heartless bastard."

That last was a little over the top, but I was full of adrenaline. I could hear the sons yanking on all the van doors.

The father's eyes narrowed to slits and his face darkened. "Shut your face, you insolent harlot." He moved fast and again I was sprawled in the mud. The black Boxer mix appeared out of nowhere, barking in my face like the hound of hell. Shit. Where were all those deputies and sergeants and inspectors?

Tipton yelled, "Jeff, Tom, you idiots. It's locked, and she's got the key. Get over here and take it away from her."

The sons closed in, one on either side. Still on my rump, I looked around for a branch or rock and found nothing within reach. My options seemed to be flinging moss or hurling my weight at one of them in hopes he slipped and fell. Before I tried either, the father stopped yelling. He wavered a little and sank to his knees by the front bumper.

Even the dog froze.

"Huhnnn," Tipton said in the vibrating silence. "Not now," he whispered to something only he could see. He crossed his heavy arms in front of his chest, weaving back and forth in the muddy gravel. He began to sag and, with glacial inevitability, fell onto his face.

No one moved. Snowflakes sparkled as they floated onto his dark jacket and winked out.

I got to my feet and grabbed his arm, trying to pull him onto his side. The dog went nuts, lunging and snarling at me. The smaller son grabbed the dog around the neck. The bearded son pushed me aside and pulled his father onto his back. He leaned over, clutched the front of his jacket, and shook him. "Wake up! What's the matter? What should we do?"

Denny crouched next to him. "He's not breathing."

We looked at each other. What was our responsibility here? I shoved the son out of the way, sank to my knees astride the father, and started chest compressions. Two-handed, straight-arm shove, let up, shove, let up, shove, one hundred times a minute. It didn't feel like the dummy we'd practiced on in first aid class. This guy was big and he was fat and he had several layers of clothing on. I'm not petite, but my weight was barely adequate to budge his chest. I was sweating almost immediately.

Denny fumbled with his cell phone.

"One-of-you-start-breathing," I said to the sons, one word per compression.

The bearded one stood wild-eyed and paralyzed. The smaller one crouched with one arm around the dog. I sacrificed my rhythm to yell, "Get down here and start blowing in his mouth."

They looked terrified. The smaller one said, "We don't know how."

"Put your mouth tight over his and blow. Right *now*."

Neither moved.

"I can't get a signal," Denny said. "You—go to the house and call 911."

The smaller son loped off in the right direction, the dog following. The other winked—an eye twitch—and ran after him. Denny knelt beside me and blew hard into the beard, then again.

I held up a hand when the man moved. His lips twitched. His chest rose on its own. Could this have actually worked? We'd restored him to life? He coughed a little and wheezed. Denny and I crouched over him. I wondered if I should turn him onto his side.

"Look...after...stridd...er," and the eyes closed again. Snow flecks disappeared into his beard.

No more breathing. I resumed chest compressions, and Denny blew into his mouth, an endless cycle.

A deputy skidded to a stop next to me, followed by another. I relinquished my position and got to my feet, arms trembling. The two of them were smooth and skillful and, better yet, they had a CPR mask. The one doing chest compressions said, "Defibrillator in a minute."

But I was pretty sure it was over.

I glimpsed the two sons standing at the road's edge like lost sheep waiting for a shepherd. A wailing ambulance arrived bearing paramedics, who disembarked with their gear, knelt over the father for a minute or two, and straightened back up. The deputies nodded and one reached for his radio.

When I looked again, the sons were shadows backing away from the angled light beams and erratic clots of snowflakes. They stepped through tall ferns and vanished among close-spaced trunks.

Chapter Five

Denny drove hunched over the steering wheel staring into the wipers. Wet snow made raspberries on the windshield, obliterated in a steady rhythm. Sad little chirps came from the rear of the van, also small chewing and scratching noises. I was shivering from cold and lingering adrenaline, unable to decide whether unzipping my jacket and letting in the heater blast was a better option than keeping it zipped. I struggled with my boots and finally got them off, wet socks, too. Boots that leaked were the curse of my profession. "Why would a judge let these guys out on bail? What was he *thinking?*"

Denny threw open a hand, focused on me instead of the road. "Only one possible reason—that family's got connections. Mover and shaker customers for hash or meth. Or they're part of some religious group. Maybe they spent all that drug money on extremist politicians and the judge is connected with that. Or—"

"I'm still freezing. Turn the heater up, will you? My pants are soaked."

"Ire, it's ninety degrees in here. It's maxed out. Take your pants off and use the towels in back."

I knew he was right. Bare skin is warmer than wet clothes. My feet were proving that. Still…

Denny glanced at me sidelong. "I've seen you naked. I can take it."

Also true, although that was long ago and a different Iris Oakley.

I unclipped the seatbelt and wriggled out of my damp jacket, tossing it in back over an animal carrier. Then the pants. I grabbed a towel covering the mesh door of one of the carriers. Seatbelt back on, towel over my knees. No dignity, but slowly warmer. "They pushed me in the mud. Twice."

"Yeah, I thought we were doomed. Jumped us out of nowhere."

"That Jerome Tipton is a piece of work. Was." Despite his anger and power, death had come and taken him. "Once he was out of commission, those sons were useless." I pulled out my cell phone for the third time to check that it still worked and wiped a little more mud off.

"Robotic storm troopers obeying their commander. I'd bet my next paycheck they skip bail. They're probably heading for Idaho. That farm needs a good exorcism. Doesn't always work, but sometimes it makes a difference."

I drew a deep, halting breath. "Denny, kudos for mouth-breathing that ugly bastard. Don't know if I could have done it. I feel like we should get vaccinated."

"I rinsed my mouth from my water bottle. If he'd been chewing tobacco…"

Heat was seeping in. "I guess I should feel bad that it didn't work. I wonder if CPR ever does."

"Sure. When I was a kid, a friend of mine got stoned and fell in the river. My mom's boyfriend pulled him out and held him upside down to drain. Then he did the CPR thing. Kid was fine."

"How old was he?"

"The kid? Fourteen or fifteen."

"This was on the commune where you and your mother lived."

"Yeah, before she moved to Jack's farm, my step-dad. He was a pretty cool guy—Crow, the guy who did the rescue. He turned me on to snakes. He used to drop acid and play with his baby rattlesnake. He wouldn't let me near it. But we found garter snakes in the meadow and a king snake once. He knew a lot about frogs and fish and stuff like that. I was really sorry when he left for Baja."

I chewed on this. "That scene was about separating from regular society. Follow your own bliss and use a lot of drugs."

Denny made a face. "Don't go thinking it was like that hostile outfit we just left. Boss Tipton was totally autocratic and rageful. Strictly ego-driven. No one at Aquilegia Farm would have put up with him. They were all about therapeutic acceptance, but they knew when to tell someone to hit the road."

I hadn't heard Denny talk about his upbringing for a long time. It beat reliving the helplessness of sitting in the mud waiting for the Tiptons to grab me. I remembered something. "You saw that photographer? In the black jacket with the knit cap. He came back when the ambulance did and took a bunch of pictures. I bet he has a scanner and heard the 911 call. We might end up in the papers." That could cost me professional points.

"Neal can't harp on us for that. Not like we had a choice."

True. The curator disapproved of his staff talking to the press without approval. But someone snapping our pictures while we performed CPR on a dying man wasn't quite the same as an in-depth interview. It shouldn't be a problem.

We pushed through the night without talking for a little time. The weather gods switched to hail mixed with rain, then shut everything off. In half a daze, I stared at the road. White dashes against wet dark asphalt were mesmerizing. The van hit a pothole, and I jerked awake. I stretched my back. "We'd better stop to eat and buy gas. Keep an eye out for a café or something."

"Robby?"

"With my parents."

After a silence, I said, "I wonder if he knew his daughter was shot. Does the mother know? Any of them?"

Wanda Tipton had lost a husband and a daughter. Her home was overrun with strangers. A lonely future lay ahead. Or maybe widowhood from the tyrannical Tipton was a net improvement. No, losing a child trumped everything. If Robby died, I would flat-out never recover.

Obsessing about ways my child might die was not what was needed. I diverted myself onto the Doberman. Maybe Ken from Animal Control would catch her tomorrow. I hoped the brothers wouldn't get her back or any of the other dogs. I'd seen their dog food, and it was the cheapest available. The dog houses were a joke.

Here I was worrying about dogs when a girl lay dead.

Denny said, "I can't believe no one noticed her for two days. Laying there half frozen all that time."

So young...dead before she had any chance to dodge poverty and crime. I remembered peeking into what had to be her bedroom. Crumpled on the polyester bed cover was a picture torn from a magazine—William and Kate in their wedding finery. I guessed that cops had searched the room and pulled the photo of royalty out of a hiding place. Jerome would not have approved of a girl's fascination with fame and glamour.

We ate at a pizza place in Battle Ground, my still-damp pants back on. Denny told me a great deal about a frog, Darwin's frog. "The male has this hole below his tongue."

"To his lungs. Birds have that."

"No, not to his lungs. To his vocal sac. After the eggs hatch, he sucks the tadpoles inside the sac and keeps them there. When they metamorphose into little frogs, he coughs them out."

"Is this relevant to tonight?" I asked. "Some analogy to Old Man Tipton? If so, I don't get it."

He ignored me, helped himself to a cherry tomato from my salad, and detoured onto turtles that never age. "There's this rumor about alligator snappers. People catch them to eat and sometimes really big ones have a musket ball or stone spear tip in them. They might be hundreds of years old, way older than anyone thought they would live."

"Just a rumor?"

"Yeah. I've tried to confirm it. No luck so far. But this one *is* true. Blandings turtles in Michigan: If they make it to adult size, the only thing that stops them is getting run over by a car. Or maybe a bear. Something with powerful jaws. They live forever and keep on reproducing, too. No senility at all."

He was talking to keep from thinking. I let him ramble. It made me feel better, too. A good time to talk about Marcie? Not when I was this wrecked.

We pulled into the employee lot at the zoo about eight o'clock. I'd called the night guard, who met us and opened up the hospital. The quarantine room was nicely set up with perches, food, and water pans. Each bird flew a circuit of the room when I released it, then settled on a perch. They sat erect with their feathers sleeked down tight, holding themselves rigid and ready to bolt. I turned the lights out and left them with my fingers crossed, grateful that they had all survived the day.

Denny returned from checking on the tortoises.

"Everyone good?" I asked.

He shrugged. "For now. Tortoises die slow."

"What are we going to do about the macaw pair?"

"Not our problem. We've dealt with enough Tipton crap, and I'm way behind here."

"They'll die unless we get them out of there. I'd rather give a wolverine an enema, but somebody's got to do it."

"Call Neal. He can send someone else out. Pete maybe. Or Arnie."

I didn't have Neal's personal cell, but the night guard did. I stood in the hallway outside the quarantine room, leaning against the wall, and dialed while Denny and the night guard waited. Neal answered with a suspicious, "Yeah?"

I recapped the day—Amazon parrots loaded and now in quarantine, one murdered girl discovered, an attack by drug dealers, a dead patriarch. "We got out ahead of the ninja assassins," I said, gallows humor to steady the hand that held the phone.

A silence. "For some reason, I believe all this."

"The ninja assassins part isn't really true." I was too tired to stand up. I slid down to the floor and sat with my legs stuck out. My pants were still damp at the waist.

"You and Denny are in one piece?"

"Yeah."

Denny squatted next to me so he could hear both sides of the conversation.

"The van?"

I assured Neal that the van was fine.

"You can give me the details tomorrow. Thanks for the update. Go home."

Not so fast. "Somebody has to go back and get two macaws tomorrow."

"Nope. Mission accomplished. The feds can deal."

"We can't trust the Tipton boys to feed them. The electrician shut the heat off at the barns, and he might shut it off at the house." My heart sank at the thought, but my mouth kept on. "We have to go back."

"I'll call the feds. They can step up to this one."

"Neal, you told them we'd take care of it. These are big, bad macaws, and we're the experts. We just have to throw two birds in the van and get out." A girl can dream.

A long pause. I could hear him moving around, pacing maybe. "Only if you have a police escort every single minute."

"Absolutely." No way was I doing this without backup. "I need someone to go with me."

"Denny. Call me tomorrow as soon as you get back."

◇◇◇

The house I grew up in had never seemed nicer. My parents trended toward comfortable and practical rather than elegant, a house full of places to set a coffee cup and turn on a reading light. My father's sign painting magazines had a dedicated shelf within reach of his recliner. Often a gardening book lay on the kitchen counter, sometimes held open with a muddy hand trowel. Winter was a frustrating time for my mother, the season of not-gardening. In the living room, a handsome toy-box my father had constructed held educational toys guaranteed to produce a genius. My mother worked part-time as an elementary-school math specialist, and she knew her toys.

They both adored Robby, probably seeing him as a second chance to rear a child that would turn out the way they had expected back when I was two. My schedule required working weekends, when the day care center was closed. I was fortunate to have them take him on Saturdays and Sundays and the rare times, like tonight, when I worked late.

"You look so tired," my mother said. "I saved you a lamb chop. How about a glass of wine?" Gray threaded through her hair and a wrinkle showed here and there, but she still seemed tireless, two women's worth of energy in one short package. Tonight she wore her yellow sweatshirt with wildflowers, an old favorite.

My father was immersed in a basketball game, the reason my mother hadn't seen the news and wasn't full of alarm about the Tiptons. That would happen tomorrow.

"I wish I could. We stopped for pizza and I don't dare drink when I'm this beat. Robby's asleep? I'm sorry I'm so late."

"He was fine. How did the animal rescue go?"

"We had a few setbacks. I have to go back tomorrow. I'll give you the full story when I can think straight." Telling her about a dead girl and failed CPR would keep me there all night.

"We'll take Robby to the Children's Museum this Saturday. That is, if it's all right with you."

"That would be awesome."

My mother's focus on toddler enrichment had my full support. Robby benefited and so did I, since that left her with less energy for nudging my life into shape.

My father was the calm center of our small family. He was tall and quiet. I inherited only the tall part, that and his dark hair. His hands were skilled and sure, trained by a lifetime as a sign painter and home handyman.

I climbed the stairs to my old room, where Robby was curled asleep around his stuffed armadillo. Seeing my child did much to set my world to rights again. He was an unlikely gift to my life, conceived by accident just before my husband Rick died. I inhaled his baby scent as I leaned over to pick him up.

I needed this day to come to an end, to go home. To sleep. But Robby woke up cross-wise and pitched a fit. I hugged him and explained and did my best, but he wanted…I couldn't tell what he wanted, but being awakened was not it. Finally I gave up on sweet reason, wrestled him into the car seat, and waved good-bye to my parents, who stood watching my failings with concerned frowns.

Pete and Cheyenne's car was in the driveway, but they were upstairs in their room. I lugged Robby up to his room and tucked him in. Thankfully, he collapsed back into slumber.

My dogs, Winnie and Range, were thrilled to have me back. Range was mostly black Lab, Winnie was part German shepherd. I sat on the floor and stroked the dogs, apologizing for coming home late again. They did their best to heal the day's misery with doggy affection, and their best was quality work.

I was able to buy this house because of Rick's life insurance, but that edge of discomfort had mostly worn off. Like my parents' home, it smelled of good food—Pete's spicy cooking—and the kitchen was neither beige nor worn out. The house still had some of the "new-on-the-market" glow from when I'd bought it two and a half years ago.

Why had the Tiptons lived in such a barren house? They must have had drug profits to spend.

I pushed away recollections of the Tiptons' kitchen by calling Marcie, my best friend, for a quick check-in. She wanted to talk, but I was too exhausted. We settled for dinner on my next day off. I felt bad about that—she needed me and I'd made her wait. Denny had backed away from their three year relationship and she wasn't taking it well.

A quick shower and I was in bed.

The deep comfort of domestic routine didn't survive the darkness. In the quiet, unsettling images intruded and pushed sleep away—Liana's pale, vacant face, Tipton's collapsing body.

Tomorrow was a work day—insomnia was not an option.

Better to think about the birds I wanted for the new walk-through aviary featured in the zoo's master plan. Lady Amherst pheasants with their green and blue backs and long barred tails. Temminck's tragopan, a gorgeous red and orange pheasant. My hands on the warm bodies of parrots with broken feathers, the stab of blackberry thorns pulled aside to show a slender muzzle pressed to a bloody sweater.

I concentrated harder. Laughing thrushes in the bushes. Maybe Asian Fairy bluebirds, gorgeous. Green magpies, if Neal could find any. A wisp of detail intruded: My palms on Jerome Tipton's chest had shoved on an expensive Filson jacket like the one my mother gave my father for Christmas. His sons' jackets were cheap denim.

Demoiselle cranes. He'd worn a fancy watch, the kind with many buttons and functions. Red-breasted geese…sleep.

Chapter Six

Under thin wintery sunlight, the farm looked less desolate, transformed from squalid to merely rural. Clear sky equals cold in the Northwest in January. Frost outlined tall grass stalks along the road and rimmed the hog-wire around the vegetable garden.

I ran the van up to the house and shut it off. Denny and I emerged blinking in the unaccustomed light, grateful for air that wasn't tainted with disinfectant fumes from decontaminating the van. The Tipton place and toxic air would be forever linked in my mind. We had a solemn agreement to get in and get out—load the macaws and split.

Mud crunched underfoot, icy on top and gooey underneath. Crème brûlée of muck. I grumbled to Denny, "If I had to live here, I'd order a truckload of fir bark on Day Two and make some decent paths."

My arms ached from the night before. The black Boxer mix that had been so aggressive circled in a live trap under the eaves, barking dutifully at us. The Chow, still loose, loitered next to him and raised his nose to emit a woof now and then. No half-grown Doberman.

As the first order of business, we checked that The Law was on duty. We found Deputy Gettler amid a group standing in the dining room giving each other instructions about wrapping up the crime scene. When he confirmed that the Tipton brothers weren't back in custody, I said, "We are not facing those guys again without serious firepower on our side. I left my nets in the parrot barn, so we need someone to go with us."

Gettler seemed insulted that we asked for security he'd assumed he would provide. He led us outside. "You're not supposed to park here. That's why everyone else is parked by the gate."

"We're going to load the macaws," I said. I pointed to the VW van. "You guys checked that out? The Tiptons might have left a gas receipt or something from where they picked up the parrots and tortoises."

"We checked it."

"What did you find?"

A shrug. "I wasn't there."

He led us across ice slicks to the closer barn, clouds of our breath drifting ahead, and removed the padlock from the hasp on the door. It was dark and cold inside. He flicked on a flashlight.

"Did a huge electric bill give them away?" I asked.

"Nope. Tom Tipton sold meth to the wrong guy. That's what we came out for. The grass was a surprise."

"Like the animals," said Denny.

The deputy looked defensive. "We knew about the dogs, just not the rest. Not until we had a chance to look around."

I'd left the nets leaning against the wall in the back room. Now they lay on the floor. The night before, Denny and I had been the last ones out of the building. "Did you dump them here?"

Denny shook his head.

"Who's been in here? I thought this was locked up at night."

Gettler said, "Only one entry and you saw it was padlocked."

I looked around the back room. "That bag of parrot food was moved. I didn't leave it there."

Denny shifted from foot to foot. "Who cares? Grab the nets and let's go."

I was just as eager to leave this place behind, but he wasn't in charge, and I ignored him. Something had been bothering me for two days. "Only one exit," I said to myself.

"Yeah. Maybe not the brightest plan," the deputy agreed.

If I were growing dope in a barn, I'd have a back door as an escape hatch. We could spare five minutes to put that itch to rest. I looked around, remembering what I'd seen when the lights were on. No loft above. No possible place to hide. Experts had been over every square inch of the building.

The back room was better lit. Sun filtered through knot holes and narrow gaps between the boards. With no birds to distract me, I stopped and for the first time gave my attention to the room itself. The exterior wall that was part of the parrot cage was insulated and sheathed in plywood. But that was only two-thirds of the back wall. The rest was the only part of the barn not lined in fiberglass batts. Fir studs darkened by age supported the rough exterior boards, the barn as it was before the Tiptons tricked it out for their cash crop. I took a close look, finger tips exploring the boards. The deputy said, "Wasting your time. We checked."

"Skip it. It doesn't matter," Denny said.

"Someone's been in here messing around." If the Tiptons were using this barn for shelter, I wanted to prove it. I wanted them caught. I wanted them to explain how Liana died and then tell the law who they got the parrots and tortoises from. A girl was dead, animals had suffered, and nobody shoves me in the mud without consequences.

It took more than a few minutes and Denny was about to mutiny. What I found was simple and well done. A section of wall framed by the old studs on all sides moved a tiny bit when I jiggled it with finger in a knothole. I finally lifted just right and the section disconnected from the wall and fell outside. Bright sun and cold air streamed into the back corner through a gap that would have been a tight fit for the heavy father. A hint of a path disappeared through the blackberry vines outside. Denny and the deputy stooped and followed me out. They stood aside so I could push the panel back in place. It was invisible from inside because the cut lines were all behind studs. It was barely visible from the outside. I said, "I bet the other barn has one of these, too."

Gettler put a hand on his gun and told us to stay where we were. He vanished into the brambles, returning in a few minutes.

"The path disappears in the woods. I'd guess those boys came in here last night to get out of the weather."

We slipped back into the barn and shut the hidden door. Gettler turned the electricity on and we looked around in better light. The deputy thought the buckets of potting soil had been moved and the dirt pawed through. He unlocked the other barn, and we found a duplicate door at the back. Again, the trail petered out.

We all looked around the meth barn with fresh eyes. Denny was sure someone had disturbed the straw in the tortoise corral. It was heaped up in the middle. The deputy had frown lines on his forehead that hadn't been there before. He said, "I'll be back in a few minutes," and left toward the house. My guess was that he had a few people to consult with about access to the supposedly-secure barns.

"*Now* can we load those birds and go?" Denny asked.

"Damn straight."

We followed Gettler outside.

I glimpsed a human shape emerging from the trees behind the barn. My muscles were set to "flee," but my brain identified the woman before I bolted. It was the neighbor I'd seen before.

Today she looked less like a woods witch and more like an aging woman worn down by a hard life. Her gray hair was still wild, and again she held the shotgun in lumpy fingers, the barrel pointed down. A brown wool shawl was draped over her shoulders. Her eyes were cautious in a soft, lined face. "We met before. I'm Pluvia. I was hoping you might have learned how Wanda is getting along. Wanda Tipton." She had a nice voice, a little hesitant but clear.

"I'm Iris. This is Denny. I haven't heard anything more. Her husband died last night. A heart attack, we think."

"In prison?"

"No, here. He was released on bail."

She didn't react to the death, but her eyes widened with the news the Tiptons had been released. "I heard the ambulance. I wondered…" She scanned the yard behind us. "Tom and Jeff were released also?"

I hoped Denny would keep quiet and not scare her off. She knew more about this farm than anyone alive except the Tipton brothers. "That's the sons, right? They were here last night. Scary guys."

"Jeff can be. Neither one will pee without the father's permission. They're probably watching us. I do wish I could find out about Wanda."

She confused me—the shotgun, the mix of boldness and fear, her concern about a difficult neighbor. I wouldn't have wanted anything to do with any of the Tiptons, no matter how charming and innocent Wanda might be. "That friendship must not have been easy."

She nodded. "Jerome and the older son, Jeff, were unpleasant. But Wanda would walk to my place and we would visit. Liana brought her. Wanda stopped coming a few months ago, and I… I wasn't going to come here." She looked around the farmyard.

"You could talk to the deputies," I said. "They could tell you where she is."

"Oh, I don't think so. They came to my home. I found their questions very unpleasant."

I wanted to know much more about the Tiptons, and she looked about to take flight. "I could let you know if I hear anything about Wanda. If you gave me your phone number."

She stepped back and studied us both. "You'd be wise to stay clear of Jeff. Tom is a different story." She looked toward the house and back to us. After a hesitation, "I'm worried about Liana, too. I thought if she escaped, she'd come to my place. If you see her, I live north…" She raised her head, looking beyond us. I turned and saw the deputy approaching at a fast walk.

Denny said, not harshly, "Iris found Liana's body yesterday. She was shot during the raid."

Pluvia's eyes went distant, and she stood motionless for a few seconds. Then she walked back the way she'd come, threading her way among the blackberries, her shawl snagging a little. I could see only the top of her head when she made it to the little trail behind the parrot barn and disappeared toward the woods.

Denny said, "This is *so* not a good place."

The deputy arrived and demanded to know who we had been talking to.

"A neighbor dropped by," I said. "She's a friend of the mother."

The deputy was not mollified. "This is a crime scene, and people can't go wandering around ignoring the tape and breaking into the barns, poking their noses in everywhere. She comes back, I'm going to arrest her."

He was mad at *her?* "It could have been the brothers." I didn't add, "while we were out here alone and you were in the house," but he got my point.

Pluvia lived to the north and it was within walking distance, but what were the odds of finding her house in the woods? Not good, but no matter. We wouldn't be back after today. I'd lost my chance to learn more about the Tiptons, such as their car trips to pick up animals.

Time for the macaws. I'd brought the biggest animal carrier we had. Denny and I carried it into the dining room. I handed the birds broccoli spears and spinach leaves, which did not appeal, and more carrot sticks, which did. Their hooked beaks reminded me of a description of their genus, *Ara,* that I had once read: "can openers with feathers." I had the feeling that my bird mojo was insufficient to allow me to grab them and stuff them into a carrier without losing a finger.

I hated situations where animals had to be moved in a hurry. Given time, I could train the macaws or almost anything to shift to a smaller cage in exchange for treats—no stress or excitement. The rushed alternative was to cowboy the critter—grab it or net it or throw a towel over it—and hope that no legs or wings were broken and no one was bitten. I wasn't looking forward to grabbing the macaws, for their sake or mine. Another way finally came to me.

Denny said, "Can't we just put the whole cage in the van?"

"That's what I'm thinking." I found a piece of string and used it as a tape measure to get the width and depth of the cage. We checked the dimensions. It looked tight, but do-able.

We'd need to put the cage on its side, and then the macaws wouldn't have anything horizontal to perch on. I found a branch and stuck it through a corner of the cage at an angle. The macaws objected at volume.

Together we tipped the cage over, with me apologizing to the birds for the disruption. They hit new highs in decibels, clinging to their old perch until gravity and good sense sent them scrambling to the branch. The cage was heavy and we were leery of the birds chopping our fingers off so it was hard to know how best to grip it. Denny nicked his thumb on a projecting metal stub and stopped to wrap a handkerchief around it. Ken from Animal Control showed up and stepped in without a word, hefting my end as though I were too frail for the job. Which I had to admit, I was. I moved to Denny's end. The electrician and various agency staff offered conflicting advice and annoying opinions. We three animal pros wrestled the cage out of the house and into the van. I shut the tail gate, and we shared high fives.

The excitement over, the agency people drifted off toward the barns or inside the house. The photographer in the wool cap took pictures of us standing by our zebra-striped van. "Would you mind answering a few questions?" he asked. "It won't take long. I'm writing an article on this arrest, and I'd like to include the zoo perspective. Let's start with your names." He smiled, expectant.

I looked up and met intelligent hazel eyes. A stray shaft of sunlight lit his face and faded. I glanced away from that perceptive gaze. "The names you want are Neal Humboldt, the curator, or Dr. Crandall, the director. We can't talk to you without their okay."

He looked unsurprised. "I'll see to that. I'm Craig Darsee."

He seemed fit and competent despite the limp. In his thirties. Narrow nose, a mouth ready to smile. If he shed that cap, he'd be good looking. His clipboard was at the ready and the long-nosed black camera hung off his chest. "I should ask about talking to …."

"Iris Oakley. This is Denny Stellar."

He studied me, ignoring Denny. He reached out his hand. "Iris. Very glad to meet you." I shook it. He turned and Denny shook it. He said, "I'll be in touch" and stepped back, still looking at me.

While Denny and Ken tied the unused animal carrier to the rack on top of the van, I went back to the living room for the bag of parrot food. It's best to transition to a new food gradually, so I'd need the old food. The cage had been set tight in a corner. Left behind was the inevitable residue of spilled birdseed, peanut shells, feathers, and dried bird poop that had drifted down and stacked up between the cage and the wall. It was a sprawling pile now that the cage wasn't supporting it. It had been out of sight behind the metal skirt around the bottom of the cage, and the tidiest housekeeper couldn't have reached it.

I wanted to leave, but I was more or less responsible for this. Out of a dim sense of respect for Liana or whoever had toiled to keep this sad house clean, I searched out the broom and dustpan. My first pass uncovered …what? I grasped a corner and shook the detritus off. It was a quart-size plastic bag, the kind with a seal you press shut along the top. Inside was a small water glass and inside that was a wadded up tissue. I opened it and looked closer. The tissue was dirty, a smear. Something put down and forgotten when the cage was originally set up?

"What cha' got?" asked the electrician.

"Beats me." I shouldn't have touched it. Too late now. I sealed the bag back up and stuck it in a pocket. The house was empty of law enforcement. I swept the carpet as best I could and dumped the mess into the kitchen trash.

Denny stood in the cold by the van yakking with Ken. I waved the bag. "Found this behind the cage. A bag with a glass in it."

Denny gave it a glance and didn't try to care. "Let's go."

Deputy Gettler emerged from the barn and tromped over to the photographer who stood watching us. "You again? You want to get yourself arrested? Keep on doing what you're doing, because I am *that* close. You get yourself behind that crime scene tape right now."

Craig saluted and headed toward the driveway with the deputy close behind him. Ken followed them. I could hear Gettler's radio mumbling in Navaho or Sanskrit on his hip.

I checked the macaws and the carrier on the roof while Denny visited the bathroom. Denny climbed in on the passenger side, and I started the motor. "I need to show this bag to the cops." But all the patrol cars were gone from the parking lot. Only the electric company van remained. "Damn. Where's a cop when you need one?"

Denny was preoccupied with his thumb injury. "Call them tomorrow. Or tonight. We are done with this place. I can't remember my last tetanus shot."

"The date will be on file in the office with your TB tests." I tucked the bag behind his seat where we wouldn't kick it and the macaws couldn't chew it. I'd deal with it at the zoo.

Two men in parkas, jeans, and boots wandered the driveway between the road and the parking area. Denny and I tensed, but they ignored us, focused on the metal detectors they each waved along the ground. Looking for some sort of evidence? Nothing they wore displayed an agency logo. The log that had trapped us the night before was gone.

"Outta here!" Denny said.

"Too right." I gunned the van onto the road. It skidded on an icy patch and I wrestled it back into the right lane. Getting creamed just as we were escaping the Tipton farm would fit right in.

Even in daylight, the road seemed ominous. Thick, moss-padded limbs of big-leaf maple hung over the highway. Sword ferns and evergreen shrubs prevented any view inside the forest. A raven followed the road ahead of us for half a mile, flying easily at our speed before veering off on unknowable raven business. We passed a tangle of logs on a naked hillside; a yellow log loader rusted amid the stumps.

After a few miles, Denny said, "Nothing is ever totally bad. Those birds will end up in a better place, and we got these amazing torts. I'm going to talk to Neal and see if we can set up a whole tortoise unit. This is golden—we'd never see these guys otherwise. A few will be good for Asian Experience, and we could set up a whole Madagascar exhibit. I'll look at the master plan with Neal maybe next week and see what we can do."

"Golden?" I said. "*Golden?* Two people are dead and you're celebrating? And may I remind you, that these are *stolen* reptiles?" Anger felt good. It flushed out some of the impotence and fear of the last three days. "How many of those animals died before they got to the Tiptons'? Most of the rest could croak despite everything Dr. Reynolds can do. Golden, my ass." A macaw squawked behind me.

Denny cocked his head, considering my perspective as if it really hadn't crossed his mind. "Probably true, but no one can change what already came down. All we can do is deal with the new reality and improve the trajectory. We could do a ton of conservation messaging. Between the pet trade and the food markets, tortoises are getting vacuumed up everywhere." He wound up, "*And* if we learn more about breeding them, collectors won't need to take them out of the wild."

"Messaging, sure. Breeding, mostly bullshit. Those Amazon parrots? Neal told me plenty of people breed them. They're *common.* Anybody can buy a legal one. The wild ones are just *cheaper.*"

"Huh. That sucks swamp water." He took a moment to think. "Captive bred ones are healthier, so it's stupid anyway. But nothing we can do about it now. Seriously."

"Yes, there is. We can figure out where they came from, who the importer is, and shut down the pipeline."

Denny looked at me sideways. "Uh, what have you got in mind?"

"Nothing. Yet."

We rode on in what would have been silence if Denny hadn't lapsed into muttering. "Different antibiotic…Show Marion how to soak them…Humidity…Ban cold meds…Legalize to strip out the profit…"

The macaws also muttered, but didn't release the full power of their vocalizations. The van would have been intolerable. I rolled down the window to clear the disinfectant smell and soon rolled it back up because it was cold out there.

I waited until we were on the freeway and the van was settled in the middle lane. Letting go of annoyance at Denny was an old challenge. I squared my shoulders, took a breath. This week, we'd worked together, been in danger together. We were both calm. Well, he was calm. There was no reason to think we'd be alone together any time soon. A better opportunity wasn't likely. "Denny. Life doesn't offer up unlimited opportunities, you know. They don't circle back if you miss them the first time."

Any normal person would have said, "Huh? What the hell are you talking about?"

What Denny said was, "That's true and it's not true. Karmic debts don't go away until they're paid. And some life lessons keep repeating until you get them."

He had a talent for derailing me, but I wasn't having it. "You won't find someone like Marcie again. You should make it work."

He shifted in his seat, not looking at me. "We decided to separate for awhile and see how it goes."

It sounded rehearsed. "Not what I'm hearing. She's pretty broken up." I kept my own tone reasonable.

"Why am I talking to *you* about this? This is between her and me."

"I'm collateral damage. She's my best friend." The silence that followed didn't feel quite right. "And you and I, we go way back." *There* was a muddle. What were Denny and I to each other? Co-workers, sure. Ex-lovers from long ago. Friends? Yeah, sort of. With Marcie, I needed to know she was solid and there for me when I fell apart. Pure self-interest. No, not just that. I hurt when she hurt. With Denny—

"I talked to her two days ago. We're friends. She's fine." His voice was firm, but stress leaked out in the line of his mouth.

"Yeah. I heard about that. Not fine."

Silence.

I adjusted the rear-view mirror to check on the birds and set it back. All I could tell was that they hadn't escaped. "Her dad split when she was four and she hardly ever hears from him. She had this abusive boyfriend when we were college roommates. He used to tell her she was fat and stupid. You were her first boyfriend after that—it took her four years to try again. Now you bail on her. She's hurting."

"It's not like that."

"What *is* it like?" When he didn't answer—"She told me she never used the M word, but something flushed you like a pheasant. She's good enough for hooking up now and then, but not for a real commitment. Is that it?"

"Bullshit. You know that's not true, and it disrespects us both."

He sounded angry and he had a right to be. I'd lost patience and gone to goading him.

After a pause, he said, "She's into mellow music, like Jack Johnson. I like Unknown Mortal Orchestra. She's super tidy and clean. I'm not. But the big thing? Whatever she thinks I should do or say, I don't get it right, and she's nice about it. She's always nice about it. She has to *transcend* us both to make it work. We can't keep misaligning and pretending it doesn't matter." Denny's eyes were locked on the Costco truck ahead of us. "You never wanted us together. So what's your beef now?"

He had me there.

Chapter Seven

We were almost to the zoo, in a leaden silence, when I realized the lack of a next step. Where were we supposed to deliver these macaws? Denny called Neal to see what he and Dr. Reynolds had decided. He figured out which button to push to turn on the speaker phone, something I'd never managed.

A tinny little version of Neal's voice said, "You're done out there? No drama?"

"Denny cut his finger. He might need a tetanus shot."

Neal said, "That's an improvement." He was his usual wound-up self. "This favor we're doing wasn't supposed to take two keepers for three days. It's costing us overtime, and lord knows if we'll ever get compensated for it. And the fact that it turned out to be that dangerous for you two has me wondering what the hell our taxes are paying for. I am not happy with the police performance."

His concern for our safety was touching, until I wondered if that had to do with the downside of injured keepers—OSHA investigations, hiring temps, and so on. No doubt I was being unjust. Denny assured him we would never set foot on the Tiptons' farm again and asked, "Where do you want the macaws?"

He said to put them in the quarantine room with the Amazon parrots. Then he remembered that the Amazons were probably wild and the macaws weren't and that the quarantine regulations were different. So use another quarantine room. No, they were all full or about to be. Apparently he and Dr. Reynolds hadn't connected and gotten this settled.

We waited while he told us to put them in various places, proposing and rejecting options. "Hell," he finally said, "where *are* we going to put them? I shoulda figured this out already, but I've been buried in elephant barn meetings, and Fish and Wildlife keeps calling. You got any ideas?"

"Hap has parrots," I said toward the phone. "He might take them." Hap, the zoo's Commissary manager, kept birds at home in elaborate aviaries. "No, cancel that. Disease risk."

Silence as we all thought. "Well, there's always my basement." I meant that as sarcasm, but knew it was a mistake the instant the words were out.

"Good idea. It'll be temporary. You and Denny set them up today, and we'll figure it out tomorrow. Best we can do."

Dead air.

Denny thought this was fine. Not his basement, after all.

How were the two of us going to unload the heavy cage? Damn.

Finley Memorial Zoo is off Interstate 5, south of the Tipton farm and north of Vancouver, Washington. My house is farther south across the Columbia River in Portland, Oregon. We took the zoo exit off Interstate 5 and drove to the employee parking lot, where Denny's van and my car were parked. I explained that he had to drive the zoo van to my house while I drove my car because it held Robby's car seat. He could drive the zoo van back to pick up his vehicle.

Denny headed for the hospital to argue his way into the tortoises' quarantine room and check on his babies, and I left to find Hap and see if he would come along to help unload.

Late afternoon, and Hap was where I expected him, in the Commissary. He sat on the metal counter talking on the phone, a big, scarred man with tattoos up and down his arms. Bald-headed with a closely-cropped beard, he looked tough, which he was. We had a solid, if cautious, friendship.

He finally finished with his produce order. "Iris. You're back to civilization."

"How'd you like to leave early to help us unload the mother of all cages? At my house."

"Me and who else? Will Pete be there?"

"No. Me and Denny. It's their night for dinner out and tango class."

Hap snorted. "Tango? Benita keeps ragging on me to learn that shit with her. You checked with Neal?"

I called Neal and told him I was hijacking Hap. He didn't object.

Hap looked at the sky. "Snow or ice storm by tomorrow. Benita's got to quit driving the Mini Cooper or pop for snow tires." Benita was his petite and ferocious wife.

"I don't think so. The weather report's almost always wrong."

We wrangled our way to the parking lot. Hap and Denny would unload the macaws. I'd pick Robby up on time, and we'd have a quiet dinner at home, just the two of us.

Hap set off toward his vintage Crown Victoria, me toward my Honda. Hap had history with law enforcement—ancient history, to be fair—and thought that driving a retired patrol car was a hoot. I could only imagine what it cost to fill the tank. The zoo van was still in the lot since Denny was still messing with tortoises. Its passenger door wasn't closed right; I could see the seatbelt was out of place and in the way. The macaws would get chilled.

"Hey, wait," I called to Hap and opened the door to look around inside the van. The GPS device was still there. The macaws were fine. Maybe I was imagining things. But I was pretty sure Denny wouldn't have left the door that way. I looked for the plastic bag and couldn't find it.

Damn.

Hap came over to find out what was holding me up.

"Someone broke in."

"You left it unlocked?"

"I guess so." I couldn't remember hearing the chirp. Double damn. "Now this…thing…a bag…from the Tipton house is missing." Why would anyone swipe that? I couldn't believe someone had followed us from the Tipton farm, broken into the zoo, probably thanked his lucky stars that the van was unlocked, and stolen the bag.

I searched the van again, with the same results.

Hap walked over to examine the gate. "Jimmied to keep it from latching." He pointed to the short chunk of two-by-four that kept the gate from closing enough to latch.

Anyone who drove up to the gate from Finley Road had to stop and enter a pass code at a keypad. Then a motor opened the gate. To leave, all you had to do was pull up to the gate and a sensor opened it. The chunk of wood had kept the gate from latching, which meant it could easily be pushed open from either side. Hide in the bushes, wait for a vehicle to come along with a driver who knew the pass code—that would be me—then shove the piece of wood in place. Once everyone had left the lot, push the gate open and walk or drive in.

I got Hap to search the van, which upset the macaws. Denny showed up and confirmed he hadn't touched the bag. I called 911 and told them that what might have been evidence from the Tipton bust had just been stolen, but I didn't really know what it was. I felt like a fool.

We followed instructions to wait. Eventually a patrol car showed up outside the gate. I waved an arm at the sensor inside, the gate opened, and the car pulled in. A few minutes later, I'd told the deputy all I could.

He didn't believe a word of it. "No idea what was in that bag, huh? No idea who stole it? Are you sure?"

Confused and annoyed, I said, "What's the matter with you? I *told* you what happened."

"Iris," Hap said, "he thinks you had a drug buy turn sour."

"Drugs? What? *Listen*, you—"

Hap put a hand on my arm. "We'd better get those birds to your house. Are we done here?"

The deputy said, "I guess so."

I certainly was. "Tell Deputy Gil Gettler about this. Please."

He nodded unconvincingly and lost interest entirely when his radio muttered something comprehensible only to him. He hopped back into the patrol car and took off.

I headed south, alone in my car with my outrage. Hap followed in his Crown Vic, Denny in the zoo van.

Unloading the macaw cage was way worse than getting it into the van in the first place. We never would have gotten it out without Hap. No plastic bag showed up. The three of us wrestled the cage, with the birds horrified into silence, down the steps into the basement. Robby was in day care, which helped. My dogs couldn't stop barking, which didn't. We tilted the cage upright and it barely cleared the basement ceiling. The macaws scrambled for a new perch. Denny and I were breathing hard, Hap wasn't.

We rested in the kitchen with beers for Hap and Denny and a glass of cabernet for me. We spent a few minutes trying to figure out why the Tipton brothers cared about a little glass and a tissue in a bag.

Hap wanted to know how they knew we had it. I said, "Anyone could have been hiding in the woods watching us. I showed it to Denny outside. It wasn't a secret."

Hap opened a second beer. "Maybe not them. A random car prowler might have thought it had something valuable."

"A car prowler would have taken the GPS," I said.

"Maybe that bag is what they were looking for when they searched the barns at night"—Denny's only useful contribution.

I checked my watch. Plenty of time to get Robby. "I wish I knew what was wrapped up in that tissue." Denny was off and running: a safe deposit box key, jewels, a thumb drive with all their sources and customers. "No, thumb drives are too big. I'd have noticed that. Something fragile and tiny, put inside the glass to protect it."

"You should have searched the roadsides in case he threw it away," Denny said. "You can do that tomorrow."

That bag was gone forever and the Tiptons took it. I knew it in my bones.

Chapter Eight

The next day, gratitude coursed through my veins as I clocked in at the Commissary, as welcome as caffeine. I was back to being a mom and an animal keeper, in my own world where the worst problem I would face was a toddler tantrum or a penguin refusing its vitamin-enhanced fish. If both roles meant cleaning up doo-doo, well, that was what I signed up for. Ordinary routine suited me fine. I looked for Hap to thank him again for his help loading the macaw cage the day before, but he wasn't around.

"Iris! You're back." My friend Linda, senior feline keeper, smiled at me. Sturdy and solid, she had let her thick hair grow out to its natural color, an enviable red. "I thought you were on a one-day boondoggle and now I hear all kinds of stories."

"I am totally behind on everything, and I don't want to repeat the same story a dozen times. I'll tell all at lunch. What's been happening here? Quick version."

"That's not fair." She fake-pouted for thirty seconds before bringing me up to date.

We walked and talked. I'd started as the feline keeper and could never entirely let go of the cats. "Have you put Losa and Yuri together yet?" I asked. Our clouded leopard pair had bred successfully two years ago, and we were eager for a repeat.

"It's the right time of year, but so far she's not interested. Maybe in a month."

"And the tiger girls?"

"Fat and sassy. Come by on break. They'll be out."

Nadia and Katrina were Amur tigers, two-year-old sisters. They lived where my old tiger buddy, Rajah, now deceased, had resided for his long life.

What a pleasure to talk with a friend about the ordinary joys of my job.

This was a Saturday. I was always assigned to Birds on Saturday and Sunday, when Calvin Lorenz, the senior bird keeper, was off. I usually worked Birds with him two or three additional days a week as well. Pete had filled in while I dealt with crises at the Tipton farm.

Linda's path diverged from mine and I headed for the Penguinarium kitchen. No ice storm had materialized nor had snow, aside from a light dusting, which was being eradicated by the rain.

Underfoot was asphalt, not mud, and there wasn't a law officer or crime technician in sight. An ordinary day at the zoo. Perfect.

Except that I remembered my first task was reporting to Neal, which wasn't routine. I swerved off to his office.

My boss was a little taller than I, maybe five-foot-nine, but he projected six-foot-six worth of impatience. Short brown hair, piercing blue eyes, great posture with square shoulders. His background was a complicated history of military, corporate, and zoo positions. I'd seen him laugh, but never relax.

"The macaws are settled in my basement," I said. "Mission really accomplished." Then I had to tell him about the stolen bag in the parking lot, which made me look like an idiot. I couldn't keep it a secret—he'd find out eventually.

His reaction managed to combine alarm and disbelief. "I'm going to have Maintenance search that van again. This makes no sense."

I dodged further discussion by asking where I should take the macaws. He massaged the bridge of his nose between thumb and forefinger. "I'm working on it. It should come in for a landing soon."

"They're close-banded, so I'm pretty sure they're pet birds."

"Agreed. They aren't part of the parrot and tortoise hairball that's giving me ulcers. Every agency in every form of government for miles around has a stake in one or the other."

"And where is it that you want the macaws to end up, exactly?"

He tapped his fingers on his desk. "I appreciate that you went the extra mile in a really tough situation. I know I can count on you to manage the gap for now."

The bullshit was a signal he was stumped—he hadn't a clue where he could park the macaws other than my basement. I felt duped. That gave me the right to press him a little. "Everyone agrees that the Amazon parrots are illegal, right?"

"I'm told there's no record of any permits to import them."

"So what's happening to catch the smugglers? Is Fish and Wildlife tracking them back to the source?"

He made a little tent with his fingers resting on the desk. "You may be surprised to learn that law enforcement doesn't copy me on their internal reports of investigations. We don't meet for coffee and bran muffins. I'm just supposed keep the birds alive until they decide what to do with them."

"But are they going after these guys or not?"

"The Tiptons, the surviving ones, are in hot water up to their red necks already. So maybe not. But I have no idea. Aren't you assigned to Birds today? If you don't have enough to do…"

I plowed on. "The Tiptons were the middlemen. There's no reason to think they went to Mexico and caught the birds and brought them across the border themselves. Someone else did that and sold them to someone who sold to the Tiptons. That's a chain that needs to be broken."

"I couldn't agree with you more. Now if you'll excuse me, I've got work to do and so do you. And, by the way, those tortoises are the big deal. They're worth a wad to collectors, some of them are from Madagascar, and it's pretty strange that they ended up with a family that never made a blip before with Fish and Wildlife."

"They'd been selling weed for years and no one noticed that."

I left in a sulk, depressed about the smugglers and sullen about the macaws. I had nothing against the macaws personally, but they were noisy, their cage was guilt-inspiring, the feather plucking was dismaying, and Robby had to be kept away from them lest they nip off a hand. Not my first choice for house guests, and I seemed to be stuck with them.

I ran into Marion, the veterinary technician, on the way to the Penguinarium. She was young and round with ruddy cheeks and looked like she should be herding geese with bows around their necks through some bucolic, sun-lit pasture. She wore a standard brown uniform accessorized with a dozen enamel pins on her chest, mostly big-eyed baby animals. This demure exterior often misled the unwary.

"How are the parrots in quarantine?" I asked.

"Eating like there's no tomorrow. There's ca-ca everywhere in that room."

"What about the tortoises? Is that little one any better?"

"Still sick."

A little more of my delight in a normal day faded.

She wanted to know all about the Tiptons, and I told her, "Details at noon."

Marion chose not to pass up the opportunity to bitch as we stood with our arms wrapped across our chests in a chilly wind. "Denny is driving me nuts about those tortoises. Dr. Reynolds says no way can he hang out at the hospital, which he knows perfectly well, the idiot. Can he spell 'quarantine'? No, he cannot. He's fixated on substrates and humidity and UV light, nagging at me nonstop. They're all eating now. He should go be happy someplace and get off my case."

I backed away making sympathetic noises.

At the Penguinarium, I spent half an hour reviewing the notes Calvin left for me plus the standard records of each minor event or anomaly from the previous three days. One penguin had declined her vitamin fish two days running, but ate fine otherwise. The Bali mynahs were not happy about the new low-iron pellets. The female nene, or Hawaiian goose, in the aviary was limping, but her foot looked fine. Calvin's guess, and mine, was arthritis since she was a geriatric bird. All of this was wonderfully normal and my spirits lifted again.

I stood at the baby gate set across the door between the kitchen and the African penguin exhibit and examined each bird for a few minutes. Nobody limped or bled or sat hunched up. I set to work stuffing vitamin pills into fish as the penguins brayed orders to hurry it up. Even the heavy scent of fish eaters was a comfort.

After the morning feeding, I scrubbed the aviary pond and wondered what was in that wretched bag and why the Tiptons thought it was so important. Was there a connection to Liana's death? For the life of me, I couldn't see one. Or a connection to the smugglers, either.

At lunch time, I ducked into the administration building and down the steps to the basement. This was the new employee break room—"new" as in newly designated for our use. The zoo café manager had wearied of us clustering at the indoor tables all winter, leaving his "real" customers, the visitors, to eat their hot dogs while standing. Worse, they could overhear our discussions of fecal matter, insects, and sex habits of exotic species. Now the keepers were privileged to eat in this basement at a table next to the copy machine. The room was airless and the décor dispiriting, but it was warm and dry, characteristics we all valued highly in winter. And no one interrupted lunch to ask us where the bathrooms were or why we didn't have pandas.

Denny and Linda, the feline keeper, were there already. My housemates Pete and Cheyenne were eating also, as was Marion with her Bambi jewelry, so the little room was nearly at capacity. Pete was working Primates today. Cheyenne was always on Elephants because it was so specialized, although Elephants included the giraffes and other hoof stock.

Ian, the lead elephant keeper, and Arnie, the bear keeper, rarely joined us. Ian was shy to the edge of catatonia, and flaky Arnie long ago discovered that he'd had used up my tolerance as well as Linda's.

Denny had already shared most of the disasters at the Tiptons' farm to a fascinated audience. I wasn't eager to revisit Jerome and Liana Tipton's deaths, but there was no escaping it. Hearing Denny describe how I'd found Liana's body depressed me all over again. It also reminded me that the circumstances didn't make sense.

I was correcting details about moving the parrots when Jackie, the zoo's office manager since fish crawled onto land, dropped in with a local newspaper.

"This is great stuff," she said. "Best news since that huge travel trailer fell off the freeway into the river." Reality rarely satisfied Jackie's thirst for drama. Her poofy hair was an unconvincing jet black, which somehow suited her sharp features and inquisitive dark eyes.

I skimmed the articles about the Tiptons. It described the shooting death of a teenage girl believed to be their daughter, nothing new. The pictures were mug shots of the sons. Jefferson Davis Tipton looked like a frightened Cape Buffalo, a burly guy ready to bolt or charge. Thomas Jefferson Tipton seemed to have a little more cognition going on, but he didn't look like Citizen of the Year either. They were wanted for questioning in regard to the death of their sister, but were believed to have fled to California. I found no mention of myself or Denny. I handed the paper to Linda.

Denny ticked off items on his fingertips. "We've got drugs. We've got illegal wildlife. What goes with that kind of criminal pipeline? Weapons. Human trafficking."

"Whoa! I didn't see any sex slaves in the barns," I said.

Jackie and Linda stared at him. Pete and Cheyenne looked at each other, one of those couple things. Marion snickered.

Denny chewed on his veggie burger. We watched his Adam's apple as he swallowed and regained his voice. "Same criminal networks run all of those. Not always, but they overlap. These are the big dollar international crimes, billions and billions." Denny had a weakness for conspiracy theories, but he was on target with this. "The Tiptons are the tip of the iceberg. The cops missed a weapons stash is my guess." No longer on target.

"Well. Ain't we got fun?" Jackie said. "This zoo business gets more exciting all the time." She rolled her eyes at me and reclaimed her paper. I grabbed it back and checked the byline before I relinquished it. Not Craig Darsee.

I ate and climbed up the stairs to get back to work, only to find Officer Gil Gettler waiting for me. Jackie ushered us into the tiny conference room between Neal and Mr. Crandal's offices, located near enough to her desk to permit eavesdropping through the thin wall. We both declined coffee. The office coffee was always terrible.

"I'm here about your recent incident. Could you tell me about this stolen evidence?" He'd been a fixture at the farm, but I'd never really looked at him. He was trim and tidy in a crisp uniform with chunks of lethal-looking black gear hanging off his belt. He looked to be about forty, with arms and shoulders that implied he worked out. I braced myself for criticism.

We sat around a rectangular table and I walked through finding the bag, failing to find anyone to turn it over to, and what the bag and its contents looked like. "It was an ordinary plastic bag and a boring little water glass. Not exactly Waterford crystal." I showed dimensions with my hands and, as requested, sketched the glass in his notebook. "The tissue was wadded up inside. I didn't take it out so I can't say what was hidden there, but I think there might have been something. The tissue wasn't very clean."

"You said it was behind the bird cage against the wall."

"Yeah. This cage—I can show it to you—is pretty old and I think it's homemade. It sits flat on the floor instead of raised up on legs with coasters. It's hard to move. No one could have gotten at the bag without some work. I didn't see it until I went back to sweep up."

"You took the cage?"

"It's at my house." Gettler looked surprised, so I explained why the macaws were in my basement. I assured him he was free to discuss the matter with Neal and suggest a different home for them.

"How could this bag have gotten where you found it?"

I'd been thinking about that. "One way would be when the cage was first set up. But it wouldn't be that hard to do later. The cage has small doors so you can reach in to feed and water from either side. The door on the far side wasn't hard against the wall. You could reach in, unlatch it from the inside, and push it open three or four inches. Then you could drop the bag down between the cage and the wall. If you wanted to hide it, toss some birdseed and feathers after it. Then close the latch again."

"So anyone could have put it there."

"Not really. Whoever did it had to stick their hand in with the macaws. They're likely to bite."

"How bad would that be? What if you wore gloves?"

I shook my head. "With gloves, you couldn't unlatch the far door. Without them, you could get chomped pretty good. But if the birds knew and liked you, you could try it without gloves."

His eyebrows went up. "Who knew you'd found this?"

"I can't remember who was around when I brought it outside and showed it to Denny. It was a bright day. Someone could have watched us from the woods and seen me bring the bag out. You could hide an army around that place." Pluvia had said that Tom and Jeff watched from the woods.

He moved on to the van robbery in the employee parking lot. If he didn't believe me, at least he was polite about it. He said, "That bag might have nothing to do with the Tiptons, but if you find it, we'd like to see it. It's a murder investigation, and we have to follow up on all the leads. Thank you for your time."

He was being dutiful and doubtful, and I couldn't blame him. I moved to another concern. "Um, are you looking into the wildlife smuggling? Where they got the parrots and tortoises?"

"That would be the Feds. You could contact US Fish and Wildlife."

I might have to do that.

"Uh, one more thing."

He waited, eyes alert.

"Liana wasn't killed during the bust, right? She didn't die where I found her."

A stiff smile. "Let me know if you remember anything else of significance." And he took his leave.

When I clocked out at the Commissary building, I looked for Hap and found him in a back corner at his computer, his bald head bent close to the screen, thick fingers poking at the keyboard. "Who the hell boosts canned marmoset diet?" he demanded. "Is there a black market for canned monkey food nobody ever told me about?"

"Inventory program savaging you again?" I tried to be sympathetic. Hap hated that program, mostly because he didn't like Neal, and Neal was the one who insisted he keep it up to date. "Maybe Kip took a couple of cans and forgot to tell you."

"It's a whole carton short. And it shows an extra carton of turtle diet."

I debated saying the obvious and finally went for it. "Sounds like it was logged in wrong when they were delivered."

"Get outa here. Go home and feed our kid."

"Our kid" was Hap's little joke, based on me wearing his uniform in the last stages of pregnancy because no one else's would fit. It was not anything to be mentioned around his wife, Benita. She was highly territorial in regards to Hap, who in his less conventional years had given her excellent reasons for suspicion. I wondered from time to time why they never had children. The zoo staff overall had a very low rate of reproduction, and my co-workers seemed to regard Robby as an example of a rare and fascinating species.

"Hap, I want you to come over again. Bring Benita. I'll buy cookies. That macaw setup isn't great, and one of them is chewing on his feathers. Neal's got no plan to get them out of my basement any time soon." I'd read that at least a quarter of captive macaws pull out their own feathers. Smart, active birds confined to a tiny world get bored and frustrated.

"There's half a dozen macaw sanctuaries he could call." Hap poked a key and swore.

"It's probably held up by the court case."

"That would be his story. I'll come by tonight, but it may be late. Benita slid on the ice and creamed the side mirror on her Mini. I gotta fix it. Shouldn't be too bad."

"Great. Call if it doesn't work out. I turn back into stone about ten o'clock."

Hap pointed to his computer. "Where am I supposed to get dandelion greens in January? Denny can grow his own weeds for those tortoises."

I clocked out and wasted half an hour walking the road to and from the freeway looking for the lost bag. I found plenty of beer cans, a sofa cushion, and a smashed pizza box. Duty done, I drove to my parents' and found Robby engrossed at the kitchen sink. He demonstrated that a plastic triceratops would not float and provided a lengthy and mostly incomprehensible narrative as I helped him into his coat.

At home, Pete was cooking eggplant with green curry and tofu. That was one of the major benefits of having him and Cheyenne as housemates—he loved to cook. They had lived with me since I was pregnant with Robby and paid half the mortgage payment and utilities in return for a bedroom and the run of the place. I found Cheyenne a little tough to live with, but she and Pete were good to Robby and overall, they were a huge plus.

I offered Robby a sample of Pete's creation, a peanut butter sandwich, and some peas. I dove into the curry.

Cheyenne seemed subdued.

"Don't like it?" Pete asked.

"No, it's fine." She opened a second beer, which wasn't common. "We got the blood test results on Nakri. Not pregnant."

I looked up from collecting the eggplant Robby was rejecting. "Oh, that's too bad. It all went so well."

Six months ago, Cheyenne had predicted Finley Zoo would have its first elephant birth. The younger of our two Asian elephant cows, Nakri, had been the recipient of semen a veterinarian had brought from a bull at another zoo. The artificial insemination had gone "perfectly" according to Cheyenne, meaning Nakri had stood still for the expert, something the elephant keepers had spent months training her to do. The procedure had gone according to plan. Except that egg and sperm had stood each other up.

Artificial insemination was the only way Nakri would ever know motherhood since Finley Zoo lacked the facilities to house a bull elephant. No one wanted to ship her away from Damrey, her blind companion, to mate with a bull the usual way. I picked peas off Robby's shirt. "Will they try again?" Nakri would probably vote "yes"—she would earn a steady stream of treats for the insemination and the regular blood draws to track her hormones.

"I guess. If we can afford it. Neal's going to look at the budget. Pete, I found Irish music at this coffee house on Division. Let's eat and go."

Pete said he was too tired. Cheyenne took the stairs to their room in a huff.

Hap showed up, alone, right as I was starting the bedtime routine. He ignored me and my parrot concerns. Instead, he said "hi" to Pete, who was on his way upstairs, and then crawled around on the floor trotting and bucking with Robby on his back. He rolled Robby, already choking with laugher, onto the rug and tickled his belly. The dogs circled and barked, trying to figure out how to join the fun.

I kept myself from telling Hap to dial it back. Robby was loving it, and Hap wasn't going to break him. My boy didn't have a father, and he spent most of his time with me, my mother, and his day care provider—women who tried hard to be calm and gentle with him. My dad was more physical, although Pete wasn't. Hap was taking it to a new level. Guy time. Gender appropriate. A Good Thing.

When I couldn't take it any longer, I said, "Hap, he needs to calm down or I'll never get him to bed."

Robby voted against calming down, but Hap backed off and settled on the sofa with him and the farm animals. Robby slowly lost momentum as he showed Hap the correct way to arrange chickens and pigs so the triceratops could eat them. I left Hap to evaluate the macaws in the basement while I carted him up to bed.

Hap was watching "Dancing with the Stars" when I made it back to the living room. He clicked the TV off, reluctantly, and we talked about the birds—toys and other entertainment, diet, a bigger cage. He said he'd bring over a spare cage he had and connect it to the existing one. He'd figured out a structure that would occupy most of my basement and allow them to fly a little.

"We can do better than what you've got right now," he said, "but it's still piss poor. The sanctuary I'm thinking of has this huge flight cage. Get Neal to send them there, with a donation to pay for expenses. It ain't free, housing dozens of rejected parrots."

"Sure, Hap. All I have to do is ask. Neal always does whatever I want."

He ignored this and leaned back on the sofa, his elbows resting on its back. "So, Iris. You seeing anybody yet? With your looks, it shouldn't be that hard."

"What? No, not right now." Where was this coming from? Thankfully, he didn't sound like he was offering himself as a candidate. "Better not let Benita hear you talk like that."

Hap grinned. "She was the one who pointed out what a babe you are. Me, I never notice that sort of thing. So…What's holding up the parade?"

"Excuse me? You're taking charge of my love life?"

"Nope. Just asking why you aren't out there."

"Mind your own business" was on the tip of my tongue, but Hap was a friend and parenting had taught me not to give irritation its head. And he was helping with the macaws. "I'll get around to it. I'm busy, in case you hadn't noticed."

"No pressure. Benita wants me to ask if you'd like to meet a guy she knows. He's good."

"Hap, I'll tell you when I need you to pimp…to find blind dates for me."

"Sure you will. Well, I had to ask. Don't keep your mad on for too long."

"Not mad. Just busy."

I puttered around after he left, closing down the house. Romping with my kid and helping me with Birds didn't earn Hap a license to remodel my life. My mother had exclusive rights to that. Ah—playing with Robby triggered this. He thought Robby should have a daddy.

Hap wasn't the first to raise the issue of my social life. A few months ago, Linda suggested ditching the wedding ring. "You'll never get paired up again if you keep that on." I'd mulled it over—loyalty to Rick, people thinking I was an unwed mother, no time or energy for dating—and decided to try living without it.

Mr. Right, whoever he was, hadn't noticed. Now the universe was nudging again.

The more I thought about the guys I'd met at Hap and Benita's parties, the funnier it got. Their circle of friends did not run to people with steady jobs and parenting potential. I pictured myself test-driving part-time roofers and shade-tree mechanics, men who who spent their weekends drinking beer at motorcycle rallies.

Pete was coming out of the bathroom when I climbed upstairs. I was still laughing and wouldn't tell him why.

Chapter Nine

You don't get to sleep in on your day off if you live with a toddler. We were all up at the usual six o'clock. Pete and Cheyenne went off to work. Faced with a day at home with his mother, Robby tugged at my sleeve and said, "Pay wit' Hap." I couldn't compete with a bronco ride from Hap, but I did my best.

At the off-leash area in Laurelhurst Park, I tossed a foam ball to Robby and tennis balls to Winnie and Range. When the dogs were panting hard enough, we moved across the road to the playground. The dogs flopped down and panted away while Robby and two bigger girls clambered about on the elaborate bright blue climbing structure. It was a reasonably dry and satisfying morning, ending with a flushed and cheerful Robby and two contented dogs.

After lunch, I suggested that he exercise his creative side. "Let's draw with the new markers. This one smells like grape." My celebration of normal life was over and unfinished business from the Tipton farm had swept back into my awareness. I had an agenda.

While Robby unleashed the right side of his brain, I found the scrap of paper Ken from Animal Control had handed me when I'd asked for his card. I made a phone call to ease my mind. It seemed to be his personal number, and he wasn't in. I hesitated about the voice message—leaving my own number might be misconstrued as—what? A come-on? I left my name and the number anyway and asked whether he'd gotten the Doberman pup out of the rain. I hung up and stood with my hand on the phone wondering whether I did have a subconscious motive. No, I'd meant to call him before Hap had messed with my mind.

I intended to make a second call, but good sense intervened. Neal would not appreciate me contacting US Fish and Wildlife directly about their intentions and strategies in regard to certain illegal wildlife now held at the zoo. I'd try asking Neal again. I paced around for a few minutes trying to think how I could strike a blow for conservation and came up empty. I had nothing to help track the animals back to the wholesaler. Wildlife crimes had happened under my nose, and there wasn't a thing I could do about it, any more than I could nail whoever had murdered Liana.

Robby and I burned the rest of the day with grocery shopping and housekeeping, which included adding branches to the macaw cage for them to destroy. Everyone needs a hobby and my vine maple needed trimming.

I'd invited Marcie for dinner because Cheyenne told me she and Pete were going out to try a new restaurant. I put a chicken in the oven to pot-roast and laid out sweet potatoes as a reminder to stick them in the oven later. A salad, carrots to microwave for Robby, a bag of organic cookies, and dinner was checked off.

Robby roared around the living room on the red train engine my parents had gotten him for Christmas until I drafted him to help set the table. He trotted back and forth from where I stood at the silverware drawer to the dining room table, toting one fork or spoon or knife at a time. After I released him back to his train engine, I arranged the flatware in the conventional pattern. The dogs announced Marcie's arrival.

"Mar, come pay wit me!" Robby scooted past at an alarming velocity.

"Coming, honey." To me, "You swore you were going to deep-six that thing."

"But he loves it. I took the batteries out so now it's mute, and I don't have to hate it. Ask him about his drawings."

Marcie toiled in a clean, warm corporate cubicle writing technical things. She liked her job and it paid well, but she never risked a talon in the eye or a hoof in the mouth, and she seemed to feel she was missing out. We'd been best buds since my unsuccessful attempt at college, discontinued after my second year. She'd gone on to graduate, but we'd stayed close. A few months ago, she'd urged me to work toward a promotion. "You need the income and someday you'll get bored with routine and being second-fiddle."

She was sane and calm when I wasn't and had seen me through a lot of rough weather. I wanted to do the same for her, even if my skill set didn't skew that way.

She looked better than she had the week before, not as grim and weary. She had come straight from work dressed in white pants and pink blouse with a little silvery jacket. Robby abandoned the train to show her his art work. I was slow, and he clipped her knee with a felt-tip pen, a peppermint-scented green slash. "It's washable," I assured her, hoping that was true.

During dinner, the macaws started vocalizing, which I used to introduce my misadventures at the Tipton farm. Drama was one of my important contributions to our friendship. I soft-pedaled the scarier parts as well as Denny's role to avoid stirring up negative emotions.

Marcie was horrified anyway. "Finding that poor girl sounds awful. Who would shoot her? Her brothers wouldn't, and they were in prison anyway."

"They could have done it. They were out of prison the day before I found her."

"They wouldn't kill their *sister*."

Who knew what the Tipton family dynamics were all about? Marcie and I were both only children. We had zip experience with sibling rivalry. "The cops are focused on the death and the drugs. They'll find them and figure out which one killed her and why. I want them to trace the smuggling pipeline, too, but I don't see any way to make sure that happens. It bugs me. After days of having those animals in my face, it's back to routine."

I helped Robby out of his highchair. I started to sit down, but he climbed up the back of the sofa, the better to help a plastic sheep fly. I hauled him off and explained once again that the back of the sofa was forbidden territory—too tippy. He crawled under a chair to track down his sheep. Winnie joined him and almost knocked over the floor lamp. I caught it in time and scolded her. The macaws screamed.

Marcie said, "Routine, huh?"

I gave her a look.

"The chicken was great," she said, changing the subject. "Dill and thyme."

I shrugged modestly as I stroked Winnie to console her for being scolded. I couldn't remember for the life of me which jars of leafy stuff I'd used. "An old family recipe."

"Is not. I showed you that method, only with tarragon."

Whatever. It was good to have her all to myself again, after two years of accommodating Denny. The realization incited a throb of guilt. Heartbreak therapy was my role, not taking advantage.

Marcie looked thoughtful. "So those awful men are in California. Maybe they'll try for a fresh start. Maybe that's what I should do, try another state."

My heart constricted. "I thought maybe…things were better."

She gave a dismissive hand wave. "I'm fine. Let's watch a movie. I brought three—you choose."

"I tried to talk to him when we were driving back from the Tiptons the last time. I told him he was making a big mistake."

"Iris, I appreciate the thought, but you'd better stay out of it." She held her hands up to show she meant it.

"I just want you to have someone who makes you happy. He's so goofy and unpredictable…"

"Enough!"

"Right. Sorry. Sit tight while I put Robby down."

Half an hour later, I returned to find her staring at the TV, her face blank. I chose *New Moon* from the Twilight saga. I'd missed it when it came out and knew Marcie wanted to see it again. I got it set up and found the remote.

Marcie said, "So...what did he say?" Her voice was casual, her hands folded tight in her lap.

"When I told Denny he was making a big mistake? Um, that you were too different from each other and were both trying too hard. Aren't there any nice guys where you work or at your gym? Normal people?"

"Iris. You are locked into an out-of-date understanding of Denny. You never got why we...I..." Her eyes filled up. "He dumped ...left ...because ...never mind. Just let it alone and watch the damned movie with me."

So we did. Marcie was rapt, but I couldn't get into the doomed romance between Edward, the youthful-but-ancient vampire, and high school girl Bella. I snorted when Bella half-drowned herself so that he would have to show up and save her and she could see him again. When the fuzzy werewolves galloped in, I laughed out loud. Too late, I saw Marcie flinch.

She stood up, said, "Thanks very much for the dinner. I have to go now," grabbed her coat, and walked out.

Chapter Ten

I felt like banging my head against the wall when Marcie was gone. Stupid, stupid, stupid. She wanted to see that movie again because she loved it, and she loved it because of the doomed romance, and I had laughed and ruined it. I waited until she had time to drive home, then called. She didn't pick up. I left a message to please, please call me.

I was wrestling Robby out of his clothes for a bath when the phone rang. I grabbed it as he ran around the living room in just a diaper, giggling hysterically. It wasn't Marcie. "Oh. Ken," I said. "You're working late."

"Nope. I'm at home. You called about that little black-and-tan. She surrendered yesterday. Safe and warm at the humane society."

His voice was not sluggish—*easy*. That was the word. Easy.

"Oh, good. Thanks for letting me know. She's pretty—somebody will adopt her, right?" Please let something good come out of the Tipton disasters.

Robby climbed on his engine and scooted around the living room. Winnie took a notion to frisk alongside, barking. I tried to focus on the call.

"Oh, she'll find a home. Which reminds me…You live in Portland? There's a barbeque place I've been wanting to try. Podners. Texas-style smoked ribs. Care to join me Friday night?"

I was the one who paused this time. A date? Yes, he was talking about a date. "Ahhh…Um…Sure. I think so. I have a kid, did I mention that? A two-year-old."

"So. Married?"

"Widowed."

"You could bring the kid."

"No, no. I think I can find a sitter…But I need to make it an early evening, 'cause I work weekends."

"No problem. Should I pick you up or do you want to meet there?"

Meeting there sounded good. He gave me the address and hung up.

Why did I tell him about Robby as if my child were a case of herpes? Why did Ken hang in there while I sputtered? Why had I said yes? This was Hap's fault.

And maybe it was a mistake. Ken had a great voice and that chipped front tooth was cute and he seemed smart and pleasant, but…

But what? I was just nervous. Out of practice. Chicken-livered.

I snagged a squealing Robby off the engine and lugged him upstairs to the bathtub.

When he was asleep, I let go of first-date jitters, fired up my laptop, and poked around on the Internet looking for information about wildlife trafficking. This had been on my to-do list since visiting the Tipton farm. The volume of animals and the dollars the conservation sites reported made me want to weep. Tortoises were especially hard-hit. I confirmed that the United States is a huge importer of wildlife, much of it for pets. Some of the animals shipped here left their home country with permits obtained by bribes or just plain faked. I logged on to Multnomah County Library and reserved a couple of recent books on the subject.

Winnie and Range pushed outside through the doggy door and started barking as if a cougar lurked in the back yard. The outside light revealed the dogs yelling by the back fence. I stuck my head out and called them, which they ignored. The front door opened, and I jumped, but it was Pete and Cheyenne. The dogs blustered inside with the hair along their spines bristling. Probably a raccoon on the prowl. Still, it was strange to see them so aroused.

"How was the new restaurant?" I asked. "You stayed late."

Pete gave Cheyenne a quick glance.

"It wasn't that good," she said. "We went shopping afterward. I'm off to bed."

I shut down the computer, checked that all the doors were locked, and grabbed the first shower. I lay in bed and sought calming thoughts to encourage sleep, something to override smuggled animals. I revisited Birds for the new aviary. Would Demoiselle cranes need to be kept separate from visitors? I'd read that they could be aggressive…The date with Ken rose to the surface. Why was I so skittish about a dinner date? Not just loyalty to Rick—worry about how dating would affect Robby, concern about finding the time and energy. I fell asleep wondering whatever happened to the Iris who leapt into relationships without a thought.

I was off work the next day as well. Marcie did not call. In the afternoon, Hap showed up in a huge black pickup that he'd borrowed. He lugged wire panels into the basement and banged around installing them. When he presented the results with a beer-bottle flourish, I found that I had a passage to the washing machine and dryer and access to the basement door. The rest of the basement was a ginormous macaw palace, as long and wide as the foundation walls permitted. The birds still had their old cage, with one door wired open for access to the new structure. They stuck tight to their familiar perch, looking alarmed and outraged.

Hap inserted branches strategically to encourage them to move around. "When they get used to it, pull out some of these so that they have to fly to get from one end to the other."

I hung a nice fruit kabob in the new space. "Come on, guys," I said to the birds. "Be happy. It's new and a little scary, but it's better. Truly." We left them to adjust.

I considered telling Hap about my date and decided I wouldn't give him the satisfaction. I did give him a six-pack of his favorite beer, and he had another wild romp with Robby.

◇◇◇

When I clocked in on Wednesday, my Monday, I found out I was scheduled for Primates instead of Birds. That was unexpected, but not unprecedented. Kip Harrison, the senior primate keeper, was already chopping fruit in the primate kitchen. Small, skinny, and tough, built like a strip of jerky and just as salty, she grunted a greeting and cut to the news. "Violet popped last night." Violet was a female mandrill monkey who had been bulging as if she were gestating a litter.

"All good?" I asked. "Just one?" Mandrill twins are rare, but they do happen.

"Just one, a big boy, but not so good. When I came in, it was on the floor. She sat next to it, but she didn't hold it."

Bad sign. Humans are unusual among primate species because we put our newborns down. As a rule, ape and monkey mothers carry their babies twenty-four/seven for months, until the baby is ambitious enough to let go and try moving around on its own. "And now?"

"She's still in her own night den. Dr. Reynolds is coming by to check her out."

"This is her first, right? Has she ever been around a baby?"

Kip shrugged. "Maybe when she was little, before she came here. Maybe not."

I didn't say what we were both thinking, that Violet had better pull this together or we'd be hand-raising a baby monkey. Or mourning one. Motherhood isn't as instinctual as we'd like to think. Experience matters.

I fed the new father, Sky, and Carmine, the troop's other female. The mandrill mom had already received her breakfast. With Kip's permission, I dropped by to pay my respects. Violet looked exhausted. Never as vivid as her mate's, her blue muzzle with a pink stripe seemed even more faded today. She sat with the baby draped face-down over her thigh, the infant making an effort to hang on. He was doing his part in the tricky interplay of mother and infant, where if one doesn't follow the script of normal behavior, the other won't either. Violet glanced at him now and then without touching him. I offered a bite of cantaloupe through the mesh. She took it in her dark, delicate fingers and sucked on it, watching me with distant brown eyes.

"I know how you feel," I told her. "Trust me, it gets better. It's never easy, but it gets better. Put him on your chest, girl, that's where he belongs." She looked away, and I left her to rest.

Kip set me to work cleaning the Diana monkey exhibit while the animals ate breakfast in their night quarters. I swept and bagged straw bedding in the tall, narrow exhibit, doing a careful job because I'd learned the hard way that little bits of straw would gang up and clog the drain when I hosed. The work was peaceful in a mindless way.

After lunch, I found Kip and asked if I could check on Violet and her baby again before I started fixing the afternoon diets.

"Leave her alone for now. Dr. Reynolds wants her separated in the night den for tonight. I saw the baby try to nurse, but she doesn't like it. She better get with the program soon—we can't keep her separated for very long."

"You're worried Sky will beat her up when she goes back in."

"Or Carmine. Carmine was a real bitch to her when they were first together."

Kip had to attend a senior keeper meeting at 2:30, so she was forced to ask me to do what she clearly would rather have done herself. She handed me a little deli container of blueberries. "When you're done with the diets, go sit by Violet and give her one of these when she lets the baby nurse."

Fresh blueberries in January? Kip must have spent her lunch hour at a grocery store, not to mention five or six bucks.

The baby was hanging on to Violet's belly—progress. I didn't mind spending an hour sitting on cold concrete with my butt going to sleep, handing her a treat whenever he managed to suckle a little. She seemed too out of it to notice why she was being rewarded—tolerating suckling—but the fruit did distract her from pulling the baby off. Poor mom. I felt her pain. Her rear end hurt, she hadn't gotten any sleep, and this weird little creature was messing with her. The baby sported a dark cap, a wrinkled little muzzle, and big, dark, liquid eyes. His pink skin shone through a thin fuzz of gray hair. When he gave up trying to nurse and fell asleep, Violet's head sagged and her eyelids drooped. The baby woke up and started suckling again while his mother slept sitting up. I sat still, afraid to move.

If she wouldn't let the baby nurse enough, we'd have to remove him. Bottle-raising would produce a monkey that knew more about humans than about mandrills, a monkey that would be the rejected loser in the troop.

When Kip returned, Violet woke up and pulled the baby off her teat. "Honey, do not *do* that," I said, creaking to my feet.

"She'll get the hang of it," Kip said without conviction. "I'll drop by tonight to check on them."

I expected this—that was the sort of thing she did. That was the sort of thing *I* did, before Robby.

Kip said she had to catch up on animal records, and I should scrub out the rest of the night dens. That's what I get paid the big bucks for.

Chapter Eleven

Thursday I was assigned to Birds, but I dropped by Primates to visit the mandrills and see how Violet was doing. She looked a little perkier. She was back with her troop, Sky and Carmine. Kip gave the new mom a passing grade. The baby was nursing and being carried properly. Kip didn't say anything about naming the baby. Usually the director, Mr. Crandall, made a big hullabaloo over that. He liked naming baby animals after big donors or city councilmen or letting one of them choose the name. This wasn't happening yet, which might imply that he and Neal and Kip weren't all that confident about the baby surviving.

On morning break, I watched the group from the visitor area, staying quiet and a little back so that the animals wouldn't worry about my uniform. They know that regular visitors are irrelevant to their lives and treat them like television or ignore them. Keepers are a different matter, especially if they aren't behaving normally, which to them means the daily routine.

The inside exhibit was fairly roomy, with lots of rocks and a concrete tree. Their outside yard was closed off due to the weather. Violet huddled in a corner with her baby. Carmine puttered around foraging in the straw bedding. Sky, over twice the size of the females, sat above them on a tree limb. He yawned at me, displaying his huge canine teeth, and closed his mouth with care, fitting those choppers into his gums just right. Kip said that his yawn was a threat or sometimes just a sign he was feeling tense.

After a few minutes, he climbed down and approached Violet, moving slowly. She didn't notice him until he was about ten feet away. The instant she saw him, she pulled the baby off her nipple, held him to her belly with one hand, and scooted away on three legs. I could hear the baby's eh-eh-eh of protest. Sky stared hard at Violet and slapped the ground with a hand, a clear threat. He backed it up with a head bob. Violet crammed herself into a high corner as far away from him as she could get and shot nervous glances his way. Sky walked to where she'd been sitting, lowered his massive muzzle, and sniffed at the spot. He climbed with hands and feet back up the artificial tree to his perch on a broad limb. Violet scrambled down and tried another corner.

I didn't like the looks of this interaction—threatening the mother and baby—and described it to Kip. "He's always cranky," she said, "and he's never seen a baby either. Probably just curious. I don't think he'd hurt the baby."

She knew them far better than I did.

Calvin and I expected a busy day at Birds. Dr. Reynolds had scheduled physicals for the penguins. We'd wrangled penguins for her many a time, and it went smoothly. Which is to say, after it was over, I stank of fish, had a swelling lump on my knee where I'd fallen in the slippery exhibit, and was bleeding from a chomp on my left thumb courtesy of Mr. Brown/White. Mr. B/W was a youngster with a two-tone band on his wing because we'd run out of colors and had to double up. He wasn't any more resentful of physical restraint than the other birds, I just got careless. Under Dr. Reynolds' watchful eye, I'd rinsed and ointmented and bandaged my wound. The smart money said I'd survive.

The birds had donated blood samples, been vaccinated, and endured a fair amount of poking and prodding. Nothing serious had turned up, and we'd soon know the gender of the three unsexed chicks thanks to the blood work. Calvin had assigned Mr. or Miss to each of them, based on intuition, and I was eager to see how accurate he was.

The Penguinarium was a beneficiary of the bond passed a few years earlier by the good citizens of Vancouver, Washington. The "island" in the pool was resurfaced to seal it against bacteria and reduce abrasiveness on tender penguin feet. An expensive new air filter system slightly improved the tang and greatly improved the chances of avoiding fungal diseases. Neal muttered about tearing down the whole building and starting over, but Calvin and I saw little hope of that. Other areas of the zoo had more pressing needs. Other areas of Birds had more pressing needs, such as the decrepit walk-through aviary that would be replaced someday with the glorious one I envisioned.

The exams put us behind schedule. I was striding toward the Children's Zoo to tend to the birds that lived there when I ran into Neal. It was too soon to lean on him again about the macaws, so I meant to smile, nod, and go about my business.

But he stopped in front of me. "Okay, okay," he said. "I've got a deal cooking to try and get those Amazon parrots sent back to Mexico, but it's complicated as hell. It might not work. Especially not if they turn out to be full of viruses."

"Mexico as in a zoo or as Mexico as in free in a forest?"

"Not yet established."

"Still, that's great. When?"

"Also not yet determined."

"How about the smugglers?"

"Like I said before, I have to read it in the papers like everyone else. We look after the animals until the court case is settled, then the agencies tell us what to do with them."

"Right," I said to be polite.

"I've got no juice with these people. I just wish I did. Doc Reynolds is looking into where those tortoises were stolen from, and that's about all we have the resources for."

"Got it," I said. Good news about the parrots, no news about the smugglers. Did I dare bring up the macaws? But he was off.

I stopped by the mandrill exhibit again after work and found Kip there. We studied the monkeys in silence. Sky yawned, flashing his canines, and watched us out of the corner of his eye. He wandered around the exhibit poking his fingers into clumps of straw. Violet kept getting up to stay out of his path, yanking the baby off the nipple each time. "*Stop that*," I muttered. "Does the baby seem weaker?"

Kip shrugged. "Not really."

"Violet's not getting any rest, and the baby's not getting to nurse much."

Kip shook her head. "Can't tell what's going on when we're here for just a few minutes."

"What if we got one of the Education volunteers in civilian clothes to hang out and take notes for a few hours?" I should have taken longer to think about it. Kip was quick to conclude that her inferiors were trespassing.

"Either it's working or it isn't and we have to pull the baby. We'll know in another day or two."

I pushed my luck. "Right now, Sky's reacting to us, and Violet's reacting to him. Couldn't hurt to see what they do when we're not around."

Kip looked unconvinced. "Those volunteers aren't trained in behavioral observation."

"Some are. They watched the clouded leopards for Linda. We know which ones have the most experience."

Kip looked irritated, which was not unusual. We watched the monkeys for a few more minutes, but nothing much happened. I was surprised when she said, "Go ahead if you want to. Can't do any harm."

I took this as a sign that Kip was more concerned than she was letting on. I left a message for Karen Belsky, the head of the Education Department.

At home, I found Pete immersed in a cloud of spicy scents and steam rising from a wok. He loved Thai and Chinese food and used to cook four or five nights a week, although he and Cheyenne had been eating out most nights lately. I cooked on my days off—meatloaf or spaghetti or roast chicken. Cheyenne cleaned up the kitchen, and I did the rest of the housework, which suited us all reasonably well.

"Where's Cheyenne?" I asked, looking in the fridge for a snack for Robby. I washed his hands and gave him a chunk of string cheese.

"She's returning some stuff she bought at the Jantzen Beach mall. She should be here soon."

Pete was a good-looking guy, tight-curled black hair and complex tattoos on his dark skin. He looked like he'd be a player at a bar or music scene, but he was steadfastly domestic. Cheyenne was the risk taker, and I worried that she'd get bored with Pete. I liked them as a couple, liked the idea that their relationship had lasted for years, through jobs at several zoos, travel in Thailand and Cambodia, and living with a child who wasn't theirs. They were affectionate with Robby, but I knew better than to use them as live-in babysitters. I might be the landlord, but Cheyenne had a sharp tongue and a clear idea of who was responsible for what.

I called Marcie, who didn't pick up, and left another message apologizing and asking her to call me. After feeding the dogs, I spent a little time with the macaws, who were edging into their new space one perch at a time. They let me reach into their cage and swap out three toys I'd bought, replacing them with three others. Toys get stale when they're available all the time. I tossed in some Brazil nuts in the shell. "Put those beaks to work," I suggested.

I hadn't yet read their scratched-up bands. I'd need to be close, maybe with the bird perching on my hand. With luck, I could use the codes to trace them back to their breeder and maybe learn how old they were and what gender. I sighed. The birds needed more attention and hand-fed treats to learn to trust me and tolerate handling. Where was the time for that?

"Dinner's on," Pete called and I washed up and came to the table.

Cheyenne showed up before we were finished, in high spirits. She smooched Pete and filled her plate, talking non-stop about cool shoes she'd seen at the mall and plans for the new elephant barn and news about Ian—the strange and silent keeper she shared Elephants with. "I think he's got a girl friend, can you believe it? She came to Elephants today and he managed to introduce her. Bridget. Tough looking chick, but she acts like she owns him. That's what he needs, he's got no initiative *whatsoever*. He just pines after unavailable women." Ian was inarticulate and socially incompetent. I had to admit that he came across as a little creepy.

I glanced at Pete, who seemed puzzled by the ebullience. Normally Cheyenne was a little on the dour side. Whatever, her mood was contagious. I was glad to hear that Ian had found a legitimate romantic interest. If he took to mooning over Cheyenne, Pete had made it clear he would either flatten the guy or else they would pull up stakes and head for another zoo. None of us wanted that.

Robby was asleep and I was brushing my teeth when Cheyenne hollered up the stairs, "Iris, get down here. The news is going to have 'startling Tipton developments.'"

I stood behind the sofa where she and Pete sat and heard about a near-miss airplane incident, a gigantic mud slide in Honduras, and another impasse in Congress. The local news finally came on.

The woman newscaster announced, "The Clark County sheriff's department has released information about the girl initially identified as Liana Tipton." With wide eyes expressing shock and amazement, she said, "The teenager found dead at the Jerome Tipton residence during a recent drug arrest was not the Tipton's daughter as believed. Fingerprints have identified her as seventeen-year-old Shelby Adamson, who ran away from her home in Fort Dodge, Iowa, when she was fifteen." A quick shot showed a stubby, weary couple with expressionless faces—her parents.

"And now this word from the sheriff's department." A uniformed spokesman said in a flat voice that Shelby/Liana had died from a gunshot fired between twelve hours and thirty-six hours after the Tiptons were arrested. Moreover, she was killed somewhere else and moved to where her body was discovered outside the Tipton home. Back to the newscaster, who flashed the mug shots of Jeff and Tom Tipton and a phone number to report any sightings. Cut to a commercial for a drug that would make a depressed woman laugh and square dance. Cheyenne shut the sound off.

"You thought she was their daughter," Pete said.

Liana, Liana—how did you end up with the Tiptons? "Everybody did. The Tipton mother was asking for her daughter. A neighbor said she was missing. She *lived* there. How did she get from Iowa to the middle of nowhere in Washington? This is unbelievable."

Cheyenne said, "The killed-elsewhere-and-staged part is what *I* think is unbelievable. Lugging her body around? Sick."

I stood up and paced, wide awake. "I saw the spot after they took her body away. No blood on the ground. There should have been a lot of it if she'd been left where she'd fallen. Somebody shot her and tried to blame it on the bust." This didn't make sense. "How could anyone expect something that dumb to fool the cops? Anybody who's ever seen a crime show would know it wouldn't work. The cops must have kept quiet about it while they tried to find the Tiptons, maybe so they wouldn't run as far."

The Tiptons didn't have a television set. Did Tom or Jeff have a clue about forensics? Maybe they were the last two Americans who didn't. That pale freckled face…"Why would they murder her? She was just a kid." But not their sister.

Cheyenne clicked the set off. "Maybe they think she turned them in."

I considered. "One of the cops at the farm said Tom sold meth to the wrong person and that's what got them busted. But Jeff and Tom might not know that. They might have thought it was her." Shooting a girl…"A neighbor said the mother was really dependent on her. She was part of the family."

"Maybe the sons fought over her, or she two-timed one of them."

I couldn't come up with anything better. All I knew was that the Tipton ugliness had touched her and she'd died.

Cheyenne got up and stretched her arms up and back. "The media will milk this dry."

Chapter Twelve

Cheyenne was so right. The radio on the way to work was abuzz with Tipton news. I didn't hear my name, which was heartening. I had slept badly and could barely cope with Robby and Cheyenne, much less the media. It was Pete's day off and he slept in.

I was assigned to Birds, but interrupted my routine to rendezvous in front of the mandrill enclosure with three Education Department volunteers Karen had rounded up on short notice—after I had explained and apologized to her for hogging the Education van for three days. If school children never became conservationists, it was the Tiptons' fault, not mine, I insisted. Karen said she'd be big about it and contact her group.

I told the volunteers what we wanted them to look for. Three female heads nodded—two gray-haired women and one college student. They had clip-boards and pens and a hastily constructed checklist. They seemed delighted to help out and were concerned but not emotional about the situation. Perfect. I confirmed their schedules—two hours each, six hours total today—and turned away to leave them to it.

And found myself facing the photographer in the black jacket. "Iris, it's Craig. You remember?"

"I do." He'd stuck in my brain as the only appealing feature of the Tipton calamities. He and Ken.

The jacket was unbuttoned, showing a dark tee shirt and an indifference to cold. The knit cap was gone. Brown hair with a clean shine. Jeans and black sport shoes. Those hazel eyes. "Can you talk for a minute?"

I shook my head with regret. "If my boss had okayed an interview, he would have told me. So, no. Sorry."

He looked away and back. "How about this? I'd like to ask you to lunch. Rosemary Café, on me." His smile implied a joint conspiracy, a good time, a world of possibilities. "I promise not to talk about the Tiptons."

"Why would you do that?" I knew the café in downtown Vancouver and liked it. I liked the smile, too, but that was irrelevant. I wasn't *that* easy.

"Why wouldn't a guy ask you to lunch?" A frown. "You *are* single, right?"

The volunteers weren't hiding their fascination.

He folded his arms across his chest. "All I'm asking for is expertise on the zoo part, background only. We can keep it off-record. I don't want to get the animal parts wrong."

"Talk to Neal Humboldt. His office is in the Administration building. He'll want to see your credentials."

"You are one tough lady to get to know. Here's my card. It's good for a free lunch any day." He gave a finger wave to the volunteers and moved off toward the zoo's entrance.

One of the older ladies said, "If I were you, I'd just say yes."

"Yum," said the young one. "Give him *my* phone number if you aren't interested."

Whoa. I'd almost forgotten I had a real date that night, dinner with Ken. Liana turning into Shelby had jolted it out of my brain.

A date. Uh-oh, no child care. My top priority after lunch.

In our claustrophobic little break room, Denny out-did the broadcasters with speculation about Liana/Shelby and the Tiptons. Linda, Cheyenne, and Marion chewed their lunch and watched him roll. I didn't pay much attention until he started in again about human trafficking.

"Denny! Stop it. Liana walked over to visit Pluvia with Wanda. She wasn't a prisoner."

"Could have been emotionally subjugated."

"Yeah. But she was warmly dressed and didn't look starved, and the mother was really concerned about her. Liana could have walked to the road and thumbed a ride if she wanted out."

Denny actually stopped to think. I steered him toward something that bothered me. "The Tiptons grew weed for years and stayed under the radar. Then a few months ago, they set up the second barn and started cooking meth. The animal enclosures we saw looked new, so the wildlife trafficking was recent, too. What set them off? Why change a system that was working fine?"

Cheyenne said, "Maybe it was Liana. Maybe she had bigger ideas for bigger bucks."

Denny said, "That neighbor, Pluvia. She and Liana and Wanda, the mother, could have come up with a plan to overthrow Boss Tipton."

I waited to see how he could possibly create a coherent explanation out of this.

He didn't even try. "Or it's the younger son—Tom? He wants to establish himself in the hierarchy, not be bottom tier any more. So he came up with all the changes. But Liana didn't like it and …Probably Tom and the other one, Jeff, both wanted her and she played them off against each other and it went bad."

He had soared well beyond the few facts we had. I gave up, finished my lunch, and checked in with Neal. I told him Craig wanted to interview me and asked if that was okay. He said he'd prefer I didn't. That was as expected, but disappointing. I wouldn't have minded a little one-on-one with Craig. I refrained from asking about re-homing the macaws, but only because he took a phone call.

I called my father at his shop and asked if he and my mother could keep Robby for dinner and an hour or so after.

"Don't see why not," he said. "I'm not going anywhere. I'll pick him up on my way home."

I was reasonably certain that he understood I'd called him instead of my mother because I didn't want to answer questions about my plans. Bless him, he didn't ask any. I'd tell them about Ken when I picked Robby up afterward.

I went back to work, finished up with Birds, and stopped by Primates to de-brief the last of the mandrill volunteers. The three of them had diligently checked the checklist and noted the notes, but they'd also put their heads together at some point during the day and come up with a theory. The silver-haired woman on the last shift said, "She's scared of him, but he wants to see the baby. He comes to take a look, so she runs away and that makes the baby cry and then he gets grouchy so she runs away some more. She's frazzled and so is the baby. The other female just sits there and ignores the whole thing."

I couldn't fault their analysis, since it supported my own. The question was, what could we do to de-stress the mandrill family? I had an idea, but blurting out ideas sometimes worked and sometimes didn't. Dr. Reynolds' approval was necessary and she would likely say yes, but it was Kip's area. If I went to Dr. Reynolds first, Kip would consider that sneaking around her back. But Kip wasn't convinced we had a problem and would likely say no. Worse, Kip was already annoyed with Dr. Reynolds for reducing the fruit in most of the primates' diets and substituting more leafy greens— better for their teeth, digestion, and weight control. Monkeys love fruit, and Kip loved giving them treats.

Persuasion and politics: not my strengths.

I gave it my best shot. Kip was wrapping up her reports when I dropped the data sheets on her desk. She glanced at them while I summarized the observations. "I've got an idea that might help," I said. "If you like it."

Her attention stayed on the reports. "We're not pulling Violet out of the group. It could turn into a nightmare reintroducing her. Sky might think he has to beat her up to remind her who's boss. And Carmine was awful to her when they were first together. So forget that."

"Not what I was going to suggest."

"We aren't pulling Sky out for the same reasons."

"I get that."

She looked up. "And I'm not sure we have a problem. It's a little hectic in there, but not all that bad. They could use more exercise."

"Can I say what I had in mind?" I tried to keep the annoyance down.

"Sure." She sat back and crossed her arms, her mouth a thin, straight line. "Let's hear it."

I hate doomed endeavors when the only possible reward is to say, "I told you so. I tried to get you to do something." I reached deep for positive energy. "Let's give Sky something to do so that he's occupied for a couple hours a day. A puzzle feeder. If it works out, he'll sit in one place giving the feeder all his attention and Violet can relax."

"He'll get fat."

"His daily ration, not extra."

"By the time Maintenance gets the thing built, the baby will be breeding age."

"Not if we get Neal behind it. And Dr. Reynolds. If *you* tell them it's crucial to keeping the baby alive, they'll make it a priority." The emphasis on "*you*" was inspired, my subconscious coming through in a pinch. Was it enough? "Mr. Crandall must be putting out a press release about the birth. He won't want to announce it died."

Kip's mouth twisted. "It's not going to die. Don't be dramatic."

But she didn't dismiss the concept. She pushed out her lips a little and thought. "Like I got nothing else to do. But I'll talk to Dr. Reynolds tomorrow and see what she says."

I did not pump the air with my fist. I said, "Sounds good."

Kip added, "We've done that kind of thing before, you know. I'm not convinced it's really necessary in this case."

Whatever.

Warmed by the tingle of triumph, I headed off to clock out and prepare for my first date since I'd married Rick.

Chapter Thirteen

Linda was describing a promising hint of flirtation between the clouded leopards when Cheyenne joined us at the time clock and interrupted. "Pete and I are going out tonight. You're on your own for dinner. We've got some shopping to do, then a friend's in a gamelon performance."

"Gamelon?"

"Indonesian. Bunch of people whacking on weird musical instruments. Strange and cool."

"Have fun." No need to mention that I wouldn't be dining at home either, so I didn't have to explain. I was on a roll. When Cheyenne was gone, I said, "They've been out almost every night for weeks. Expensive way to get private time together."

Linda said, "You remember how to manage without them, right?"

"No problem. In fact, I'm going out tonight myself."

"That sounds like a date. Unless it's a lecture on potty training."

I looked around. No one else was within earshot. "Dinner with an Animal Control guy. I met him at the Tipton place. Don't tell anyone."

She did a little jig in place. "Hot damn! The price of my silence is full disclosure. Tomorrow without fail."

"No way. You never tell me about your dates."

She blushed. "That's different."

The blush was too intense. My eyes narrowed. "Who is she?"

"I'll tell you later, if it keeps working."

"Tell her that if she trifles with your affections, I'll come hurt her."

"Tell your dog catcher the same."

And I had to be satisfied with that. I crossed my fingers for luck, hoping for a happy ending to Linda's long, hesitant search for a partner. And crossed them again for myself.

In the parking lot, I sat in my car and called Marcie, hoping to catch her before she left work. This was a desperation move since calling her house wasn't working. She picked up, said she was fine, much better, thank you, and it wasn't a good time to talk. "Let's get together soon," I said, and we hung up.

I'd planned to coax her toward our normal relationship by talking about my date with Ken, but, on second thought, hearing about my romantic ventures was not what she needed.

She'd said it wasn't a good time to talk. She hadn't suggested a better time. I started the car feeling as uneasy about her as before.

After taking the dogs on a short walk, I put out the kibble, fed the macaws, and took a shower. I let go of Marcie and focused on courtship. A first date. How about that. If I owned any perfume, I might have put some on. "Mountain Meadow" scented deodorant would have to do. What to wear? Jeans and a sweater were the obvious choices, given the weather and venue. My old black dress boots, still decent. Gold hoop earrings with a sparkly bead sliding on each. Lipstick.

What else? I glanced around the house, which was reasonably tidy. I wouldn't be bringing him home, so that didn't matter. I wasn't going to his place either. This was a long shot, an opportunity at friendship. Or a small disaster if one of us was enthusiastic and the other wasn't.

I'd pay for my dinner to avoid any sense of obligation. One glass of wine only.

What could we talk about besides dogs? Ah—Liana. Maybe he would have an insight that had escaped me.

Why was I wishing he were Craig?

My fussing was cut off by the doorbell. My neighborhood is popular with door-to-door solicitors for political candidates and environmental causes. It wasn't election season, so probably a college student collecting for some outfit that saves endangered species or scrutinizes logging. Thanks to Pete and Cheyenne's rent, I could make a contribution now and then. But not tonight. I hadn't time or patience to listen to a pitch.

It wasn't a canvasser.

It was Thomas Jefferson Tipton.

Astonishment hadn't time to turn to fear and action before he nudged his way in and shut the door behind him. The dogs ran up to us and barked, but when a wrenching crunch came from the kitchen, they bounded that direction hollering their lungs out.

Jefferson Davis Tipton stood in my kitchen, a pry bar in his hand.

I froze, feeling blood drain from my head, trapped between them.

The dogs kept barking. I wasn't welcoming these strangers, and they didn't know what to do. Neither did I. They subsided into uneasy bursts.

"Ma'am. We just wanted to talk to you for a minute." The younger one, Tom.

Jeff waved the pry bar at the dogs, a mild warning. The dogs didn't scare them—they were used to big dogs that barked. Denim jackets, heavy cotton shirts, dirty jeans, muddy leather work boots, no hats. The macaws screeched in the basement. The brothers glanced at each other.

I took a ragged breath. "Sure. Have a seat." I walked to the kitchen table and stood on rubbery legs by a chair.

I could look for a chance to pull out my cell phone, dial 911, and leave it open and hidden in hopes that the emergency operator would send someone by to check on us. They could track a cell phone. Or was that just on TV?

They were watching me. Tom said, "You remember who we are? We don't mean no harm. *Any* harm."

I nodded.

Cheyenne and Pete wouldn't be back for several hours. No one was likely to drop by. What the hell did these guys want? I waved them to chairs. Tom sat. Jeff stood. My empty brain channeled my mother's reflexes. "Would you like coffee?"

"Coffee would be real nice, ma'am." From Tom.

I filled the kettle at the sink and put it on.

I could smell them—stale sweat, wood smoke. Jeff's beard was ratty, Tom hadn't shaved for a couple of days. Neither took his eyes off me. Wide-spaced blue eyes in broad foreheads. Pale skin. Broad shoulders and big hands, although Jeff was taller and heavier. Jeff had yanked me out of the van and pushed me into the mud.

Tom said, "Sorry to bust in on you like this, but we're sort of on the run. We just want to talk to you."

I could throw boiling water on them. That might buy me enough time to get out of the house. No, it wouldn't.

At least Robby was safe with my parents. I had only me to save. I sat down at the table. "So talk."

Jeff finally sat down. His left eye twitched.

Tom said, "We wanted to thank you for trying to save our father. We didn't know what to do and you and that other guy tried hard. We appreciate it."

Right. They broke into my house to thank me. I waited.

Tom shifted in his chair. "And we wanted to ask if maybe he said anything, there at the end. Last words, I mean."

Ah. That was it. I thought back. Mostly I remembered the feel of the thick body under my palms, Denny stepping up to the mouth breathing, all in slanting, unreliable illumination from the headlights.

Tipton *had* said something. "I think he said, 'Look after slither,' something like that. It didn't make any sense to me."

Tom and Jeff looked at each other. Tom was apparently the designated spokesman. "Look after Stridder?"

"Yeah. That sounds right."

"Like I keep telling you," Tom said to his brother with sudden venom, "all he cared about was those birds. He didn't give a wad of spit about his family."

Jeff shook his head. "He was dyin'. You can't blame him."

"It's always been that way. You know it and I know it. He treated us worse than dogs and treated himself just fine."

Jeff flushed and started to rise.

The kettle whistled and I got up. Jeff settled back. I set up the French press under watchful eyes. "Who's Stridder?" I leaned against the counter while the coffee steeped.

Tom looked surprised. "The parrot. The other one's Stanley."

The macaws, then. Old Man Tipton's last words were to take care of his pets. I'd be pissed, too.

I pulled half-and-half out of the fridge and set it on the table. "So what's the story with the parrots in the barn? And the tortoises?"

Jeff frowned a warning at Tom. Tom said, "What about them? Lots of people have birds and turtles."

I gave him a look. "I work in a zoo. I know about this stuff. They were illegal. You were going to sell them. And they were suffering and dying because you weren't taking good care of them."

Tom shrugged. "They're *birds* and *turtles*. It's not like dogs. They don't feel things. People have dominance over them anyway, it's in the Bible."

Jeff cut off this line of bullshit with one of his own. "We came here to see that his birds was taken care of properly. Stridder and Stanley."

I couldn't hide how lame this sounded. Tom looked embarrassed.

"They're in the basement. Go take a look if you like."

Neither budged.

Jeff said, apparently to mollify me, "The big birds, they were different. He could do anything with them. He'd pet 'em and hold them on his lap. They like peanuts. Popcorn, too. He had a lot of fun with them."

"Do they talk?" I wasn't sure where this was going, but conversation was better than any action they might have in mind. The dogs were lying down, panting from worry.

"Nah. He tried to teach them, but they never talked back."

"He thought we had them in the van," I said.

They looked at their coffee cups. Tom said, "He liked those turtles, too. Liked them a lot. Are they here?"

"Nope. They're at the zoo."

Tom wrinkled his brow at me, an attempt at sincerity? "We'd like to go see them, see that they're all right. If you could tell us where they are."

"Locked up somewhere in a back room. I don't really know. I'm a bird keeper."

They looked at each other, defeated. Good grief, they really were smart as hemlock stumps. On the other hand, they had eluded the police for a week and had tracked me down. How? My name hadn't been in the news as far as I knew. I poured out the coffee and set down the sugar bowl. They used lots of sugar and cream.

Tom was a lousy liar, but he had persistence going for him. "Do you know how we could talk to the people in the ambulance? He might of said something to them."

I thought about it. "I can't remember which ambulance company it was. You could make some calls and find out."

I might as well suggest they don magic helmets and use telepathy.

Tom reached out toward Winnie, who slid back away from his hand. "Would that guy who was helping you, would he of heard any last words maybe?"

"Nothing I didn't hear. I'm sorry, but that's all there was. Your dad was in bad shape." What were they hoping for? Proof that their father loved them? Instructions for surviving without him? The password to his brokerage account?

Jeff spoke to himself as much as to Tom or me. "He's dead, and Liana's dead. He said that's what the government would do if they came. They shot her and got him so stirred up that his heart quit." His eyelid spasmed.

Liana hadn't been shot during the bust. I considered pointing this out, but they were the top candidates for her killer. Instead, I said, "Sorry for your loss."

The men acknowledged my cliché with subdued nods. Tom cradled his coffee cup in both hands. "He never knew. He thought she got away."

My head felt full of helium, floating into some universe where this was a normal conversation.

Jeff said, "He found her at a highway rest area. He felt sorry for her and brought her home. He saved her from a life of disrespect and danger. She was going to be my wife when she turned eighteen." He seemed to be defending his father's memory. "The birds liked her, too. They bit at me and Tom, but they liked her."

Tom's mouth twisted. "You couldn't even buy her a ring."

Jeff sat back in his chair, his cheekbones turning an angry red.

I tried to shift the topic before this escalated. "So how did you make bail?"

Jeff shot Tom a clear "shut up" look.

Tom ignored it. "He had money. He just liked to keep us poor. He was giving it away to certain people and…Well, he had some set aside."

Jeff's mouth was set in a grim line. "That's enough out of you. I mean it."

"What's the big secret?" Tom said. "Everyone knows what he—"

The phone in my pocket rang. I reached for it and Jeff half-stood, his face determined. I put my hand back on the table. I watched my fingers quiver and let it ring. When it stopped, I sought to regain some leverage. "How's your mother?" Surely that would nudge them away from violence.

They both stiffened. "We got no way to know. Government's got her locked up," Tom said.

I spoke carefully. "I heard she's in a hospital, not in jail. Once you turn yourselves in, you can probably talk to her on the phone or get a doctor's report."

Jeff snorted. "Hospital? That's just another word for prison. She's locked up tight. And we aren't never going to turn ourselves in because we'd be dead. The government men shot Liana, and they'll kill us just as quick."

I looked for the eye twitch, but it didn't happen.

"Besides, they brainwash people in the hospital," Tom explained. "Modern medicine poisons people so they don't ever revolt. They stay tame and quiet because of the drugs. That's what they're doing with our mom, and we can't do nothing about it. We don't even know where she's at."

And just as well, I thought. They were both getting worked up. I was familiar with this type of logic from working with Denny, but Denny never seemed to take his theories all that seriously. These guys believed.

The phone blared in my pocket and was silent, announcing a voice message. We all jumped.

"More coffee?" I asked, and they split the last of it. Getting them wired was not my first choice, but I didn't have a lot of options. I took a breath and pushed my luck. "I can make you some sandwiches, but then you'll need to leave. Friends of mine will be showing up soon, and things could get complicated."

That got nods, so I threw together two peanut butter and jam sandwiches at lightning speed and shoved them into a paper bag. Tom stood up and took the bag. "Thank you, ma'am, for the coffee and food. Sorry to be beggars, but we got nothing." He looked embarrassed, and I took advantage of it.

"You guys leave now and stay away. You pushed me in the mud before and tonight you scared me again. You broke my door. Don't *ever* come here again." My voice barely trembled.

"We'd better get back before we catch hell," Jeff said. His eye twitched.

Tom nodded, shame-faced. "Yes, ma'am. We won't bother you again." He picked up the pry bar off the kitchen table and stuck it in his rear pocket.

Jeff examined the door latch on his way out. "It's not so bad. A little glue and it'll be fine."

Pete and Cheyenne walked in an hour later and found a Portland Police officer finishing up his questions. His partner returned from a stroll around the neighborhood and reported that a neighbor had seen a green VW van driving away. I remembered to tell them about the dogs barking in the back yard a night or two ago. I was still shaking. What if Robby had been home? It was pure luck he wasn't. What if Cheyenne and Pete had showed up before they left? The brothers might have panicked or gotten aggressive, who knew?

One of the officers said, "We'll have a patrol car check the house every hour or so. Call 911 if anything happens."

I reminded them to coordinate with Gil Gettler.

Robby and I spent the night at my parents' house, and I didn't remember my date with Ken until I pulled my earrings off to go to bed, too late to call back.

Chapter Fourteen

I sat in my car in the employee parking lot as the sun considered whether it was worth the effort to rise and listened to Ken's calm, puzzled voice message on my cell phone. I figured he'd be up by seven thirty so I pushed Send to call him back. I got his voice mail. "It's Iris. I was on my way out the door last night to meet you when the Tiptons broke in." That should short-circuit any hard feelings. "I had to deal with them and then the police. I'm really sorry. Call me, would you?"

The call and sleep-deprived sluggishness had made me late. Hap hovered at the time clock like a thundercloud. "Listen, you. We're buying you a hand gun after work today."

The onslaught wasn't a real attack, and I tried not to slip into defensive mode. "Pete and Cheyenne told you about my visitors."

"Yup. Let's do this. I'll meet you here after work, and we'll go shopping."

"I've never even fired a gun." I swiped my badge at the timeclock.

"About time then. We'll go to a range and I'll show you."

Hap knew things I never would, from the years that left him scarred and an expert on motorcycles and bar fights. I knew different realities, different disasters. "Hap, I have a kid. No way can I have a gun in the house."

"You can lock it up."

"If I do that, it's useless if someone breaks in."

"No, you get a fingerprint safe. Sits on your nightstand and opens fast. Reads your fingertips. That's what people use if they have kids."

"No way. I could shoot the wrong person or somebody could yank it away from me."

"So you'll just sit here and wait to see what happens?" Frustration warped his face into a vicious scowl. The snake tattoo climbing his arm swelled. "Look, there's sheep and there's wolves. The guard dogs aren't keeping the wolves away, so you need to do better than sit around and grow wool."

I took a breath and a step away. "Robby's safe for now. I'm figuring out what to do. I'll put a piece of iron pipe by my pillow."

Hap's head waggle said this was totally unsatisfactory. "You've got suspected killers breaking into your house. You've got a kid to protect."

"Hap, I know that. Give me some space. I'm figuring this out."

Options and obstacles preoccupied me as I worked birds, the routine absorbed into muscle memory. I could feed and evaluate the penguin colony, which had returned to normal after the previous day's medical ordeal, and also ponder a heavy, dark gun in my hand. Would I shoot someone to protect myself, to save Robby? I didn't know, and it didn't matter. I couldn't have it around for my child to find and investigate.

Did Jeff and Tom have reason to return? Had I convinced them I didn't know anything useful? No way to tell. Old Man Tipton had not raised them to be competent and confident. He'd raised them to obey orders. I'd feared them as dangerous adults, but they were also nervous and uncertain. Country boys in the big city, out of their comfort zone. Unpredictable.

They had enough initiative to follow the zoo van and take that accursed plastic bag. I wished I'd challenged them about the bag. No, that would have been too confrontational.

I wished I could talk to Marcie about what I should do. Maybe call my mother instead? But I already knew what she'd say—"You and Robby are staying here until those men are in prison."

One of the Bali mynahs was fluffed up and sluggish. I spared a little brainpower for my job and put in a call to Dr. Reynolds with the radio at my hip. My cell phone rang while I was talking with her about the mynah. I wrapped it up abruptly and barely caught the call.

Ken didn't sound angry or shocked. "I guess I can't compete with drug dealers. Did they really break into your house?"

"Yup. Can we reschedule? I'll tell you all about it."

We set up dinner for the next evening and I hung up. It was more than a date now. He had spent time at the Tipton farm. Maybe he could help me figure out how to get them apprehended. That would be a first step in justice for Liana and the smuggled animals, not to mention the possibility of getting my life back. Ken and I had plenty to talk about.

On the way to lunch, I swung out of my way to the maintenance barn to have a chat with Ralph and José, who were deep into the guts of a giant riding lawnmower. "You guys get a work order for a mandrill feeder?"

Ralph, who looked about sixteen but had been at the zoo longer than I had, pulled his head out of the cab. "Kip came by with a design. We're on it."

"How long?"

José said, "Oh, probably three-four weeks. We're pretty busy."

An instant before I lost it, I caught the way he was watching me out of the corner of his eye. "Don't toy with me, you heartless gear heads. That baby's life is at stake."

José grinned. "I think we put it up tomorrow morning."

"That's better."

Ralph was smiling, too. I was an easy mark on a boring morning.

"You're welcome," José called as I left.

I turned and blew him a kiss, then one for Ralph. They hooted.

I'd almost forgotten how to smile.

I called Linda and asked her to eat with me at Felines instead of the basement lunch room. To avoid running into co-workers and sharing my indecision, I bought lunch early. The burrito was cooling when I caught Feline's steel door to keep it from slamming behind me.

The old concrete box was hers now, her posters and cartoons on the wall, her food in the fridge, but it still smelled and sounded the same as when I was the feline keeper—cat smells, cougar chirps, lion grunts. It always felt like a home I'd abandoned. We sat at the metal table in the kitchen. I unwrapped the burrito and popped the lid off the coleslaw container. "I need to hear myself talk."

"I'm told your date with the dog guy was pre-empted by the Tiptons." She'd already pulled cottage cheese and sliced peaches out of the fridge.

"Pete, Cheyenne, or Hap?"

"Pete. It was on the news, too—'broke into a Portland house and fled.' No mention of your name or address."

"Good. Here's the thing. I have to keep Robby far, far away from them. Hap wants me to buy a gun, but that's a non-starter. Pete and Cheyenne are mostly home when we are, but it's not fair to ask them to go up against criminals. I don't know what to do."

"So is your house safe or not? I'm thinking the evidence is pretty clear."

"Damn it, why should I have to wrench my entire life around and move out because of those bastards? I would take the risk, if it was just me, but letting Robby stay there is unthinkable."

"Hello? *You* can't afford it either. Who's going to raise him if they shoot you?"

"Where on earth can I take Robby and two dogs? I wouldn't feel any safer in a motel, and it's too expensive. My parents have their own lives, and I can't keep spreading the disruption."

Linda raised an eyebrow. "My keen intuition tells me you have made a decision and are just stalling."

"Pete and Cheyenne should leave, too. It keeps rippling out."

"Call your parents. I'll come with you to pack."

"*No!*" I sulked for a moment. "All right. Yes. Where can Pete and Cheyenne go?"

Linda thought about it. "Denny's, I suppose. He's got room. All I've got is a sofa."

"They can train that dog of his and clean up the place. Then all this might be worth it."

It was a weak joke, and Linda ignored it.

I finished my food, ranted some more, and departed in search of Pete. Cheyenne would probably refuse to hide out, so best to start with him. He was working Bears since Arnie, the regular bear keeper, was off. I found him on the platform above and behind the black bear exhibit, hosing down. "Pete," I called, "need you for a minute." He shut the water off and climbed down. He agreed that it made sense for all of us to move out for awhile and that Denny's place would be their best bet. I said, "I'm leaving it to you to persuade Cheyenne."

He looked glum.

I called my mother and explained the situation. She's at her best in a crisis and assured me that I was doing the right thing and that "we'll have a good time." What if Jeff and Tom had been raised by two warm-hearted, capable parents? I wished I could clone mine and assign all the sad, frightened toddlers in the world to better homes.

Hap waited at the time clock at day's end. He wanted to share that Oregon doesn't allow bail bondsmen or bounty hunters. "That means you can jump bail in Washington and hop over to Oregon, the state where *you* live, and no one but the police can haul you back to Washington. That means…"

"Yeah, I get it. The Tipton boys might stay in Portland, and they could come back to my place."

"You need protection."

"No, I need to hide out for awhile. I'm going home to pack."

"Where will you go?"

"Somewhere else."

He considered being offended that I wouldn't tell him and decided to pass on it. Or else he figured out that it had to be my parents'.

He met me at the house after work "just in case." He checked the inside, then hung out in the living room as Linda and I rounded up stuffed animals, clothing, and dog food. Pete and Cheyenne showed up with a load of groceries and put them away in a strained silence. I raised an eyebrow at Pete. He shook his head.

"So," Cheyenne said when she finished tucking away the coconut milk and lemon grass, "you're bailing?"

"Yeah. Until the Tiptons are back in jail. And you?"

"We'll be fine here."

I considered arguing and gave it up. My own problems were more than enough. "Pete, would you feed the macaws while I'm gone? I'll write out instructions."

"No problem. Show me where the food is."

"We can feed them together now, before I go."

Hap took a break from guard duty and the three of us fed the macaws, with minor disputes about the proportion of fruit to pellets and whether the basement was warm enough at about sixty degrees. Since one of them—I didn't know which was Stanley and which was Stridder—was half naked from feather-plucking, I had set up a heat lamp to radiate on a perch. Pete said he'd keep an eye on the bulb.

"Pete," I said, "if you talk Cheyenne into moving out, just call me. I'll come feed them. I won't be that far away. Don't let her use this as an excuse."

He nodded. "It could happen. Elephants could sing opera."

"Look at those two," Hap said. "Crammed into that cage side by side for years, and now they can't get far enough away from each other."

True. The birds perched at opposite ends of the remodeled cage. "Too bad. They'd be happier paired up," I said. Happier flying free in a tropical jungle, but that was really beyond my powers. And only a fantasy since they couldn't have a clue how to survive in the wild.

Hap said, "I'll send you an email with links to local sanctuaries. If you can get them in. They get lots of big parrots that people can't keep or don't want. I don't breed mine anymore, not since I tracked down what became of half a dozen birds I bred and sold. Too many of them resold and vanished or given away or stuck in a basement."

I said, "This basement was *so* not my idea."

"I know that."

Pete went upstairs to start dinner and fight with Cheyenne, Hap to see if by any chance our fridge held a beer. I stayed a moment, watching the birds pick through our offerings.

Jerome Tipton had been outraged that we were hauling them off to the zoo. When he hollered to "get my birds," I was sure he meant Stridder and Stanley and not the Amazon parrots. He and his sons were facing trial, his wife was in the hospital, his "daughter" was missing—assuming he didn't know she was dead—and his property was invaded. Yet he was desperate to get his birds back. His last words were about them.

The unplucked macaw put his face to the mesh, and I scratched his forehead. "What are you not telling me?"

Chapter Fifteen

My mother had put basil in something and dinner smelled like summer, a promise that winter would end someday. I scooted Robby up to the table on the booster seat. The parents had already eaten, so my mother hovered, offering me hot tea, lemon slices for the fish, rice vinegar for the beets, a salad dressing. My father sat with his wrists on the table. They both looked tired, probably from tearing around setting the house up for me, my son, and two dogs. Winnie and Range sprawled where people would be mostly likely to trip over them.

"You are the best ever," I said to both. "I could not make it without you, and I'm sorry for everything I ever did that worried you, and for being an awful teenager, and not turning the compost last fall like I promised, and for not growing up to be a teacher or a sign painter. I will make this invasion as short as I can, I promise."

They gave each other a look, and my mother said, "Relax. You're doing the smart thing."

I thought she might add, "For once," but she didn't.

My father said, "We'll sleep better with you here and safe."

That night I lay again in my adolescent bed with Robby curled up asleep—at last—on a crib mattress on the floor nearby. The dogs snuffled unhappily in the hallway outside the door when they weren't barking at unfamiliar noises. The bedroom was chaotic, suitcases and tote bags everywhere. I was evicted, stressed out, and desperate.

In the morning, I pulled on a clean uniform without disturbing Robby. Today he would stay with his grandparents, so I could let him sleep.

I walked into the empty living room carrying my rubber boots and dialed Officer Gil Gettler. Whether he had an early shift or a late one, I couldn't say, but he did pick up and I suppose he was sorry to find me at the other end. No, the Tiptons weren't in custody. No, he couldn't say when they would be. Yes, he would let me know as soon as it happened.

"They were driving around in their own van," I said. "How does that happen? They show up at the farm and just drive it away and nobody notices?"

"We're stretched thin and their place is out on the edge. We've got a murder/suicide and a bank robbery in the last couple of days."

"So they get to wander around until somebody trips over them? Look, are you sure they aren't sleeping in one of those barns? Or at Pluvia's, that neighbor woman?"

"They haven't been in either of the barns or the house, and we know there's been no vehicular traffic in that neighbor's driveway."

"And how do you know all that when no one spotted them driving away?"

"Trust me, we know. It's just a matter of time until we find them."

Trust me. I hung up in an angry panic.

I found my mother, wearing the green velvet robe I'd given her for Christmas, in the kitchen making coffee.

"Mom, go back to bed. It's Sunday. I can feed myself. Robby's still asleep."

"No, it's fine. Here." She handed me a mug.

I sagged at the kitchen table, trying to let go of the frustration and fear. "I'm really sorry to crash on you like this. I have no idea when I can go home."

"It's not so terrible to have you back. You used to live here, if you recall."

"Not with two dogs and a little kid." Was I bringing my troubles to them? If the Tiptons wanted to find me, maybe they could track me here. The thought made my head hurt.

My mother puttered around while I ate. I expected advice or warnings or pleas, but she just puttered while I ate my cereal. She pulled up a chair next to me. "Tell me about that girl you found."

I told her about following the dog to Liana's body. "I don't know why, exactly, but I feel really bad for her. I have this notion that she escaped from something awful, like a vicious pimp. Maybe the Tipton farm was a place to hide, although it was pretty awful, too. I keep seeing her walking through the woods to visit her friend. Trying to make a home out of that skanky house. Playing with the Doberman puppy. And then someone shot her before she had a chance at a better life."

"Do you think her pimp found her and killed her?"

"At the same time as the drug bust? That seems too coincidental. I have no idea. But I keep thinking about her."

"I wondered how you'd handle motherhood." She patted my hand.

I wasn't at all sure what that meant, but it seemed to be a compliment. "I don't think I'm ready to feel motherly toward a teenager, not yet. Let me get through toilet training first. Or maybe you're right."

A quiet conversation between equals. How odd.

I had my hand on the front door knob, ready to leave, when I remembered. "Mom, I know this isn't the best timing, but I have a date for tonight. I already canceled on him once. I can see if Amanda's daughter will watch Robby. Courtney's good with him."

"You have a *date*? Is his head shaved? Is he tattooed?"

It was almost a relief to have my real mother back. "*Mom…*"

"I'm only asking."

A few dubious choices in high school stick like gum to my shoe. "He's got hair and a job. I'll let you know about the tattoos if it goes well."

She blushed. "Robby will be fine with us. Have fun."

"I'll be home to change before I go out." I'm not a big hugger, but gratitude and affection got the best of me.

◇◇◇

Sky was really, really pissed off. We keepers had conspired to play a cruel trick on him, humiliated him in front of his wives, and, far worse, deprived him of his rightful food. The big monkey stared a mean stare toward where I observed from the visitor viewpoint. He followed up with a head bob and slapped the ground with a palm to show he meant it.

How did he know this was my fault?

The mandrill stormed back and forth at the keeper door to his exhibit, which had grown a contraption overnight. A box made of close-spaced metal bars, about a foot square and two inches deep, was welded flat to the metal door. It was full of monkey chow, and he couldn't get at it. He stopped now and then to poke his fingers into the box. He could touch the hard little biscuits as well as see and smell them, but he couldn't get them out. This was *his* monkey chow, in the wrong place. Violet and Carmine wouldn't dream of claiming it. They stayed as far away as they could get.

It had taken all my will power to wait until break to leave Birds and check out the mandrills. This wasn't what I'd hoped for.

Sky emitted frustration like a fumarole. He applied his teeth to the steel bars and got one of the uppers stuck, his head at a weird angle. My heart stopped. If he broke a canine…or his neck…He yanked it out intact and went back to pacing.

"Figure it out, dummy," I muttered. "Calm down and *think*."

"He's really got his macho on."

Craig again. He raised a hand. "Neal says it's okay for you to talk to me. True story."

He looked good in that black jacket. Pale brown dress shirt, dark pants. "Sorry, but I have to confirm that." Why was I apologizing?

"Of course. Tell me what's going on here."

I explained we were trying to keep Sky busy so that Violet could relax and focus on her new baby. He stood beside me, a little closer than strangers stand. I was a little more aware of him than I should have been. But then Sky vented his feelings by charging Carmine, who fled shrieking. Violet screamed also and the three of them, four counting the baby clinging for his life, tore around for what seemed like a very long time, but was probably only seconds. Sky broke off and went back to cursing at the puzzle feeder.

"Good grief," Craig said. "I would not want to be trapped in there with him."

"He doesn't actually hurt them." So far.

"What's supposed to be happening? With that gismo."

I put aside the thought that this might be one of my worst ideas ever. "See that hole near the top of the box? The idea is that he uses his fingers to walk a piece of chow up the side and out the hole." Sky obliged by sticking two fingers down the hole, which accomplished nothing. "It's tricky, and he's never seen anything like it."

"A guy with big teeth doesn't usually need brains."

"Not until this."

"And his color scheme?"

Visitors were always riveted by Sky's vivid pink-and-blue muzzle and rump. "Indicates he's a mature male, a major stud. The bright colors might help mandrills find each other in thick jungle, but no one really knows." I'd spent all the time watching mandrills that I could afford. "I have to get to work. As long as you're at the zoo, have a look around."

"I'll be at the front entrance at noon with lunch."

"Um, 11:30 is better. And I only get thirty minutes."

"That will work." He gave me a little tap on the shoulder and ambled toward the gibbons. I stared after him, bemused that my blood was racing just a trifle.

He was so different from Ken. Denny could probably explain that I had a dual personality and that it was perfectly logical to be attracted to both, but I didn't plan to consult him.

I concentrated on feeding birds and cleaning the Penguinarium and fixing a weak spot in the aviary fencing, lugging tools and food pans from one side of the zoo to the other in fitful rain. Both Bali mynahs looked fine today. At 11:15, I called Neal.

Who said, "Yeah, he came in and talked to me. He's a freelancer, used to work for some Florida newspaper. Talk to him if you want. He'll just bug Crandall if you don't, and Crandall always says yes to anyone from the press."

So Neal had folded.

Fine with me. Craig was persistent. He might find Jeff and Tom before the police did. That was a good reason to establish contact. Reason? Excuse, maybe.

He was waiting at the visitor entrance, toting a white paper bag with "Rosemary Café & Espresso Bar" written on it. "Hey," he said, hazel eyes alight, "He got one! I only saw one, but I had to leave to get the food. He's figuring it out!" He had a fine grin.

We celebrated Sky's victory with a high five.

"I think one of those other monkeys, a female, I guess, has a problem with her teeth. Not the one with the baby, the other one. She shoves at her lower jaw with her hand and grinds her teeth. I saw her do it twice."

He'd actually watched the mandrills. Most visitors take a quick look and move on as if they'll get a prize for checking off every animal at the zoo. "Cheek pouches. She stuffed her breakfast down alongside her jaw. She shoves a chunk of monkey chow up with her fist and chews on it when she's hungry. It's normal."

Craig raised his eyebrows and nodded, apparently impressed by my expertise and reassured about mandrill tooth decay.

We settled at a table in the café, Craig sticking his bad leg out carefully. I received a frown from the manager, who would probably complain to Neal, who wouldn't care. We weren't displacing paying customers since there weren't any. It was raining and cold and only 11:30.

Craig pulled out containers of soups and salads, paper-wrapped sandwiches, and two big cookies. My good will is so easily won...

We tucked in to the chow, which was excellent. Instead of asking questions, he told me about reporting from the civil war in Liberia where he ended up under a jeep with a broken leg. "Wrong place, wrong time, and by the time I got hauled out of there, the leg was really screwed up." If he ever got a job with health insurance, surgery might help. "We might as well get that out of the way. People always want to know, and you're probably too polite to ask."

I nodded and chewed and thought that I couldn't find Liberia on a map. The more my blood sugar rose, the more interesting Craig became.

He summarized his reporter job in Florida, massive layoffs throughout the news industry, and moving to Vancouver for a job that vanished when he arrived. "Now I'm working on a feature-length article about the Tiptons and their family businesses." He was sure he could sell to any number of publications. "*Winter's Bone* set in the Northwest."

He had a touch of "not from around here" accent, but I couldn't pin it down further than "East Coast." He was a riveting story teller, but I began to wonder whether he wanted an interview or just an audience.

We were down to the cookies—oatmeal/raisin and chocolate chip, which we divided and shared—before he asked me about the Tiptons. He took notes while I gave him a brief account of why the zoo was involved and the current status of the parrots and tortoises.

He looked up when I stopped. "You really don't like talking to reporters."

True fact. "I've got nothing to gain, aside from a nice lunch, and this one's a first. Usually reporters misquote me, and the other keepers make jokes about it. Or I say things carelessly, and they make jokes about it. Or I say something really stupid, and my boss doesn't make a joke about it at all. So it's downside all the way. We try to make the zoo look good and not put our foot in it."

"Most people like to see their name in the papers, as long as it's not for an arrest."

I shook my head.

He put his palms flat on the table and looked me in the eye. "My recorder broke or I would have brought it, but I take good notes. I will do my best not to embarrass you in any way."

I appreciated that. He wanted to know about old man Tipton dying, and I gave the short version, wishing he hadn't asked. I changed the subject. "Have you learned anything about Liana? The girl who died."

He nodded. "A year ago, she was picked up on a prostitution charge in Los Angeles and released. Somehow she made it to Vancouver and ended up on the farm. I think she was there for several months, but no one seems to know for sure. Apparently she was plying her trade in the towns around the farm. Getting information about the Tiptons has been really tough. The mother won't talk to me, and I can't find the sons any better than the police can."

"Plying her trade. How do you know? Is that from the police?"

"No, they aren't interested in talking to me, but I've got a scanner. Plus a few tricks up my sleeve."

Oh, Liana, perhaps I misjudged you. "Do you think one of the sons shot her?"

He wadded up our trash, thinking. "Could be. But Jerome was funding some home-grown terrorist groups. They can get pretty violent. We really don't have enough information to make an educated guess."

Craig asked about the parrots and, once I got started, I fulminated more than I should have about the illegal pet trade and how it can eliminate a species from most of its range, just so the animals can sit in someone's house until they die. "Parrots are smart, social birds—they're meant to bond with each other and be together every minute of every day. We want them to bond with us, then we go off and leave them alone all day. Some European countries require that they be kept in pairs, not singly. They have *laws* about it."

"And the tortoises?"

"Same conservation issues, different problems as pets. They're being wiped out globally, partly for eating, partly for pets. Collectors pay a fortune for anything rare. Denny says they're tricky to keep alive. He goes on about humidity and how each kind has these picky requirements or the shells get deformed."

"Iris, I can use this. The animal angle will add a fresh dimension and amp up the emotion. This is great stuff."

Go, Craig! "Tell people how hard smuggling is on the animals, the humane side and the conservation side both."

"You really light up when you talk about this. I want to capture that passion." He smiled at me, then went thoughtful. "I never got any shots of the tortoises. Do you think you could set that up? It wouldn't take long."

"You should have started with Denny."

"Yes, but you're a lot better looking." His grin was unrepentant. "Seriously, can you help me here?"

"They're in quarantine. Off limits."

"You could ask, right?"

"I could ask. The vet might surprise me."

"You've still got my card? My cell phone's on it."

I did.

"Call me. Anytime." His voice had dropped.

We weren't talking about tortoises anymore.

I started to get up and sat back. "Look, if you find the Tiptons, please, please tell me right away. They broke into my house, and now I have to hide out. I want them in jail."

Craig sat bolt upright. "You *saw* them? *That* was the Portland sighting?" He looked at me with reproach. "You didn't mention that."

My lunch hour was over and then some. "Yeah, they busted in two nights ago and asked a bunch of bullshit questions. They wanted to know their father's last words. He said to take care of his parrots. That hurt their feelings. I tried to talk them into turning themselves in, but Old Man Tipton filled them full of paranoia and they won't."

He asked for more details, and I gave them.

He leaned toward me with a frown. "Are you safe in your house?"

"I've moved out for now."

He nodded, but didn't seem all that reassured. "I'll let you and the police know if I track them down. I can interview them from jail just as well. Can I contact you to confirm details of what we talked about today?"

"Sure. Bring food like this and I'm available any time."

"I'll remember that. Good luck with the baby monkey."

I felt his eyes on me as I walked away.

Cranes dance together. Ducks bob their heads in a certain pattern. Bali mynahs preen each other's faces. Humans share food. A pleasant fizz in my blood sent worries off-stage for a little while.

By the end of the day, I'd come back to earth. Food and flirting were part of Craig's reporter toolkit, useful for relaxing the subject. Fun, but not to be taken seriously.

Looking for good news, I checked up on Sky. The puzzle feeder was empty and the troop was dozing, the monkeys scattered in different corners of the exhibit. I wondered if he'd gotten all the monkey chow on his own or if Kip had helped. I'd ask her tomorrow.

The baby was wadded up on Violet's belly with his eyes closed. She had an arm around him. Picture perfect.

Chapter Sixteen

On the way home, I clicked on the local news, hoping to hear that the Tiptons' house call had led to their capture. After several minutes of national and international disasters, malfeasance, and trivia, a local talk show came on. The Tiptons were in the news all right, but not what I expected. The host was delighted to report a much more sensational development in the Tipton saga than housebreaking—lost treasure.

"We've learned that drug king-pin Jerome Tipton, now deceased, made bail with—wait for it, folks—gold coins! Canadian Maple Leafs, for you gold bugs. And, folks, unconfirmed rumors say that Tipton kept his drug money in *more* gold coins. Here's the best part—he *buried* them. Or so the rumor goes. Nobody knows where—nobody who's telling, anyway. Those of you hit by this tough economy can sympathize, right? Gold's what you want when the economy is in shambles. Let's talk with long-time treasure hunter Ted McDermott. Ted, you've been out to the Tipton place, right? With a metal detector. Did you find anything?"

After an awkward pause, a slow, reluctant voice said, "Well, I can't say as I did. There's people looking around the area. Most of them are sweeping, but some are just poking the mud with a metal rod. I figure they hope to hit something that way."

"Tell us what 'sweeping' means, Ted."

"Using your metal detector." The tone implied, "you idiot."

"You let us know, Ted, if you find something good. We all want to hear that you struck it rich."

"Sure thing." That verged on sarcasm.

Of course. Anyone who found something valuable wasn't going to let out a peep, unless they were brain-dead or a rank amateur.

After a spell of dead air, the host realized Ted had said all he was going to say. "Thanks, and good luck out there in this cold, wet weather. Nothing like buried treasure to get folks out of their warm houses. Next up: those two skiers lost on Mount Hood. Did the search parties find them? After this word…"

I clicked it off. That's what had been happening in the Tipton driveway on our last visit. Not a search for evidence. Denny and I had seen the beginning of the gold stampede, the two men with metal detectors. Now it was in full gallop. Did Craig know about this? He would soon enough, assuming he tracked the local news. He would love it. I turned into my parents' street wondering who started the gold rumor. The bail bondsman seemed the best candidate.

The brothers had searched the barns looking for shelter, looking for the gold, either or both. I could see the old autocrat keeping his stash secret. That was why Jeff and Tom wanted to hear about his last words. That conversation made a lot more sense now. They were in a race to find the gold. Maybe someone already had and was quietly figuring out how to convert it to cash. A lot of people might be cold and wet and risking a trespassing charge for nothing.

Where was a good place to hide gold coins? I set that aside. I had bigger problems. Also a date.

◇◇◇

Podners was new and pretty, red walls except for a window wall that provided a fine view of the weather, floors of wide planks. Ken sat in a boxy wood chair at a little table made from trendy old-growth fir, salvaged of course. With a Hawaiian shirt and tan cotton pants, he looked unfamiliar. In a uniform, around dogs, I felt a common bond. Here, he was a stranger, one who pretended it wasn't January in Portland. The short sleeves showed muscular arms. He'd not had any difficulty with the heavy macaw cage. He gave me a cautious smile showing that eye-catching front tooth.

I wasn't late—he'd arrived early. Freshly shaved, a whiff of aftershave. A first date for him, too. I apologized again for standing him up, which he brushed off. I ordered a glass of wine. Ken tossed off the last of the beer he had in front of him and accepted another from a waitress who reserved her smile for him and not me. "Back again," she purred.

He looked unfamiliar, yes, but aside from that dumb shirt, he looked good. My body alerted to his. Primed by lunch with Craig? I imagined subtle signals and messages sent and received, a whole conversation without words, our brains not even listening in. I smiled, then succumbed without warning to a shy-attack.

He ordered the pulled pork. I asked for the smoked chicken.

I was out of practice and couldn't remember the script. "Um, have you checked in on the Tipton dogs?"

He seemed perfectly relaxed. "No, they're the Humane Society's problem now. They'll try to work with the mother. If they can't pull a plan together, they'll release the dogs for adoption." He studied his beer bottle. "If people paid their dog and cat license fees, we wouldn't be short-staffed and I could follow up." A little smile at me. "Anyway, we're tied up with horses now. The economy's bad. Hay's expensive. Lots of bony horses to check out."

Work talk. A little slow paced, but that was fine for now. My social courage was returning. "If the Tiptons get those dogs back, I'm stealing them."

"I'll help."

So far, so good. "You're not married? No kids?" Get the basics out of the way.

He shifted in his chair. "Getting divorced. Not final yet. No kids."

"'Not final'. What does that mean, exactly?" My bullshit detector switched on.

"It's filed. We're waiting for paperwork." He considered for a moment. "She's already moved on. A guy with 'manager' in his title. 'Dog catcher' bugged her." Matter-of-fact tone.

Too soon to dig into that. "I've got the same problem. 'Animal janitor' hasn't carried a lot of weight with my mother. You know I'm widowed?"

"Not divorced?"

"My husband died in a zoo accident almost three years ago."

He nodded. He didn't ask how it happened and how I felt about it and how could I still work at the zoo, yadda yadda. Good.

Food arrived and rescued us.

Ken was comfortable with pauses in the conversation. We talked about the Trail Blazers and the proposed new bridge across the Columbia River as excellent piles of meat disappeared, along with beans and coleslaw. He ate and spoke deliberately, with the same relaxed attention that he'd shown with the dogs he'd talked into cooperating.

"How'd you end up in Animal Control?" I asked.

After a moment of reflection, "Not much demand for a bachelor's in chemistry. I tried sales and found out I'm no good at that. So now I'm trying this, not that it was easy to get the job. I had experience—summer jobs at a boarding kennel and some vet tech work—and I know a woman who works there, so I got an interview."

He had finished his degree, more than I'd done. "Do you like it?"

He considered. "It's good work. I like talking to people. Most of them don't *want* to neglect their animals. They're just broke and overwhelmed. They're usually relieved that, one way or another, I get the animals fed and under shelter. Haven't been bitten yet or punched out. That might change my mind. But so far, yes."

"You're good with dogs. I saw you with that pit bull. I'll bet you're good with people, too. The Tiptons would have been a real test."

He sopped up juice with a piece of bread. "My boyish charm doesn't work on them." He cocked his head at me. "You said they broke into your place."

I remembered my agenda: find out if he knew anything I didn't about Liana or the Tiptons. I told him about the break-in without mentioning that I'd moved out of my house. "That family has made my life hell for almost two weeks. The cops say they aren't at the house or in the barns. They've got their van, so they could be anywhere. Any ideas?"

Ken shook his head. "Not a clue. I'd be pretty upset if I were in your shoes."

"No kidding. Keeping my kid safe shouldn't be this hard."

The waitress swung by with an offer of more beer, which he considered and declined.

I spooned up the last of my beans. "They looked like they were living rough—hungry and dirty. What worries me is their next move. They won't turn themselves in. They think the cops will shoot them."

The waitress cleared our plates and asked about dessert. I was prepared to be virtuous and decline, but Ken jumped for the pecan pie and assumed I'd want it, too. We both ordered decaf.

He added cream and sugar to his coffee and stirred it thoroughly. "You'd think the old man would have told the wife where he kept his money. Or his kids. They were his partners in crime, after all."

"He wasn't much of a father. His last words were to look after the birds, not his family."

"Cold."

I'd brought it up, but I was tired of the Tiptons. "I want those rotten sons busted—now, today—so I can quit worrying about them popping up. And I want them grilled about Liana's death and where they got those parrots and tortoises. But nothing is happening."

"The animals probably came in through LAX. Somebody must have done a good job of hiding them or had a lucky day with customs."

"Good guess."

"No, I heard cops talking at the Tiptons. After awhile, they forget you're around. Just the dog catcher…" A wry smile.

"Yeah. I felt some of that."

We finished up the pie and the waitress brought the tab. I tried to split it. He shook his head, laid out bills, and waved away the change. A good tipper.

Something earlier in the conversation came back to me. "You said your charm doesn't work on the Tiptons. You sounded as if you'd already tried it."

A slow nod. "I went to middle school with Jeff. We didn't get along."

"*What?* You *know* him?"

Ken looked—chagrined? "Just for a year or two. In Amboy. Then we moved away."

We'd settled back into our seats, the last customers. The waitress asked if she could bring us anything else, the implication being that she'd like the table freed up. We declined and I didn't budge. "What were they like when you knew them?"

"You sound like a reporter."

Not the time to think about Craig. "I need to understand these guys."

Ken straightened up a little and looked to one side, remembering. "They were kids when I last saw them. Everybody liked Tom because he was cute and nice. The teachers wanted to save him from turning into his brother. Nobody liked Jeff. He wasn't any good at school and he was mean. Not entirely his fault. We called him "Zitchy," for zits and twitchy. His eye still twitch?"

"Indeed it does. Mean, how?"

"Chewing gum in the girls' hair, stupid nicknames, tripping people. He picked fights and he was big, so he won. Looking at it now, the teachers could have done more to include him and make all of us behave better. Maybe it would have helped." He grinned at me. "I've been accused of excessive forgiveness."

I noted an edge to his grin and wondered what it meant. "Too darned nice for your own good?"

"That's my ex's diagnosis. She mistook it for not caring."

That was interesting. "My diagnosis is foot-in-mouth disease."

"Not so far."

We looked at each other for a minute. I felt my face flush and skittered back to safe ground. "Ah, those Tiptons—did any of them have the brains to set up the meth and animal smuggling?"

"My guess would be that girl. Liana or whatever her real name was."

"Why her?" I didn't want it to be her.

"Where'd they learn all that? Plenty of dim bulbs figure it out, but it feels like a stretch."

"She was helping the mother and keeping house for the rest of them. I can't see it."

"Because she was young and a girl? We don't know why she was there or what she was doing before. She's more likely to be the brains behind the meth than any of those Tipton losers."

"That reporter who was hanging around the Tiptons said she went into town to turn tricks." I was helping trash a person who couldn't defend herself.

"For pocket money or maybe Jerome was exploring another profit center."

I pushed my chair back a little. He was making sense, but I didn't have to like it. "So who killed her?" The buzz I'd felt between us had cooled.

"Beats me. Someone from her old life maybe."

I stood up, surprised at how upset I was at the idea of Liana as a master criminal.

We stepped outside into the cold night, a full moon glowing faintly behind the clouds. He walked me to my car and shook my hand, the first physical contact, awkward and electric. I thanked him for a nice evening.

He said, "My pleasure. Keep safe," and left it at that.

Why didn't he press for more? A kiss? A drink at his place?

I drove away certain I'd never hear from him again, trying to talk myself out of the conviction I'd lost a round in the dating game. I was too focused on pumping information out of him, a college drop-out, an animal addict when he might be working Animal Control only until something better came along. No wonder he hadn't wanted more.

And all I'd learned was to avoid naïve emotional bonding with dead girls.

My mother stood at the sink with dripping hands. "How was it? Will you see him again?"

No pressure…"It was okay, but I don't think it's going anywhere. How was Robby? I want to ask Dad about the trip to the Children's Museum." I ducked away to the living room.

I busied myself putting Robby to bed and avoided cross examination for the time being. Not that long ago, I would have called Marcie and dissected the evening with her. I missed her. As for Ken, chalk it up to experience. He'd checked me out, and it hadn't clicked for him.

Well, Craig liked me. Mostly because he thought I had information for his article. Men. Who needed them?

Me? Something female and feral was trying to wake from a two-year hibernation, alert and hungry. I shoved it back into its cave. It was still winter.

Chapter Seventeen

Monday was my day off, a day I normally spent with Robby and my dogs, a day for household chores. Not today. Today I tried to get my life back. Child care was the first step since my parents had gone to work. Amanda was distracted and kept putting the phone down to deal with toddlers. Once she focused long enough to understand my question, she said, "Sure, you can bring him for a half day. Gabe will love that." Gabe was Robby's best buddy, an older guy who had seen his third birthday already.

"I'll drop him off about ten o'clock and pick him up about two."

"That should be fine. Katie, do you have to go potty? I think you do. Let's…"

I hung up.

Ken hadn't called. No matter.

Half an hour after I dropped Robby off, I stood on a Vancouver sidewalk with my back to the Clark County jail. Across the street were two bail bond storefronts. I picked one, the wrong one it turned out, and then the other.

After fifteen minutes with a pleasant but wary woman sitting behind a desk, I knew more about bail bond in Clark County than anyone should. Middle-aged with seen-it-all eyes, she told me, "We can't discuss the specifics of any case."

"Jerome Tipton *died* while I did CPR on him. His sons broke into my *house*. I need to know where Jeff and Tom are hiding out and get them locked up. Do you have anyone looking for them?"

She didn't react to my dramatization. "Nope. There's prob-ably a warrant out for them about that dead girl—bring them in and question them—but their court date isn't for three weeks, so we're still good with the bail. If they skip, we send out a fugi-tive recovery agent."

"A bounty hunter?"

"A fugitive recovery agent."

"Right. And if they turn up in Portland?"

"We call the police and they pick them up. They're pretty good about it."

That was different from what Hap had said, different and better. "Let's see if I've got this straight. Jerome Tipton called you to arrange bail. He signed over his property as collateral, but he still owed you ten percent of the bail as your fee. That showed up in back of this place as a box of gold coins the next day. Right so far?"

"I need a cigarette." She didn't bother with a jacket, just leaned against the outside of the building under the awning and lit up. I had the choice of breathing smoke or standing in the rain. I chose the rain.

"Everyone's looking for the rest of that gold," she said.

"Not me. I just want to be safe in my own house. How did Jerome get the coins to you? Who delivered them? And who picked the three of them up when they were released?"

She shrugged and dragged on the cigarette. "We have no idea. He told us the money would show up, and it showed up. We didn't see who delivered it. I did the paperwork, and they were released late that afternoon. Coins are unusual, but they work."

"How much was their bail?"

"No secret. $150,000 for him, $50K for each of the sons."

I did the math. "$250,000 total bail, so ten percent is twenty-five grand in gold?"

"Yup." She read my mind. "Price of gold is up. It's not as many coins as you'd think."

I left with twice as many questions as I'd arrived with. Not a good trend.

Next stop was Legacy Hospital, the Salmon Creek campus. It's several miles from downtown Vancouver, much closer to Finley Zoo. I left the car in the low-ceilinged parking structure, worried I'd never find it again.

I found myself in the midst of some swell landscaping. A large metal sculpture dominated the courtyard. It looked like an inflated kid's toy—giant blocks shaped like O's and J's. It was about as orange as a sculpture can get. It radiated orange under the blue-gray daylight, glistening in the rain. Each building around the courtyard was nicely identified by a legible sign. I flipped up the hood on my jacket and headed toward the hospital.

Inside, a man in a red polo shirt sat behind an information counter and smiled at me. I swerved away from him and up an escalator. Marble floors, wood paneling. I should have dressed better than jeans and a white sweater. This place was *fancy*. Hard to picture Wanda Tipton here. After studying the directory, I tried the fifth floor. A nurse in plain blue scrubs had no problem directing me to Wanda Tipton's room.

I was a zoo keeper, not a cop. Maybe that gave me an advantage. Something somewhere ought to, if there was any justice in the universe.

The door to room 518C was half open. What was the worst that could happen? She could yell at me. I gathered my courage and knocked. No answer. I peeked in. The bed was occupied, a woman half sitting up, with her head tilted to watch the television suspended above the bed. "Mrs. Tipton?" I asked. No response. "Wanda Tipton?" She was doughy, overweight, a Wonderbread woman whose pale scalp showed through thin dark hair. Surprisingly she wore sweats, not a hospital gown. They were green and tight at belly and thigh and ankle. Her feet were covered with thin hospital slippers.

Oprah was giving away a huge pickup to a park ranger. The studio audience applauded. A re-run. Even I knew the show was over. The woman's gaze drifted from the television screen to me. "Yes?"

"I'm Iris Oakley. Could we talk a minute?"

"Yes?"

"Could we talk? Without the TV maybe?"

"Who are you?" She didn't click the TV off, but she turned the volume down.

A pretty Hispanic woman in blue scrubs walked in and picked up a food tray next to the bed. "You're family? She doesn't talk much. Still kind of out of it." She smiled brightly at us both, didn't seem to expect an answer, and took the tray away.

Wanda Tipton's mouth slowly formed an annoyed grimace. Her lips were full and pale.

I tried again. "I'm Iris Oakley. From the zoo. I saw your sons a few days ago. I thought you might like to hear how they are."

"What were my boys doing at the zoo? I thought they ran off." Her forehead morphed into a frown.

This was heavy going. I sat in the visitor chair and tried to slow to her speed. "They came to my house. They wanted to thank me for trying to save Mr. Tipton. I used CPR, but it didn't work." I gave her a moment to digest that. "They're worried about you."

"They should be. I'm stuck here."

I couldn't resist. "What's wrong with you?"

After several seconds, "It's my thyroid. It gave out on me. I have to take these pills. And the doctors are talking about diabetes. I don't know. Doesn't make sense to me. We never had that in my family. All those pills and now they want shots." She had picked up a little speed.

"I'm sorry to hear that. Mrs. Tipton, I saw Jeff and Tom. They seem okay, but they're hungry and dirty. Wherever they're staying, it's not working out very well for them."

She looked away, a glance at the muttering TV screen, then out the window. "You want to know where they are." She stared at distant row houses backed by fir trees, a long pause. I wondered if she'd forgotten I was there. Without turning toward me, she said, "If I knew, I wouldn't tell you."

That cut to the chase. Damn. "I'm sorry about your husband and Liana. I thought you'd like to hear news about your boys."

She stayed focused on the window, possibly talking to herself. "Jerome brought me a daughter, and I loved her like my own. We had two sons and I said that was enough. He didn't listen to me. Men never listen. They do what they want and the women have to live with it. Now I haven't got anyone."

Something had set her off and I couldn't follow. What would bring her back? "Jerome brought you Liana. How did that happen?"

No response.

"I'm taking care of Stanley and Stridder. The birds. They're fine. I thought you'd like to know."

Her gaze swung toward me as though the mechanism were moving a heavy load. "Liana liked them. I never did." She thought it over. "Awful biters. Too noisy. You can keep them."

"Tell me about Liana. What was she like?"

She leaned back against the bed, a heavy, melting body. "I don't see the point." Her eyes started to close, then they widened and she turned the sound up. A truck commercial.

"I found a plastic bag with a glass in it hidden behind the macaw cage. What was that all about?"

No sign she'd heard me.

"I hope you feel better soon," I said on my way out.

The nurse's assistant was standing outside the door with a cart full of empty food trays. "I warned you," she said.

Now what? I'd done my best and learned nothing about where Jeff and Tom might be. Wanda agreed that Liana liked the birds, more reason to think that she had hidden that plastic bag. That was it.

I was floundering.

I floundered to downtown Portland to have the lunch I'd finally gotten Marcie to commit to. I had to get our friendship back on track. The breakup with Denny had plunged her into an emotional morass, and so far I'd only made it worse. She'd pulled me out of similar emotional disasters. I owed her. And I missed her. She was as close to a sister as I would ever have, and I wanted to reestablish the easy give and take, the reliable warmth and common sense.

West Café is a quiet place with semi-fancy food, one of her favorites. I'd warned her I might be late, and I was. She had her tea in place, Earl Grey, no sugar, no milk. She wore a long-sleeved pale blue blouse with cuffs and a soft bow. I glimpsed black pants. A black jacket hung over the chair back. Her earrings were a small cluster of black sparkly bits. I still wore jeans and a white cotton sweater, no earrings. She stood for a quick hug, so perhaps I was forgiven.

While she studied the menu, I studied her. A little strained, a little thinner. This break-up was still taking a toll. The waiter swung by. Always dieting, Marcie ordered the spinach salad. Always hungry, I asked for the club sandwich.

"You changed your hair. Looks cute."

She patted the neat blond side of her head gently. "I'm trying it shorter. Something different."

We worked through the standard list: how was Robby, her job, my job, her cats. The waiter delivered our food. Marcie's hands were busy with silverware and exclamations. I couldn't shake the notion that her smiles and animation were reenactments from a lost past. After her three cats and their medical problems were concluded, she said, "Good news. The manager agreed to paint my whole apartment, freshen it up. I'm working out the colors—a pale coral or apricot with bright white trim for the living room. How about you? Any house projects going?"

"I don't even *have* a house." I told her about the Tiptons breaking in and driving me out. "I feel like a prairie dog when the black-footed ferrets are in town."

She was predictably horrified, blue eyes wide. "It's so hard being a woman who lives alone. You just never feel quite safe."

My own eyes went a little wide. "Marcie, I live with Pete and Cheyenne and two big dogs, and I had to leave anyway. Your apartment has better security than my house, with that alarm system."

She nodded, but she had looped off to someplace else. "I'm sure they'll be rounded up soon. I'm thinking about transferring to corporate headquarters in Chicago. Start over somewhere else."

"Chicago. That's huge. You're still recovering. Give it some time." I didn't try to hide how appalled I was.

"Oh, I'm fine now. I've moved on. I'm not as fragile as you think." Her eyes flashed a little fire, which I hoped was a good sign. She laughed. "I need to find the right place for my life as a crazy cat lady. Don't worry, we'll Skype every day and visit when we can."

"Marcie, Marcie, Marcie. You *will* find someone else. You're young, you're beautiful, you're wonderful. Give yourself a break. This is still grief talking."

"No, no, and no. It's reality talking. I have to face the facts. I'm not going to pair up. I don't *want* another relationship. I'd just spend all my energy wondering when he was going to end it. I'm not putting myself through that again." Her smile was firm, her hands quiet on the table.

But I was pretty sure she was exactly as fragile as I thought.

"And what about you?" she said. "Are you going to look for someone?"

She was deflecting the conversation away from herself. "I'm working on it." I debated telling her about Ken—see? I'm a failure at love, too—and decided against it since I had no idea how she'd react. I used to know how she would react.

Using her to brainstorm my questions about the Tiptons was unthinkable. Instead, I told her about Violet mandrill and her baby, keeping it cute and light.

The waiter came by with the dessert list. We both passed. She asked for the check and we paid.

"I'm going to be late to work, darn it! So good to see you." She pulled on her jacket, gave me a ritual hug with three little pats on the back, and trotted out the door and away in her low black heels, hurrying back to work.

I stood at the covered entrance way of the restaurant and watched her navigate the flow of pedestrians, crossing at the corner, almost running.

◇◇◇

At day care, I gathered up Robby's jacket and penguin backpack, but he didn't want to leave. "No home now."

Okay. He and Amanda were both delighted to have me hand out orange slices, mop up spilled juice, and refill the bubble mower. After ten more minutes, I said, "Time to go. You can play at Grandma's."

"See TV," he said. "Then my home. See Pete and 'anne."

I wished.

When my mother came home from her part-time job with the school district, I handed her a glass of cabernet and a few crackers with cheese.

"Oh, Iris. You can live here forever." She sank down on the sofa and relaxed, looking tired.

It wasn't right to inflict myself and a child on her full time. I'd do what I could to make it work. "I'll fix spaghetti for dinner."

"Perfect. I'll sit here and read a magazine."

That was good for about a minute and a half. Then she was in the kitchen with her wine keeping an eye on me. "I'll just sit here and we can chat. I froze some meatballs. They're in the freezer in one of those plastic containers."

Right.

"That pan is too small for the pasta. It'll boil over."

"Mom, I'm putting the sauce in it."

"Oh. I suppose that would work. I never use that one. But you do it however you like."

Once I had the sauce bubbling and the salad made and the correct pot of water heating, I joined her with my own wine and gave her the high points of my futile day.

"I think you should let the police find them. What if you succeeded? What then?"

"I'd call the cops. That's all."

"Good plan."

Robby played happily in a low drawer full of safe kitchen utensils she'd set up for him.

She said, "You have so much on your mind right now. It's a wonder you have any energy left."

I had no problem parsing this. How best to survive her passionate interest, hopes, and fears about my love life? Maybe she wouldn't latch onto it like a mussel on a rock. "My date with Ken went fine. Not overwhelming, but pleasant."

"Really? How nice."

How cautious. Good. I summarized our dinner conversation about past relationships, jobs, and the Tiptons. "He seems so slow-paced and quiet, then he comes up with something surprising. But I don't think he was that impressed with me. He hasn't called, and I don't expect him to."

She murmured, "Pity. He sounds like a good man. You were always drawn to the wild ones. I've wondered if that would change."

"What? I did change. Rick wasn't a bad boy. He had a steady job, regular hair, and no tattoos."

She snorted. "Rick would have brought out the bad girl in Mother Theresa. I've almost forgiven you for running off to Reno to get married. We both thought he was perfect for you." Her mouth turned down. She'd liked him, she loved me, and she would rewind the clock if she could. "But you can't say he didn't have a wild side."

"Maybe so, but now I'm even older and wiser, and what's this got to do with Ken, anyway?"

"Probably not a thing. I'm sure you gave him a fair chance. It doesn't seem like you to wait for him to call, but that's your business. Robby, come here, darling. Let's wash your hands for dinner."

Chapter Eighteen

The next day was my second day off. Parking Robby in day care again meant shirking my quality time with him. Besides, I was out of ideas for tracking down Tiptons. I defaulted to routine—the park.

Watching Robby play hard always filled my heart and eased my troubles. His eyes sparkled and his cheeks were flushed from monkey bars and climbing structures. What a wonderful world to hold such a beautiful creature.

"Go home now," he announced. "My house. See Pete."

What a treacherous world to threaten his safety.

Back at my parents' house, I fixed lunch. Robby had never been a reliable napper and the whole concept was pretty much a lost cause. I stood him on a chair to wash plastic dishes at the sink, exploiting a major obsession with water and suds. With one eye on him, I called Pete and confirmed that no one had broken into my house lately, the macaws were fine, and Cheyenne still declined to move out. "Just one thing," Pete added. "Not sure it's anything real."

"Spit it out, man."

"The neighbor next door, the one who saw that VW van? He said he saw a guy looking at the house yesterday. Just one guy, not two."

"In the VW?"

"No, a beige sedan. He tried for the license plate, but he couldn't get it. It was late in the afternoon. I'm keeping an eye out. It's probably nothing."

"Let me know if you see him again." The neighbor in question was a retired salesman who kept an immaculate lawn despite an excessive fondness for whiskey. I wasn't sure how seriously to take his observations.

I addressed Robby's casual attitude toward water on the floor.

Next I dialed Deputy Gettler. I left a message and, somewhat to my surprise, he called me back an hour and a floor mopping later. No, he hadn't heard of any new Tipton sightings. I asked about activity at their farm or Pluvia's place. No one had driven in or out of either one. He did not know where Jeff and Tom were holed up, but assured me that they would be nabbed any day now.

Sure they would.

I'd spent Robby's lifetime learning to suppress frustration and impatience. Never adept, I did that as best I could and built Duplo airplanes with my son for the rest of the afternoon.

◇◇◇

Wednesday I clocked in and found Hap. I'd finally thought of another approach to my problems. Hap agreed to help on Friday, his day off. He didn't lay into me again about firearms, which I appreciated.

Next I dropped by the mandrills. Sky was sitting at the puzzle feeder working it like a gambling addict at a slot machine, total focus, his slender fingers inching monkey pellets up the feeder's bars and out the top. Grab it, chomp it to smithereens, go back for another.

Carmine sat close to Violet, deftly parting the fur on her troop-mate's back to pick out dander and debris. Violet's eyes were half-closed in pleasure at the unfamiliar courtesy. Carmine snuck a quick hand toward the baby now and then, a light touch on his back or leg. The baby suckled and dozed.

Perfect. Sky was preoccupied, Carmine was learning about babies, Violet was reaping the benefit of producing an interesting addition to the troop. The baby was doing what babies do.

Possibly it would all have happened sooner or later without the puzzle feeder, but I felt I deserved some credit anyway. Not that I'd push it with Kip.

Too bad Craig wasn't around to celebrate with me. He seemed to like the mandrills. Maybe he'd contact me to clarify details for his article. "Clarifying details" escalated into a pleasant fantasy that ended up in a bedroom.

Calvin and I worked the routine at birds in an easy rapport. Dr. Reynolds had given him the results from the penguin blood samples. He'd gotten the gender of two out of three penguin chicks correct.

Calvin ate at the Penguinarium alone or with Arnie and never joined the group at the basement break room. When I pulled on my jacket to leave for lunch, he stopped me.

"Thought you might want to know I'm putting in for retirement." He looked at me sidelong.

I sat down across from him at the Penguinarium's dented table. "You're bluffing, right? You've been saying this for years."

His big hands with square-tipped fingers rested on the edge of the table. One of the nails was split. His steel-rimmed glasses were smudgy. "I gotta give these knees a break. Good time to stop. I've given thirty days notice."

I didn't know what to say. I said, "You can't do this to me!"

He grinned. "You bet I can. You can handle it just fine. You'll do better with Neal than I ever did. Maybe get that new aviary built."

"Have you told anyone?"

"Just you and Neal. No need to make a fuss over it."

I shook my head. "I hate change. I can't imagine Birds without you." I got up. "Will they downgrade the position or replace you with another senior keeper?"

"Neal said senior keeper."

It took me a minute to climb out of the implications for my own life. "If you go for the knee replacement, you'll need some help. I can drop by after work every day. I'll make you my famous meatloaf."

"I would appreciate a meatloaf, but my daughter will look after me fine."

I'd met Janet neé Lorenz and wouldn't trust her to look after a duck decoy. "Calvin, I'd like to help. Keep me in the loop."

"Sure thing. You go off to lunch now or you'll be late getting back."

Which meant he didn't want to talk about it anymore.

On the walk to the Administration building, two thoughts solidified. "Don't tell anyone. Calvin wants it kept quiet," and "This is it. Time to go for a senior keeper position." I'd had that opportunity when I was pregnant with Robby and chose not to apply. Arnie had gotten the position—senior keeper for Felines and Bears. Everyone who worked with him had been astonished. Neal, who had just started at Finley, had spent months regaining the keepers' respect. After Arnie came to his senses and stepped back down to regular keeper, Linda got the job.

Here came another rare opportunity, and I'd thought I was ready. Aside from realizing how much I'd miss Calvin, I should have been celebrating, not twitching with second thoughts and self-doubt.

Denny was quiet and preoccupied at lunch. Cheyenne and Marion were bitching about Neal's rapid-fire changes. The first-annual Halloween pumpkin frenzy three months past was still vivid—smashed pumpkins in the elephant yard, the tiger and lion exhibits, the primate house. The animals and the visitors had loved it and the mess was unreal. He announced new developments at every keeper meeting. He had contracted out for camel rides and a walk-in parakeet display starting in spring. Every exhibit was to be evaluated for its photography opportunities and for viewing from a wheelchair. Keepers were to work with the education staff to improve their animal talks, and oh-by-the-way, he wanted visitors hand-feeding animals, under supervision.

Cheyenne said, "He told me he's planning sleep-overs for kids, maybe at the elephant barn, which is insane. He's thinking about a beer tasting. He wants a blues concert. It's idea-diarrhea.

He can't rest unless he's got this place turned upside down a new way every week."

I experimented with a senior keeper persona. "He's pulling more visitors in. That's what pays the bills."

"As long as it doesn't hurt the animals, what's the harm?" Linda said.

Denny just chewed away at his yogurt and greens.

"Did your dog die?" I asked. "Income tax audit? High cholesterol?"

"No, he's bummed because we found the owners of some of those tortoises," Marion said. "We wanded them all for chips, and we found one. Dr. Reynolds traced the code. It turns out to be from a Madagascar breeding facility. They raise Malagasy endangered tortoises and turn them loose in protected areas. A dozen were stolen, all chipped in the hind leg."

"So we won't get to keep it," I said, thinking of the poor beast flying twice across half the world.

Marion glanced at Denny. "We think five of them belong to this outfit. No chips, but they have scars on their back legs, so probably they were chipped and the thieves dug them out. They just missed one. Those things are the size of a grain of rice and they migrate around inside the animal. Anyway, this place says the stolen ones match the species, sex, and size of four others we've got."

"Do you just box them up and ship them back?" Linda asked.

Denny woke up and looked alarmed.

Marion shook her head. "If only. It'll take months to get the paperwork done."

"You checked the parrots?" I asked.

"Yeah. Nada."

I wasn't surprised. "All of them still alive?"

Marion made a face. "All of them have mites and parasites. They still haven't calmed down. I feel like a brute every time I go in to clean, all of them crashing around. Then we had to catch them up to test and treat."

"Has Neal said anything about shipping them to Mexico soon?"

"Not to me."

Jackie joined us, bringing the latest news on the hunt for Tipton treasure. Which was that there wasn't any news, just people wandering around in the mud like squirrels who couldn't find the hidden nuts.

"How would you spend thousands of dollars in gold coins," Linda asked, "assuming there is a Tipton stash and you found it? I go first. A studio with a really good kiln and potting wheel. All the glazes I want, and time to learn how to use them."

"Since you'll be rich, you won't need to sell them," I said, "so you can give me a set of plates and bowls and cups. Oh, and serving dishes. Blue-green like the two cups you made me."

"I'd buy a Trakehner mare," Marion said. "One that's already started. I'll hire a good trainer, and we'll win dressage and show jumping events all over the country. We'll have our picture in all the horse magazines."

"What about you?" Linda asked me.

That was easy. "Pay off the house and set aside some money for Robby."

"For college," Marion said.

"Or travel or his own house. Maybe to start a business." He might not be any better at school than I was. Paying off the house—what a relief that would be. With a senior keeper salary, I could make a little extra payment even without Tipton loot.

Jackie said, "I want a brand new house. One that nobody has lived in before me, with new rugs and new furniture."

"A house in a new development?" Linda asked. She looked guileless, but I knew this for a set-up.

"Oh, yes. On a cul-de-sac, with new little trees in front and a perfect lawn. Everything fresh."

Denny could be counted on for a major rant about housing developments, something along the line of, "That's your dream? To pay someone to trash a forest or some farm land so you can have a new house instead of fixing up an old one? That's what's destroying the world today—people expanding everywhere, paving everything, wrecking ecosystems for ego satisfaction. You're gonna need more than feng shui to get over that karma."

But he didn't say a word. Linda and I shared a look, puzzled.

Someone needed to pick up the lance Denny used for tilting at windmills, but before I opened my mouth, Jackie said, "Don't you guys start with me. I was raised on hand-me-downs, and I get to dream any damn dream I want."

"*Okay* then. Let's talk about Bowling for Rhinos," Linda proposed. "I said I'd lead it, but you all have to help, or we'll be humiliated in front of AAZK."

Bowling for Rhinos used to be exactly that. Chapters of the American Association of Zoo Keepers would round up pledges, go bowling, collect the pledges, and donate the money to rhino conservation. The fundraiser had evolved beyond bowling, but had kept the rhino focus. It had raised millions over the years for reserves in their native countries, no small accomplishment for a few hundred modestly-paid animal keepers. Linda had decided Finley Memorial Zoo should wake up and join the effort.

"Do we want to bowl or do something else?" she asked.

Pete proposed charging for a dinner in the Education Department's classroom, which we would cook, followed by a behind-the-scenes tour. Cheyenne said to just ask people for money for a good cause and not make extra work for ourselves. Marion suggested selling zoodoo from the manure pile behind the elephant barn, a more organized effort than allowing individuals to load what they wanted by appointment. "We could even can it as a gift item," she said.

Selling zoodoo sounded good to Linda. "I'll ask Neal," she said, as we gathered up our lunch trash to depart.

Denny was off in some other space.

◇◇◇

He was in the employee parking lot, a tall shape leaning against my front fender, almost invisible in the dusk. "Hey," I said, once I recognized him and my heart restarted.

Denny said, "Ire. Need to talk to you. Meet me at the Roost?"

"I have to get Robby at day care. How about tomorrow morning?"

He didn't say anything.

"What's this about? Can't it wait?"

A silence. "Yeah, sure." Defeat sagged in his voice.

Shit. One more thing piled on. "Okay. I've got thirty minutes. I'll see you there."

He nodded, pried himself upright, and walked to his ancient van.

At the Vulture's Roost Tavern, we sat where we always sit, at the rustic wrap-around corner table. It seats six, eight in a pinch, and that's where we migrate when Hap rounds us up for beer therapy. Strange to be just two. I ordered a glass of their bad white wine, which beat their appalling merlot, out of habit and to have something in my hands. Denny ordered a pint of Winter Warmer.

"'sup?" I asked, afraid that I already knew. "Sorry about losing the tortoises."

He brushed that off. "I know you've got the Tiptons to deal with. So no worries if…"

"If what?"

He blew out a breath. "I saw Marcie last night. Maybe you can do some girl thing for her. I got nothin'."

Something went wrong in my stomach. "She seemed okay on Monday."

"I went over to pick up some CDs I left at her place." He gazed around the tavern, ignoring the waitress delivering his beer. "I didn't think it would be like this. I thought we could still be friends."

"And?"

"She looked…broken." His gray eyes were cloudy, and all his fizz had gone flat. "Way uncentered. She didn't make sense."

My stomach did more of that bad thing. Until this debacle, Marcie had always made sense. She had lived in the calm center, and I counted on that. It came to me that Denny had relied on her for his reality checks as much as I did. It came to me that the Marcie I'd known for years was in eclipse right now.

He picked up the beer glass and looked at it. "What did I do that was so bad? It wasn't working. It wasn't good for *her*." He put the glass back down. "I just wanted to hug her and make her stop."

But he hadn't. He'd hung tough and now he was asking me to make it all right.

I sat back in the booth. What did I know that was of any use? I'd dumped Denny when Rick came along and then leaped into marriage. Rick and I had separated and were barely reconciled when he died. Those episodes and a string of bad-judgment affairs in high school and college were the sum of my experience in pair-bonding. That, and watching my parents and Pete and Cheyenne. Surely there were lessons from the successful couples I knew, not that I was likely to figure them out here and now. I picked my way carefully. "You said you broke it off because you were too different and both trying too hard." Captain Entropy and Ms. Tidy-Time—for sure it would be hard.

He nodded, focused on the still-untouched beer.

I said, "For a social species, we're really rotten at being together." I tried the wine. It was as bad as I remembered. What did I want to have happen here? I pushed the wine away. "You talk like you're hopelessly different. But you keep evolving toward each other. Look, you've got a steady job, you're not addicted to anything, you don't steal or beat people up. You're not a crazy hippie." I never imagined myself saying that. I finished up. "She's not—she wasn't—as timid and repressed as she was, more open to new things. You did a lot for her confidence, you know."

Denny winced. He leaned back on the bench. "She bought a vegan cookbook. Before we broke up."

That was a shock. Marcie's curried chicken, her lamb chops marinated in lemon and garlic…

"I'm not even a vegan," he said. "I should be, but I try not to obsess." He drank a little beer, put the glass down, and set his elbows on the table, leaning toward me. "A month ago she pasted a little picture of a snake on every one of her chocolate bars."

Huh?

He nodded. "She wanted me to find her a lizard for a pet."

I got it. "Marcie was trying to get over being scared of reptiles. And she expanded into food she thought you might like better. Met you half-way. And that was the problem?"

"More than halfway. Like, seventy-five percent. Ninety percent."

"So…"

"She shouldn't have to do that for anybody. She is who she is and it's great. She deserves someone who can mate for life. Somebody not like me."

"All the compromising was on her side."

"It's like a cottontail rabbit and a fringed lizard, like in some stupid kids' book where nothing pairs up with its own species. We only made it this far because I've got my own place. Living together would drive us both over the edge."

True. Denny's place was a rotting rented house with an untrained Rottweiler bouncing off the walls, tanks full of reptiles and amphibians that other people had discarded, his comic book collection stacked hither and yon, and a kitchen best described as a disaster.

"You could evolve toward neater and cleaner," I said, knowing it was lame.

"Not like Marcie's."

No, that would not happen. Marcie had a white leather couch, spotless. Her cats' litter boxes never smelled. Her napkins matched the tablecloth.

Denny leaned his head back against the wall, throat bared, hands loose on the table, and stared at the ceiling. "I couldn't be what she needed, so she warped herself to make it work. I could see her own energy and how she kept shoving it down and denying it and changing it. You do that, it's going to blow out someday, like Old Faithful. Then she'd hate me."

She wanted *you*, I didn't say. She tried her hardest to make it work. Little snake drawings on candy bars, they twisted my heart. And Denny's. It was enough to penetrate his thick skull, and let him see what I'd known from the start. I studied him, wishing I could change him into Marcie's ideal match, appalled by this latest demonstration of my powerlessness.

He said, "It was taking advantage. It was unbalanced. Get her to see it."

I felt no satisfaction at being right all along. Like my toddler, I wanted what I wanted, and that was for Denny to make Marcie happy again.

What I said was, "I'll do what I can." It already felt like defeat.

◇◇◇

"Go have fun," my mother said. "Say hi to Marcie for me."

"Not fun. Not looking forward to this."

I returned within the two hours I'd promised, wrung out. Marcie hadn't wanted to talk to me, then she couldn't stop. Seeing him had shattered the control she'd shown at our lunch. I didn't understand it, I couldn't fix it, I just let her talk. I never found an opportunity to suggest how he saw it.

"Are you and Denny together now?" she asked through sobs. "You could always have any guy you wanted."

I pushed aside the hurt that she believed I would betray her and her out-sized notion of my attractiveness. "No way. In fact, I'm seeing someone else, a guy from Animal Control."

"Denny's always had feelings for you. I always knew that a part of him wasn't available for me."

"Marcie, it's just his loyalty to Rick. He's trying to be there for Robby, the only way he can honor their friendship. It's not about me. He and I are done with each other. You've seen that—we bicker non-stop. He drives me crazy."

How could she be so calm and sensible for other people's problems and fly off the rails so thoroughly with her own? My turn to be the adult was long overdue, but all I could do was witness the bleeding. I did that for an hour and a half. Somehow Denny had been the splint on her sterile childhood and her timid personality, someone who let her live with courage, even with joy. With him gone, she seemed more wounded than ever.

"You can't keep suffering like this. You remember that therapist you saw in college? Call her. Promise me you'll call her."

After she agreed and I confirmed that she still had the phone number, I hugged her and promised to be back in a day or two.

Was this what Marcie felt like after my melt-downs over Rick's drinking, his death, my fears about being a single parent? I wanted to turn the car around, go back, and apologize.

I needed someone to talk to about my fears for Robby, about the dead people in my dreams, about Calvin retiring. It wasn't going to be Marcie.

Chapter Nineteen

The parents were watching TV when I came in. "Robby went to bed okay?"

"He was fine," my mother said. "How's Marcie?"

I dropped to my hands and knees and rooted around in the liquor cabinet below the television screen until I found a bottle at the back. I took it into the kitchen and returned with a couple fingers of scotch in a water glass. Settled next to my mother on the sofa, I gulped down a good portion of it and emerged gasping.

She muted a commercial. "That bad?"

"That bad. Denny broke up with her a couple of weeks ago, and she's devastated. It's not getting any better."

In the silence that followed, out of the corner of my eye I could see emotions, advice, and observations warring on her face. She said, "I'm sorry. I like Marcie."

I was appreciating that mild comment when my father's voice startled both of us. "Good thing, if you ask me. That kid's a dingbat. She can do better."

So much for mild.

"Dad, you've hardly met him. He's full of verbal bullshit, but he's a good person. Just not the right person for her. He's done his best to help me and Robby." I surprised myself. Why was I defending him, after all the damage he'd done?

I sipped the scotch. Loyalty. Honesty. That was why.

My mother's self-control evaporated. "Dear, do you really want to drink all that? Tomorrow's a work day, isn't it?"

I finished the scotch and reached into her lap to push the mute button and reactivate the show. "I'm going upstairs to read. See you in the morning. Sleep well."

"Let me get you some aspirin…"

Upstairs, I brushed my teeth while the alcohol burn doubled back from my alimentary canal and circled up into my brain. I yielded to it, willing mind and muscles to relax. I'd never get to sleep otherwise. Marcie, Liana, Jeff and Tom—sleep wasn't going well these days. Why did scotch and toothpaste have to be such a nasty combination?

I settled into the narrow bed, careful not to wake Robby crashed out on his mattress on the floor, turned on the reading light, and opened *The Last Tortoise* by Craig Stanford. The book was good, but alcohol didn't help my focus. Was pair bonding a loser's game? Marcie had given it her best shot and flamed out. The scotch helped me convince myself that tonight Marcie might have hit bottom and tomorrow she would start rebuilding. I could hope. In the meantime, I missed my friend. I was just plain lonely.

Ken hadn't called and that was probably good. Not meant to be, et cetera. So why did I feel like a spineless loser when I thought of him?

It was only nine o'clock. I activated my laptop for a little research, then stepped out to the bathroom where I wouldn't disturb Robby. I opened up my phone and dialed. "Hey, you awake? It's Iris."

"I'm awake. What's up?"

"I found out about a reptile show that starts Friday. You said you kept box turtles as a kid. Maybe you'd like to go."

Ken said, "Never been to a reptile show. Where is it?"

"A hotel south of Portland off I-5. Starts at ten in the morning. I want to ask the vendors about customers for illegal tortoises." I gave him the hotel name and the freeway exit.

"Meet you there?"

"Yeah. That would be good." Not spineless. Sloshed and forlorn and foolish.

◇◇◇

Friday morning I stood in a Holiday Inn banquet room staring at tables with rows of small creatures in clear deli containers, like so many scoops of potato salad or slices of chocolate cake. Little snakes, lizards, hairy-legged spiders. This "show" was really a sale. Each vendor had a sign or banner at a table where his or her wares were displayed. Price tags on the containers ranged from tens to hundreds of dollars. I'd never seen animals in such barren housing in my life, and it jarred all my zoo keeper sensibilities. Those sensibilities were already bruised from telling Neal I had a family emergency and had to take the day off. I was here to seek the other end of the Tipton tangle of string—their customers.

Spotting Ken and joining up felt entirely natural. He looked good, much better in a green chamois shirt than that dubious Hawaiian thing. We edged along with the crowd, circling the room. The customers were mostly families with school-aged children, probably thanks to a teacher in-service day. A bearded man and a teenage boy both shopped with snakes wound around their necks.

"Let's get some coffee and come back," he suggested after our first circuit. "I saw a restaurant off the lobby."

Excellent idea.

Ken ordered blackberry pie and, at my nod, two pieces. He ate with a focus that matched my own. When his pie was history, he looked up. "Cool event."

"It's more fun with somebody else. Thanks for coming."

"My pleasure." He shifted on the seat. "I'd like to have a bearded dragon. Someday when I have a stable place to live."

"My husband, Rick, had a pet iguana. He was the zoo's reptile keeper."

He studied his coffee cup. "That Denny guy has the job now?"

"Right."

Ken stirred a packet of sugar into his coffee. "How are all those tortoises doing? I got the impression there were a lot of them."

"Twenty-five or so. One is pretty sick. Pneumonia, I think."

"Denny's looking after them?"

"He's micro-managing by nagging. They're all in quarantine and he's not allowed in. He's making the vet tech crazy." I finished the last of my pie.

"The zoo bit off a lot."

"You've got that right. The hospital is maxed out. But not forever. One of them was chipped and the vet found the source. We'll be able to send some of them back to Madagascar, to the breeding facility they were stolen from."

He nodded in his thoughtful way. "More coffee?"

"Nope. Ready to roll when you are." He didn't argue over splitting the bill.

My phone rang and I stood in the hallway outside the restaurant with Ken waiting at a polite distance. Craig said, "I wanted to follow up with you about photographing the tortoises. You remember from lunch? We talked about it."

"Oh, sorry. Dr. Reynolds said no, not until they're all healthy, and the quarantine period is over. I was going to call you tonight."

"I appreciate that you tried. Not everything works out."

He sounded discouraged. Surely this wasn't such a big deal?

He picked up energy. "Hey, I need to talk through this article with someone who understands the issues. I have a draft, but I'm not happy with it. Could we meet over dinner?" His voice changed, softer, serious. "I'd like to see you again."

A lonely guy in a city still new to him. "I guess I could try to help. I'm booked up today. It's a bad time to talk. Call me tomorrow, okay?"

"Sure. Bye."

Ken raised an eyebrow.

So he had been listening. Well, I would have, too. "That was Craig. The photographer from the Tiptons. He's writing an article about the whole thing. He wants to go over it with me."

A nod. He put a hand on my elbow as we walked back. A friendly touch. A tiny bit possessive? I was tempted to run my fingers through my hair and thrust my chest out. It had been a long time since I'd indulged in girl power. I was a free agent checking out two appealing men. Pair bonding might fail in the long run, but it sure was fun in the early stages. I linked my arm through Ken's and walked into the crush of potential reptile buyers.

With the worst of the culture shock over, I realized that the animals looked healthy and everything was clean. Still..."I hate these little plastic containers. Totally sterile environment."

"Same as portable dog kennels. They're just for transport."

That made sense, especially since several vendors sold habitat wares—aquariums, plastic plants, and heating equipment. I bought an expensive bulb for the macaws' heat lamp.

Only a few vendors had tortoises. At one of them, two red-footed tortoises in a big wash pan tried and failed, tried and failed to climb out. A heap of Eastern box turtles scrabbled in a bin next to them. The turtles lacked the uniform size and coloring of other groups of animals for sale. Some of their shells were nicked or scarred. The vendor, a skinny woman with ear lobe plugs and multiple piercings, told me she had bred them and that they were various ages. She described her breeding facility and management techniques in detail. My suspicions faded and we had a friendly conversation.

Before I gathered myself to ask about collectors of rare tortoises, Ken motioned from where he had drifted to the other side of the room. "Iris, over here." I edged through the throng until I stood next to him. Cute little sulcata hatchlings moved about in an open plastic container. The sign said they were African desert tortoises that grew to over eighty pounds and lived fifty years. Whoever bought these tykes would have to think about what they were getting into. Ken said, "Tell her about that woman." He indicated the other tortoise vendor with his chin.

This vendor, a small man with a frog tattoo on his neck and a blond ponytail, leaned close. "Those Eastern box turtles—the ones across the aisle? They're wild-caught. Some of them are from states where it's legal, and some of them aren't. I happen to know that an investigation is under way." He bobbed his head at me, lips compressed. "Every vendor at this sale guarantees that none of the animals are wild-caught. She won't get away with it for long."

The accusation caught me by surprise. I'd been duped by the other vendor. Or else this one was enlisting me in a feud. "I won't buy one. Thanks for the tip. Listen, what can you tell me about the customers for rare tortoises? Really valuable ones."

"Rich people who want to impress their friends. Why are you asking me?" His voice had gone cold.

I'd put my foot in it. "I'm not looking to buy anything illegal. Honest. But I am looking for people who would. If I can find the customers, I might find a person I'm looking for, someone who imports illegal tortoises."

He seemed to think this was total bullshit. "I don't know if you're with the Feds or what, but I have nothing to do with that kinda business whatsoever. You people can quit bugging me."

"What do you mean? Did somebody else ask you? Today?"

But he turned away to another customer, determined to ignore me. Ken's hand on my elbow steered me away. "Give it a rest," he whispered. "Let me try in a few minutes."

I headed back toward the box turtle vendor, this time to convince her I was a collector of rare tortoises. She was busy with customers and wouldn't meet my eye. I deduced she'd seen me talking with her competitor and probably knew what I'd been told about the box turtles. I gave her five minutes to acknowledge my existence, but she preferred to depart in the direction of a door labeled Staff Only.

I puttered around, giving Ken time to soothe the man I'd alarmed. Ken examined every molecule of that vendor's display, chatting at length. Why did his charm work when mine failed? Finally he appeared alongside me.

"What did he say? Did someone offer him illegal animals? Was it today?"

"Whoa. Not quite. Someone asked him who handled spider tortoises. I think that's the name. Northern ones."

"Today? What did he look like? Or she?"

He steered me out of the throng toward the lobby. "Yes, today. A guy. Not much of a description. Chubby, average height, glasses. Not old, not young. Didn't seem to know much about herps. What are herps?"

"Herptiles. It lumps amphibians and reptiles. Is that all you got?"

"He wore a Blazers cap."

"Great! That narrows it down to two or three million people."

We sat down on a bench in the lobby. My excitement ebbed. "Ken, both Jeff and Tom have blue eyes. Mr. Frog Tattoo would remember that they're big and young and klutzy. It wasn't one of them. It was some random tortoise beginner."

We sat and were disappointed together. I said, "I'm still glad I checked out this show. And your boyish charm is impressive." It was having its effect on me. He was good company. I *liked* him. I got up to return to the event.

Ken held up a hand. "Aren't we done? You've seen everything."

"We can't just walk away from the illegal box turtles."

He seemed amused. "What do you think we should do?"

We didn't have any evidence or any way to get it. "I don't know." This was frustrating.

"Mr. Frog Tattoo said there was already an investigation under way. And didn't you already strike a blow for reptiles by rescuing those tortoises? Not to mention the parrots?"

"I'm done when the bad guys are in jail. That sick tortoise at the zoo? It would still be fine if it hadn't been captured. Maybe the box turtle woman knows the buyers the Tiptons were dealing with." What were the odds of that? Slim. What were the odds of her telling me? Zero.

"Come on, Warrior Princess. Let's get you out of here before you slay somebody." His chipped tooth showed as he smiled. He draped an arm over my shoulders.

Was he patronizing me? I must have stiffened because he took his arm away.

A step later, I ducked down to put it back.

Chapter Twenty

Mid-afternoon, dim with cloud cover and the tedious first hints of twilight, found me many miles north of the reptile show. This trip was the second reason I'd taken the day off. Hap and I had run out of chat, and we drove in silence. That gave me time to plan how to convince Pluvia to spill everything she knew about the Tiptons. Instead I spent it thinking about Ken. He'd kissed me good-bye in the parking lot at the reptile show, a little tentative, on the cheek, but a real kiss, not a peck. He'd suggested dinner, but I had to put him off. "I can't tonight. How about Monday? I'm off Mondays." But he had to work Monday and go to a work-related class that evening. Tuesday looked better, but we agreed to talk in a day or two.

Pluvia's place was tough to find. The first driveway north of the Tiptons' was little more than an unmarked trail. At the end of it, blending into the thick-trunked fir trees close around, sat a dark cabin that I hoped was hers.

Hap's Crown Victoria stopped amid ferns and salal on the overgrown driveway. He waited in the driver's seat. The cabin was small but in decent repair, with a modern metal roof and a sturdy porch running across the front. I stepped up on the porch. The Tipton brothers could be hiding inside or in the woods nearby, watching us now. Was coming here pure insanity? No, just desperation. I'd asked Hap to stay in the car, but I wished he were closer.

"Pluvia?" I knocked again. "It's Iris Oakley. I've seen Wanda." No one answered.

An electrical line ran to the roof. I could hear a stream nearby. An open shed held neatly stacked firewood. It looked like a weekend retreat for a fisherman rather than a year-around dwelling, but I could see the appeal of the solitude and untrammeled woods. Pluvia, or whoever, kept it neat.

The porch had only a sprinkling of fir needles. That and the broom next to the door implied someone had swept it recently. A thin path led from the porch steps across a mossy clearing and into the woods. I stepped off the porch and followed it, my back to the cabin. I didn't go far. The thick, wet understory offered far too much concealment.

I turned back to the cabin, flinching at every little noise, and confirmed that no smoke rose from the metal chimney. An Adirondack chair on the porch looked like my best option. In short order I was cold despite my heavy jacket, the damp air sucking heat away. It wasn't raining at the moment, but had been recently and would be soon. The trees dripped. A bird called, one I didn't recognize. A raven croaked in the distance. After long minutes, a car hummed on the highway and faded away. If I waited in the car with Hap, I'd be warmer. But then she couldn't see to recognize me. I relaxed my focus the way my father had taught me, using peripheral vision to pick up movement.

She appeared on the trail where I'd stopped, an indistinct shape with her brown shawl and tousled hair. I waved and tried a smile. She watched for a minute, then walked up to the porch. She carried the shotgun at the ready. The muzzle wasn't quite pointed at me, but my stomach quivered.

"You're the zoo person. Iris. Who's in the car?"

"Hello, Pluvia. I wanted to see you, and I was afraid to come alone. That's my friend Hap. Do you want to meet him?"

"No. Why are you here?"

"I've seen Wanda. I went to the hospital." Pluvia had been eager for news. I didn't expect her to be this hostile. I did not like that shotgun.

She kept her eyes on the car. "Why did you do that?"

"I wanted to tell her that I'd seen her sons."

No easing of the shotgun or the suspicion. She chewed her upper lip. "Well, then. How is she?"

"May I come in? It's cold out here." I wasn't eager to be alone with her and the shotgun, out of Hap's sight, but I had to build a relationship or she'd never tell me anything. Standing on her porch wasn't going to do it. And, like it or not, I needed to see who was in that cabin.

She hesitated, lips pursed, and made a decision. "Come have some tea, as long as you're here. Will he stay there?"

"Yes." I stood up and walked through the cabin door, telling myself that she wouldn't let me inside if the Tiptons were there.

The cabin interior was open, one room except for a back corner that must have been a bathroom. It was dense with rugs and bookcases, clothing hanging from a rod set across a corner, one huge upholstered armchair, a little table with one small chair. A bed was piled with pillows and blankets. The window sills were lined with rocks and white bones. It took me a moment to identify the kitchen area, a camp stove with a propane tank and a little sink set into a short wood-plank counter. Shelving held cans and boxes of food. Pots and a skillet hung from the ceiling inches above her head, too low for mine.

Pluvia lit a fire already laid in a small wood stove. "Sit there," she said, pointing to the arm chair. I smelled wood smoke, garlic, a hint of wet wool. No sign of any large men—no big boots or denim jackets. Nothing on the table to indicate other guests.

"Just a sec." I stuck my head out the door and waved to Hap, indicating everything was okay.

Pluvia kept her shotgun handy as she put a kettle on the camp stove and set out a tea pot and a box of Twinings English Breakfast tea. "I don't have milk. Never drink it."

"No problem. How do you do your shopping? Do you have a car somewhere?"

"A friend commutes past here to work in town. He picks me up on Tuesdays and delivers me back."

"You have a cozy place," I said. She stood near the stove watching me and didn't answer. When the water boiled, she poured a little of it into a white teapot, swirled it around, and dumped it out. Then she measured three spoonfuls of loose tea into a metal basket that fit inside the pot. She poured hot water over that, set the lid on, and flipped over a little hourglass. She washed cups and saucers at the little sink, still silent.

She knew when the hourglass ran out without looking, maybe from doing this every day, and lifted out the metal strainer with the dripping tea leaves. She said at last, "I hate teabags. They make terrible tea." She filled two white porcelain cups with gold rims. I declined sugar.

She settled herself in a chair facing me. "Now tell me about Wanda."

I told her about my visit. That was the coin to compensate her for telling me what I needed to know. Was it enough?

She seemed to relax a little. "Thyroid and diabetes. I'm not surprised. Liana knew there was something wrong. She got Wanda to tell Jerome she wanted to go to a doctor, but of course he wouldn't have it."

Hap would be starting to worry, but I didn't dare rush. "Was Jerome a bully and an idiot or just crazy?"

"All of that. He wasn't too bad when he was younger, but he kept getting worse. Every now and then he'd surprise me by doing something sensible, but it got rarer and rarer. I think he was paranoid." She said "paranoid" as if the diagnosis summed up all anyone needed to know about Jerome Tipton.

I sipped tea and burned my tongue. "He left his sons in big trouble. Jeff and Tom don't seem to manage very well without him."

"Those boys... Jeff got the worst of it." She studied me before she went on. "Jerome bullied him and Wanda spoiled him. She was sweet and lenient because Jerome was so hard on him. He got caught in the crossfire. Tom did a little better because he kept away from them more. Isn't that a sad thing to say? I excuse Wanda because she tried her best and she wasn't well, not for a long time."

"You've known them since they were little boys." The tea was cool enough to sip.

She refreshed our cups. "Tom was the prettiest child, blond and bright and full of fun. He was always hungry, and Jerome never let them eat all they wanted. I'd feed him. He'd eat pasta by the quart and a loaf of bread at a sitting, if I'd let him. Oranges, bananas. He'd eat pretty much anything."

"That would be a relief. My boy is two and a half and he's a picky eater."

"Oh, he'll be like that when he's maybe thirteen. You'll see."

We sipped in a companionable silence for a moment. Hap, be patient, please. "Wanda brought Tom over?"

"He'd come by himself or with her. He's come alone since he was four or five years old."

"That sounds so young. I guess I don't know yet how much supervision a four-year-old needs."

"More than Tom got, I'll say that. Don't you hesitate to supervise your boy."

"I won't."

She sighed. "Wanda faded before my eyes. She put on weight and her brains turned to mush. Until she got so sick, she and Liana would visit when Jerome was out of town. Sometimes Tom would come, too. We'd have tea. Liana was all rough edges, but she looked after Wanda as best she could, and she didn't take any guff off Jerome. At least to hear her tell it."

"They stopped visiting because Wanda couldn't walk this far?"

"Even Tom stopped. Wanda always had to sneak out to see me. Jerome didn't like it. Then she just wore out entirely. So I had to go visit her. Jerome would go off in that van of his for weeks at a time. He always took Jeff with him. That's when I could go over."

I drank my tea and did my best to be a rapt and harmless audience. She was edging up to the present, to what I wanted of her. How long could Hap tolerate not knowing what was happening in here?

She said, "I checked a month or so ago and the van was gone, so I went up to the house and called out to Wanda. But Jeff opened the door instead of Tom. He was very ugly to me. I could hear Wanda and Liana telling him to knock it off. Liana came out onto the porch, and they yelled at each other. She was little, and I was afraid he'd hit her. The best thing to do seemed to be to leave, so I did. That's when I started carrying my shotgun. He *threatened* me."

"Two nights ago he scared me, too."

She looked sharply at me. "How's that?"

"Tom and Jeff came to visit. They broke into my house."

"Whatever for? Why would they do such a thing?"

"I was with Jerome when he died. They asked me about his last words. I think they're looking for his money. You've seen the treasure hunters?"

"I've chased them off my property. Arrogant fools." She looked at me narrowly, the fragile trust ebbing. She set down her cup. "A reporter came here asking me questions. I'm wondering if you're looking for the money. I cannot imagine those boys breaking into your house in the city."

I kept my voice even. "It's the truth. I had to move out to keep my child safe." Now for the point of this visit. "They need to turn themselves in. That would be best for *them*, not just for me. I was hoping you'd know how to contact them."

"How could I? They're hiding or else they ran away." Her eyes darted to the shotgun and back.

Pressing her was risky, but it was that or retreat empty-handed. "Pluvia, I want to tell you how I think part of this worked out."

She drew back into herself a little.

"I think Jerome called you from the jail and told you where some of his gold was buried. I think you left it at the bail bond office and came back to pick up him and the boys. I think they stayed here for a night. Am I right so far?"

Pluvia picked up the shotgun. "You're just after the money. Get out of here and don't come back."

I sat frozen, afraid to move. "I don't want the gold." The shotgun pointed at me clotted the words in my throat. "I want Jeff and Tom in jail so I can go home again."

"Do I need to prove this is loaded?"

"No." I stood up slowly. "I just want to get my life back."

"You've abused my hospitality and lied to me."

I walked out of the house with my shoulder blades tingling and opened the passenger door. I looked over the car at her. Pluvia stood on her porch with the shotgun at her shoulder, sighting along the barrel. I couldn't think of anything to say.

Hap said quietly, "A handgun isn't any good against that."

I glanced at the gun he held out of Pluvia's sight. I got in and shut the door, my knees trembling and my breath short. "Just go."

Hap started the engine and backed the car out. The shotgun never wavered. As we pulled onto the road, a patrol car passed us going the other way.

Hap drove for several minutes before he asked what had happened.

My voice sounded harsh. "I didn't learn a thing, and now she'll never talk to me again. She's lonely and she's scared. But she wouldn't tell me where they are."

"Maybe she doesn't know."

"I think she knows."

"Don't go back there."

"I won't."

Chapter Twenty-one

"Quit worrying," said my mother. "It won't help."

"I'm not worrying, I'm thinking." That wasn't strictly true. I was sitting on the floor with my back against the sofa, scratching under two dog collars at the same time and, yes, worrying. I'd failed totally with Pluvia and was no closer to returning home.

Range and Winnie weren't happy. Lack of a doggy door, muddy paws, and my mother's fragile garden beds meant they were kept inside all day. They had good bladder control, but they didn't have to like it. I'd taken them for a long walk and now they got their petting while Robby demonstrated "log rolling" and a crooked almost-somersault that Amanda had taught him today at day care. A small foot caught Range in the rear. He hopped up looking alarmed. "Careful, Robby."

It was bedtime for Robby and soon for me. Time to stand up and deal. Snack, bath, storybook. I was reluctant to cope. The security and support my parents provided had let me lapse into a half-child, half-adult stupor. The sense of being powerless over my own fate further nudged me toward a toxic state of mind. Every adult trait I'd ever struggled to acquire was slipping away. I needed to go home.

The experience with Pluvia still vibrated, fear and self-recriminations bouncing around. I hadn't seen any reason to mention the visit to my parents.

Robby climbed on the back of the sofa behind me. My mother permitted this, on the grounds that the sofa was up against a wall instead of free-standing like mine and wouldn't tip over. Robby would need to re-learn the rule when we went home. Someday.

My father had vanished to the basement. My mother hunted through the papers on the dining room buffet. "The Portland Community College catalog came today. There's a few child development classes that you might like." She flipped it into my lap.

I had to hand it to her, she played it well. I responded in kind. "Thanks. I'll take a look." Just as soon as bison tap-danced. She'd worked on me for years to go back to college and finish my degree. I recognized this catalog as the camel's nose under the tent, the renewal of her campaign. In our last exciting episode, six months ago, shouting had ensued. Then, I could just leave. Now, if this escalated—as experience guaranteed it would—I had no place to run.

Robby occupied himself running a plastic car over every inch of the sofa back and cushions.

My mother settled in the dining room and spread work papers over half the table. "Iris," she said without looking up. "Robby needs new shoes. His feet are growing so fast. I'll take him shopping tomorrow."

"Mom, I'll take care of it."

"You have so much on your mind. I don't mind doing it."

"Mom, that's *my* job."

She looked up. "Of course it is. Sorry I mentioned it. Didn't mean to over-step."

Now her feelings were hurt. I stood up. "Come on, kid. Time to pick up toys. Do you want to open the toy bin or should I?"

He climbed off the sofa and pulled up the lid to the toy bin—that was fun—and I started tossing Duplos and plastic animals in. "Robby, you help, too." I cajoled and he did the least amount of work he could get away with.

"Just leave it, Iris. I'll take care of it," my mother said.

The wrangling disrupted her work, but he needed to learn to pick up his toys. I sat back on my heels. Which half of this lose/lose equation did I dislike the least? "Kiss Grandma goodnight," I said and then led him upstairs.

◇◇◇

The plan rose up out of failure and frustration. It germinated as I lay in bed realizing that being a prey species is just too inconvenient. It flourished over breakfast as I looked for a different angle to attack my troubles. On the way to work, it still looked, if not good, at least possible. Law enforcement was a crucial piece. Could I sell it to them? I waited until lunch break and called Gettler, but had to leave a message. He called back when I was cleaning the Penguinarium kitchen. Points to the man: he returned calls.

"I know how to catch Jeff and Tom Tipton."

Gettler's voice was flat. "I'm listening."

"They're broke. They think their father hid more gold. They're looking for it and they can't find it. That's why they busted into my house—to ask me if Jerome said anything about it before he died."

"Okay."

"Here's the plan. I tell them I think their father's last words weren't about his pet birds. He was really telling where he hid the gold, but I need them to help me figure it out. I'll say we'll split whatever we find. They show up to talk to me, and you nab them. Or Portland Police. Whoever."

A pause. "Before I get too judgmental here, tell me how you think you can communicate with them."

"A note on the door of the farm. A note to Pluvia, the neighbor. The newspaper. Radio. That reporter, Craig Darsee, who's looking for them. All of them."

"Then we're supposed to follow you around twenty-four/ seven until they decide to show up. And if we miss them, they throw you in their van, and you disappear. You do know one of them might have shot that girl, right?"

Somehow I could sense he wasn't enthusiastic. "You don't think you could nail them? What would make it work better? I could wear a tracking device or a silent alarm button or—"

"What would work better is you being patient. Let us do our job. We're the ones trained to handle guys like them. I

understand that you're frustrated, and I wish we'd already apprehended them, but this idea of yours is a boatload of risk without
much chance of success."

"You got a better idea or am I supposed to wait until they
die of old age?"

"Please tell me you won't try this. No one can guarantee your
safety if you do. You have a child, as I recall."

Rats. He'd played the parent card. "Okay. Fine. I'll sit on my
rear." Growing wool, one of Hap's sheep.

"Good. Is that all?"

"No, wait. Could Pluvia, the neighbor woman, have helped
bail the Tiptons out?"

"That was you yesterday in the black Crown Vic, right?"

I remembered the patrol car we'd seen. "I went with a friend
for safety. Pluvia didn't tell me much and then she got mad and
chased me away."

"She doesn't have a car or a phone. We're reasonably sure she
didn't pick the Tiptons up at the jail, and we know they aren't
hanging out at her place, so you might as well leave her alone."

No wonder my scenario surprised and upset her.

"So who *did* deliver the money and pick them up?"

Gettler was patient. "We don't know."

"A friend of Jeff or Tom's?"

"Like I said, we don't know. They were picked up after dark
several blocks away from the jail."

If not Pluvia, who? The only person who might know was
Pluvia herself.

Dead end.

Chapter Twenty-two

The next morning, Saturday, found me lying on my belly on the edge of the penguin pool wielding a long pole with a net at the end. A chunk of herring skin clogged the screen over a filter down near the bottom, and I didn't want to drain the pool. The penguins were alarmed by the net, but fascinated by me flopping around trying to scrape the gunk off. They had a lot to say about it. I didn't fall in, but all I accomplished was to get wet and smelly. I tried again with a length of coat hanger taped to the non-net end of the pole and fished out the obstruction at last. While moving my phone to a dry pair of pants, I noticed a message from Craig. I called back and we set up dinner to talk about his article.

I scrubbed fish scales out of the sinks wondering if his goal was more than advice on his project. My female instincts said this was not really a work meeting, but they were rusty. Anyway, he would be hanging out at some up-scale bar, not wining and dining a stressed-out animal keeper. With his looks and killer smile, he shouldn't lack for company, even if the bum leg put some women off. But it was me he called and somehow I'd said yes to an early dinner.

What if Craig did have romance in mind? What about Ken? We'd shared two dates, one kiss. I was still a free agent. But now that I was "out there," as Hap put it, the reasons I hadn't pursued love emerged like elk at dusk and confronted me. Adjusting to widowhood, learning to parent, and warping myself into a thoughtful adult took all I had. A potential partner—was that more than I could handle? But loneliness and lust weren't going to stay back in the hills forever. I wiped down the stainless steel counters wishing I could stop thinking and just roll with it. But no. That's the thing about simple physical tasks—too much time to think.

Was I attracted to Ken because he was the first option in a long, long time or for better reasons? Maybe seeing Craig would clarify that, not that I felt any rush to settle on one of them. This was the most romantic excitement I'd had in years and, despite all the fretting, the truth was—I was liking it. Liking it a lot. This was the bright spot in my tattered, disrupted life. Surely I could be a responsible adult and still date two men. Besides, I didn't have to be totally prudent in every single aspect of my life. I flipped the sponge into the sink with a flourish. "Hell, no, dammit."

Oops. I couldn't keep expecting my parents to pick up child care. I called Amanda and talked to her daughter, Courtney, who helped with day care when high school was out. Courtney was happy to walk the few blocks to my parents and spend the evening in our bedroom playing with Robby. I'd need to Google directions to the restaurant and wash my hair to get the fish smell out. This dating business took a lot of preparation.

The advantage of the restaurant Craig picked was the curved booths. He met me with a smile that would have thawed a harder heart than mine and sat close enough for body heat to register. He wore a gray dress shirt, the top button undone, no tie. Black pants, a sports jacket. I wasn't used to men who dressed with style. He'd gone with the shaved-two-days-ago look. He looked quick and smart and worldly.

And I couldn't find Liberia on a map.

I ordered a glass of wine, but he overrode me.

"Bring a bottle," he told the waiter. "It's a special night."

He vanquished the initial awkwardness by leaning over the napkins and silverware to show me prints of photos for his article. "I'd like your opinion about these, which ones will have the most impact." He'd captured the bleakness and the busyness at the Tipton farm, wet people in uniforms walking here and there. Denny leaned on the zoo van, looking loose-jointed and sullen. I toted an animal carrier full of parrots out of the barn. The Boxer mix snarled at a state trooper.

I admired his photography talent as we ate and managed not to dribble sauce on the prints. Our lunch at the zoo taught me that he wasn't going to ask any hard questions until I'd eaten. Smart man. His hand brushed mine as he held my glass and refilled it without asking first. Well, I didn't have to drink two glasses. But it was good wine and I did.

For dessert, he suggested a glass of port. "Why not?" I said. Port sounded sophisticated. That wasn't my strong suit, but I could learn. Dinner had ballasted the wine—I felt full and relaxed, but not buzzed. He asked about the tortoises, and I told him about the chip that the vet found. "My boss is making the arrangements to ship them back to Madagascar. That should make a cool ending to your story."

"Good point. That's a satisfying wrap-up to the conservation theme. You've added a lot of depth, but I can't finish this thing until Jeff and Tom are in custody. I'm still looking for a connection to the groups Jerome was funding, and only the sons can tell me."

"'In custody' sounds like the perfect place for an interview."

"I'll be pleased to have them locked up and you safe." He eased an arm over my shoulders. "I've never met a woman like you. I've known women who really cared about their work, but that's usually about money or power. It's different with you, more about nurture."

I straightened up. "That sounds totally mush-brained. It's about respecting each creature for what it is. It's about..." I'd never put into words what mattered most to me about my job.

Craig said, "Never mush-brained. Tell me how that little monkey is doing."

I sipped my port, settled into his arm, and told him about the positive developments with the mandrill family. The port was delicious. This date was most excellent.

He said, "I took a few more shots of you that I like. Some from the Tipton place and one from the zoo. You photograph well. Not all attractive women do."

I checked my bullshit alarm. It seemed to be out of order. Body heat and those highwayman eyes were undoing my better judgment button by button.

The second advantage of this restaurant was that it resided in a hotel. I wasn't terribly surprised to learn that the other photos and the draft article Craig wanted to show me were in his room. How could he afford to stay in a hotel? Maybe it was just for tonight.

A glass of wine. Or two. A guy I wouldn't have to face at work the next day. A two year drought. My regression into feckless adolescence? I got into the elevator with him.

We stood apart as I consulted my adult self. She wouldn't be in that elevator—she would have told him to bring the pictures and article down. Apparently she was off duty. Inside his room, the closed door behind me, I couldn't stop the grin sliding across my face.

He stopped short. "You wanted to see the pictures, right?"

I reached around his neck and my mouth covered his. He broke away eventually and kissed my collarbone alongside my throat. He smelled so good. He felt good. Ah, *men.* What a great idea they are. I fought us both into a semblance of self control until the concept of "condom" was in place. Then we went for the buttons and belts.

He wanted to hold back like a gentleman, but I wasn't having it. After the first urgent, fumbling explosion, we tried it again his way, a slower pace. That worked just as well.

I dozed on the bed, curled within his arms. My skin had come alive. My hair, my fingernails, alive.

I'd honored Rick with grief and my level-best parenting of our son. He peered from the shadows and nodded. It was okay to get on with my life.

And get on I must. Reluctantly, I uncurled and rolled out of bed. I rummaged on the floor for my clothes in the faint street light coming through the curtains.

Craig sat up. "Hey, c'mon back here."

"Responsibility calls." I stood up clutching my good jeans and a bra. "I guess I never told you. I've got a two-year-old. I have to get back."

Seeing him leaning against the headboard, rubbing his bare chest in consternation, I wanted to kiss him again. Nope. I'd never stop.

He didn't say anything, watching as I dressed. Safely covered, I sat down next to him and trailed my fingers across his chest. "That was fantastic. Totally irresponsible and awesome."

"You're really going to walk out on me."

He wasn't angry, was he? "I failed to give satisfaction?"

"Oh, yes. But not enough of it." He reached for me, and I slipped away.

At the door, I said, "I have no idea where we go from here. I hope…" I wasn't sure what I hoped for.

He didn't say anything and I left. Maybe he *was* mad at me for walking away. Well, I had reason to think he'd had his share of fun.

And I felt just great.

Chapter Twenty-three

"Marcie. Stop crying. Breathe. Tell me what happened." Half asleep, I had the phone in a death grip. It was midnight and I stood in the upstairs bathroom hoping the call hadn't awakened my parents.

"Oh, Iris. I thought you should know. I wanted you to at least *know*. Whatever you want to do. I left all those messages."

"I was out to dinner and left the phone in the bathroom to charge. I didn't see the messages. Marcie, tell me what's happened."

"Denny's hurt. Shot. He's in surgery. I'm here with his father at the hospital outside Vancouver. Oh, Iris…"

"Shot? What do you mean?"

"Shot, with a gun. At the zoo. It's bad."

"Marcie, I'm coming. It'll be all right." It *had* to be all right. I shoved down panic.

"Don't worry if you can't come. I know you can't leave Robby. I thought I should tell you." She was crying again.

"I'll be there as quick as I can."

I dressed and left a note for my parents and aimed my car toward the hospital. I knew exactly where it was, thanks to my visit to Wanda Tipton.

I drove empty streets to the Interstate, then north across the bridge and past Vancouver, past the zoo. It was a long way, time for too much thinking. Shot at the zoo. It had to be the Tiptons.

What was Denny doing at the zoo this late? What if he died, like Liana had died? Like Rick had died. No, don't go there.

Too much time for thinking about Denny.

Our plunge into a relationship years ago—no more thoughtful than my tryst with Craig—quickly chilled by the chaos he brought to my life. I was stuck forever with guilt about banishing him and taking up with Rick the next week.

The wipers beat against the rain, brief victories, quick-spattered defeats.

Marcie wasn't at Legacy Hospital where I'd visited Wanda. Neither was Denny. The emergency room nurse told me where the Southwest Medical Center was, where trauma patients were delivered. Back on the freeway.

Too much time for thinking about Denny.

Denny's friendship with Rick and enduring sense of responsibility toward me and Robby. His high-energy, relentless brainstorming, mining the worst-case conspiracy vein. His passion for all things cold-blooded. I owed him for adopting Rick's iguana, Bessie Smith.

Ire. He was the only one who called me Ire—she of the quick temper. To get my goat, sure, but also because he had the right to call me a special name?

Fourth Plain Road, Mill Plain Road—one exit apart. How could anyone be expected to keep them straight? I made a U turn and got back on track.

I found the right hospital, certain that Marcie and I were overreacting. The emergency room staff sent me to an adjoining building. A sign told me Surgery was on the second floor.

She was huddled in the waiting area. A large man in a red and black plaid shirt sat next to her, sleeping with his head leaned back awkwardly against the top of the couch, hands folded across his round belly. A dazed young couple sat across from them, strangers in their own disaster. Marcie got up and hugged me, a real hug. We stood aside by the elevators to avoid disturbing the sleeping man, in an alcove with a glass wall between us and the darkness outside. Marcie was pale and her tidiness was breached—fine blond hair astray and lavender blouse rumpled.

"He's still in surgery. He was at the zoo when it happened. I don't know why."

"He's alive. No tears yet." Wasted words, she was sobbing on my shoulder.

Still in surgery. My mental shield of "really not that bad" shattered. "How did they know to call you?"

"He still had my number in his wallet. I tracked down his dad. He lives out by Molalla."

"That's Jack?" I'd never met Denny's stepdad. His mother was long dead, and his biological father had never been part of his life. Jack snored irregularly. He was big—thick-bodied and tall—with frizzy brown hair gone thin on top.

"Your boss is here, too. Not Mr. Crandall, the other one."

"Neal? Where?" The police or the night guard must have notified zoo management.

"I don't know. He was here a minute ago."

No sign of Neal. I talked to the person at the information station. The estimate was at least another hour before Denny was out of surgery. Since there was nothing more to say, we went back into the waiting area and sat staring at a TV set on the far wall, the volume set to a low mumble.

A security guard walked through, scanning each of us, and walked on. "Where are the police?" I asked Marcie.

"They were here. They left when I said I didn't know anything and his father was on his way. I filled out the admissions form."

The thought of Denny actually dying seeped in, a cold spot at the pit of my stomach. I knew very well that death is an intractable, indigestible lump of reality. I sat and breathed in and out, my hands twitching.

Denny's step-father roused, focused on us briefly, and slumped back into sleep. Even conked out, something about him was reassuring. I finally figured out it was the whiff of livestock from his clothes.

"You know Denny's real name?" Marcie said out of some wandering train of thought. At least she wasn't sobbing.

I did know Denny's real name and I nodded, but she didn't notice.

"It's not Dennis. It's Denali, the Native American name for Mt. McKinley. His mother named him Denali Loowit Stellar. Loowit is Mt. Saint Helens. She told him one was for his masculine side and one for his feminine side. Maybe she invented the Stellar part. She lived on one of those hippie farms in southern Oregon."

"He told me 'Stellar' was his dad's name."

"Right." She lapsed into silence.

"Oakley. Come talk to us." Neal with a Vancouver police officer, a woman. I stepped toward the alcove by the elevators, a glass-walled space with darkness beyond. Marcie's eyes followed me, wide and blue in a white face. She didn't get up, unwilling to intrude no matter how distraught she was.

"What do you know about this?" Neal asked.

The cop looked at him. "You can take a seat in the waiting area, Mr. Humboldt. I'll let you know if I need you." She had a long, angular face and square shoulders. She looked like no one to fool with.

Neal didn't do as she asked, but he stepped back and shut up, his mouth grim.

"I don't know anything," I said. "Marcie called me."

The police woman digested that. "His girlfriend, the emergency contact." Her name tag said "Hooker." No wonder she looked tough. She glanced at the waiting area, picking out Marcie. "He was at the zoo with at least two other men. Mr. Humboldt said you might have something to add."

"Where at the zoo?" But I already knew.

"The back side by Finley Road."

"Where the hospital is." I felt sick to my stomach. "That's where the illegal tortoises are, the confiscated ones that the zoo is holding in quarantine. I'd guess it was the Tipton brothers trying to steal them back. They're broke and they can sell them for a lot

of money. Gil Gettler is the deputy sheriff on the Tipton case."
Denny had been alone at his house, alone because Cheyenne
had refused to move out of my house. What if she and Pete had
been there? I could have three friends injured or dead, not just
one. "They must have grabbed Denny and forced him into their
car. Or else they tricked him into meeting them at the zoo."

"Does anyone live with him?"

"No. Just his dog." Strongbad, Denny's dog, would bark like
crazy. Unless they shot him, which might be too noisy. Poison?

The officer cocked her head. "Any other reason you can think
of that Mr. Stellar would be at the zoo?"

I shook my head.

Neal spoke in a quiet, flat voice. "He could have been bribed.
He might have been part of this, and it went wrong. We have
to consider the possibility."

"No," I said. "*No,* we don't. You know him, and I know him."
Blood rushed to my head and my knees shook. I gasped with
the effort at self control, at not punching his treacherous face.
"You would betray your own mother if you think that."

Neal flushed. "I *don't* think it. It's a possibility, a remote one.
That's all."

Hooker moved between us, her back to Neal.

I gathered myself to speak calmly. "He has a big aggressive
dog. Can you call me and let me know if he's still alive? They
might have shot him. If he's there, I'll take care of him." How
I would do that would come later. My dogs hated Strongbad.
His reptiles would be okay for a day or two.

"We'll check his house. Give me your number, and I'll call
you if I see him."

She scowled at Neal and left, cop gear jouncing on her waist. I
turned my back on him, still angry, and sat again next to Marcie.
Neal paced in the hallway.

Time became gluey and elastic, infinite, a night without end.
Two older men in rumpled suits came to see the young couple.
They talked quietly, then all four stood in a huddle with their
arms over each other's shoulders while one of the older men

prayed aloud. Marcie and I watched as dull-eyed as oxen. My romp with Craig felt like eons ago. Rain streaked the glass wall alongside us. Head and tail lights marked the road to the hospital.

A doctor emerged through doors marked Emergency Exit Only Alarm Will Sound. Marcie jumped up. The doctor approached her and we woke his stepfather. Neal had disappeared. The doctor was a woman maybe thirty-five years old, with an ID tag giving a long East Indian name full of r's and a's. She told us in medical language what damage the bullet had done to Denny. It slipped off the surface of memory into oblivion.

"So, Doc," asked Jack, "is he going to make it or not?" He folded his thick arms tight around his chest, his jaw clenched.

"I cannot promise you, much as I wish to," she said. "He is young and in good health. That is in his favor. But it is a severe injury. We won't know for a few days."

Jack nodded several times. Abruptly he stretched his elbows out to the side and rolled his shoulders, as if shaking off fear and uncertainty.

"He is in the recovery room now. He will stay there until the anesthesia wears off. Then he will be moved to the ICU on the fifth floor. You may wait there if you wish. It will be at least an hour, maybe three, before you can see him." She gave us the room number and left us.

We moved to an almost identical waiting room on the fifth floor.

I stood at the identical alcove by the elevators, looking out at the night. An ambulance wailed in the distance, silenced itself, and pulled into the ER. A few minutes later, a helicopter swung thumping overhead to drop down and land in front, bright lights, a gurney meeting it. Cars came and went from the parking lot. Denny's catastrophe was one of many.

A nurse, unnaturally awake and calm, told us we could see him. The private room with its bank of electronic equipment frightened me anew. Tubes and wires snaked from the equipment and hid under the sheet. We could see Denny's face. He seemed absent from his body, all the quirky vitality gone.

"He came through surgery," the nurse said. "Now we have to wait."

It took some doing, but I talked Marcie into going home. There was nothing she could do for Denny. I said I would deal with Strongbad and his reptiles. My parents' house was full-up, so I suggested Jack crash at my house, which he accepted. My place was much closer than his. I followed Marcie home in my car and saw her into her apartment. Jack trailed me in an old GMC pickup.

My house was dark and neither Pete nor Cheyenne woke up when we tip-toed in. The house seemed alien without Robby and the dogs, as if I were an intruder.

I fetched Jack a pillow and a sleeping bag and settled him on the living room sofa while I debated returning to my parents' house. I'd likely wake them and maybe Robby as well. I left Pete and Cheyenne a note on the fridge, then took the easiest path and collapsed into my own bed without undressing.

I woke up two hours later when Cheyenne screamed from the kitchen.

Chapter Twenty-four

Barely conscious, I looked around for a weapon and failed to find one. If the Tiptons were downstairs…Why didn't I have that gun-safe Hap wanted me to buy or at least a piece of pipe? I found my phone, dialed 911, and stepped out into the hallway.

And heard Jack's low rumble, apologizing.

Cheyenne—tough, acerbic Cheyenne—was undone by finding a large stranger standing in the living room. I told the 911 operator that it was a misunderstanding and told Pete and Cheyenne that Jack was Denny's stepfather. "What's he doing *here*?" she demanded. Pete put away the kitchen knife. Jack was embarrassed and apologetic, which made no difference. Cheyenne rounded on me. "You could have told me! You could have said something. You can't go on and on about those meth-addict murderers and then you sneak in with some guy we've never seen before without saying a word to us about it."

I pointed to the note on the fridge and tried to explain, but she wasn't listening, I hadn't had coffee, and the whole scene was hopeless. Before I could tell them about Denny, Pete nudged her out the door saying they would grab breakfast at Starbucks. She sputtered, "I can't *wait* to get our own place."

My head throbbed and coffee did not cure it.

It was Sunday and I had to go to work—Calvin wouldn't be there. Jack fled to tend his calves. I was alone in a house that would have been quiet if the macaws hadn't started screeching.

I was finishing my cereal, eight-inch chef's knife close at hand in case anyone thought this was an opportunity to jump me, when Officer Hooker called. She said that Denny's house showed no sign of a break-in, but the front door was unlocked. His kidnappers might simply have knocked and he let them in. His van was parked in front of the house. No sign of a dog. I thanked her and asked for details on what had happened at the quarantine area. She was terse. "The security guard responded to an alarm and found a break-in underway, two men and your friend. The guard called 911. There was a struggle, a shot was fired, and the two men ran away out the gate."

"The gate was blocked open with a piece of two-by-four, right?"

"What makes you think that?" The sharp tone confirmed I was right. More evidence that this was the Tiptons' work.

I explained that I'd been involved in an incident in the parking lot about ten days before and that there should be a police report about it. "Did they get any of the animals?"

"Two turtles. The others seem to be accounted for. The curator says they were valuable."

"Listen, I just realized this. If Denny...When Denny wakes up, he can identify these guys. He's not safe there without a guard."

"The hospital has a security force and they've flagged his room for just that reason."

"Oh. Good." I hoped that was enough.

She hung up.

I drank more coffee and called the hospital. No one would tell me anything about Denny's condition. I texted Marcie to call me, hoping she was still asleep and would find the message when she woke. She called a few minutes later. Her voice was strained. "They're letting me sit in his room. He's just lying here with tubes in him. He doesn't look like Denny."

"He's strong," I said, dishing out reassurance by reflex. "Give him some time." I told her I'd come to the hospital after work and asked her to call me if there was any change. It was clear she wasn't budging. I put my bowl in the dishwasher and drove to my parents' house to tell them what was going on.

They had listened to the news and were upset about Denny and frightened for my safety. Camping with them wasn't super-conscientious any more—it was a barely adequate measure. I shared what little I knew and promised to stay safe, although I was less and less confident I knew how to do that. Robby was usually with them on Sundays, so that was normal and safe, safer than day care. Or was it? I couldn't decide.

Exhausted from stress and lack of sleep, I drove to the zoo hoping to hear from Marcie that Denny had taken a turn for the better, hoping for a call from some police officer that the Tiptons were in custody.

Hoping I'd make it through the day without hurting myself or anything else. It was soon clear I wouldn't. At break, I crashed out in my car for an hour. No one busted me, and I emerged much more functional. Neal could give me grief if he wanted to. I'd tell him it beat an on-the-job injury.

At lunch time, I grabbed a sandwich at the café and started back toward Birds, planning to eat on the way and try to catch up on work. Linda emerged from the Administration building and hollered at me.

"Iris! Get in here and tell us what's going on with Denny."

Thanks to clocking in late, I hadn't talked to anybody about the night before. I turned around and walked back.

She added, "If it's not too much trouble."

Downstairs, all the chairs were full of keepers plus Jackie. I said to the accusing gazes, "You saw the memo Neal taped to the time clock. I don't know anything more. Marcie's there now." I stood in the doorway and called Marcie. I clapped my phone shut to report that there was no new news.

We pooled all the information we had. I shared what I'd seen and heard at the trauma center. Jackie said that George, the security guard, had accosted the thieves armed with his big flashlight and a loud voice. He'd seen them fleeing. "He's lucky he wasn't shot, too."

"George told me he saw two of them, wearing ski masks," Pete added. "He thinks only one of them had a gun. Denny must have let them in the gate and the hospital. The front door wasn't messed with."

I said, "Marion?"

She said, "He really shouldn't have a key. Policy says he shouldn't."

"Marion?"

She looked at me for an instant with her mouth open and thought better of it. "Two quarantine rooms were pried open," she reported. "I lock them every night. He must have pulled the fire alarm while they were using a pry bar on the first one. They popped it open, but I think he sent them to the wrong one, and they busted into the next room. They grabbed a couple of torts and ran for it."

We couldn't figure out at what point Denny had been shot. Pete said George had done his best to stop the bleeding.

"His best wasn't that good," Marion said. "I had to mop up the blood this morning. What a way to start the day."

I could picture the hallway outside the quarantine rooms, where I'd delivered animals for treatment, collected medications, yakked with Marion a hundred times. Covered with Denny's blood. It seemed like a good idea to sit down on the floor, so I did that. Someone brought me a coffee mug with water. I drank a little to pacify whoever that was while black spots came and went in front of my eyes.

I couldn't afford this. The anger that used to be my only option in tough situations was waiting. I sat and unhooked all the techniques I'd learned to keep it small and tame. When my hands were shaking from rage and not shock, I got back up, and told everyone I was fine. I put the fury aside, where I could reach it easily, and went back to work.

I didn't do the best job of my career on Birds, but by late afternoon, everything was fed, watered, and inspected, and some of the cleaning was done. I wrapped up a little early because I needed to find out whether Pete and Cheyenne planned to stay at my house, given that Jack had scared the liver out of Cheyenne and that Jeff and Tom might find some reason to come looking for me again.

I caught Pete leaving Reptiles, where he had worked Denny's routine. Cheyenne met us on the way to the Commissary, three brown uniforms in a quiet zoo. We walked and they argued about what to do—whether to stay at the house or not. They both kept looking at me sideways. Finally I said, "Okay, let's have it. I already apologized for Jack. I put a note on the fridge and it's not my fault you didn't see it. I don't know how *you* would have handled it, given that it was four in the morning, but I'm sorry you were scared. What else can I say? And I didn't tell you about Denny because I couldn't get a word in edgewise."

Cheyenne said, "Not that. Look, we weren't there when those guys came for Denny. We weren't at his house. He wouldn't have been shot if we'd gone there like you wanted." She glanced at Pete. Like Pete had wanted.

That was the issue? "Coyote crap. You two might have been shot instead. I don't hold you responsible in the slightest. Move on."

"Uh," Pete said, "that's the other thing."

Cheyenne stopped walking and so did Pete and I, on the asphalt path at the bear exhibits, the day's light ebbing. She said, "We didn't want to worry you, so we didn't say anything. We'll give thirty days notice and all that, but, well, my grandmother wanted me to have my inheritance now, most of it, so we've been shopping. We found a place we like. I don't want to move our stuff twice."

I didn't get it. I was tired, I had a lot on my mind. I stared at her.

Cheyenne said, "We're buying our own house. We can't move in until next month, then we'll be out of your hair."

The anger flared. "Out of my hair? What does that mean? I never made you feel like a nuisance."

Pete raised a hand. "Bad turn of phrase. Bad time to tell you about this. But everything's complicated enough without keeping secrets." He turned away from Cheyenne, toward me. "Where do you want us? Your place or Denny's?"

Cheyenne looked at him in surprise, then annoyance.

I shook off future problems. "Someone has to look after Denny's animals, and Strongbad is missing. I need to know if he turns up."

Cheyenne made a face. "No big loss. He's an awful dog. Maybe he moved in with someone else."

"Or maybe he's wounded and hiding," I said, feeling heat rise again. "You may not give a rip, but Denny does and so do I."

Pete said, "We'll get our stuff and go on over. I'll call you if the dog shows up. And I'll feed the macaws until things settle down."

"My parents' house is closer than Denny's. You do them tonight since you have to get your stuff anyway, then I'll feed them." I'd forgotten to keep quiet about where I was hiding out.

Cheyenne looked mutinous, but she didn't say anything.

I sat in my car and couldn't figure out what came next. I was supposed to go to my parents and look after my son. I wanted to see Denny and check on Marcie. Somebody had to drive around Denny's neighborhood and look for Strongbad. The hurt from Pete and Cheyenne's defection had to be processed later. If I weren't so tired and hungry and upset, I would know where to go and what to do when I got there.

The hospital was the closest. A guard in a uniform showed up when I got to Denny's room and looked me over. I nodded, pleased to see him. Marcie stood up from a recliner next to the bed and talked to me in the hallway. She looked almost as pale as Denny.

"You need to go home and get some sleep," I advised. "You won't be much use if you collapse."

She shook her head. "I need to be here when he wakes up. He's going to be in pain and someone needs to interface with the nurses. I can sleep in the chair."

"I can't spell you until tomorrow."

"I know. You've got Robby."

I didn't tell her about Strongbad. She didn't ask about the Tiptons. She was completely focused on willing Denny to survive. I looked through the glass door. He lay flat and limp under a sheet and a thin blanket, switched off, gone away. His eyelids looked translucent. An IV ran from his wrist to bags of fluid suspended alongside the bed.

"Go on home," Marcie said. "They don't want people around. Risk of infection. I've got it covered."

There wasn't much to do but obey.

Craig hadn't called. A whole universe of interpretations and explanations, none of them flattering, opened up. I wanted this day to be *over*.

The next morning I felt better physically and a good deal smarter. It was Monday, so I didn't have to worry about work. I called Amanda at day care and told her I was in the middle of a crisis. She was happy to take Robby for the day, and he was happy to be dropped off. Was he getting used to his mother being absent? Was I becoming superfluous?

I found Marcie hollow-eyed and wide awake at the hospital, not interested in my offer of respite vigil. "Don't you need to shower and check on your cats?" Mentioning the cats did the trick. "Take your time. Take a nap." That hadn't the same power.

I sat and read *Stolen World* by Jennie Erin Smith to stop myself from watching Denny breathe in and out. The book made it clear that the Tiptons were penny-ante beginners compared to the big-time reptile smugglers. The rarer a kind of tortoise, the more valuable they became, so the hunt accelerated in a perverse spiral to extinction. It was all so thoughtless and wasteful and short-sighted.

The big recliner could not be adjusted to a comfortable angle and my lower back ached. Denny never moved. I stood up to stretch and confirmed that his chest was rising and falling. A nurse came in and inspected him and the equipment every hour or so. I used the bathroom in a corner. When I emerged, a covey of white coats surrounded his bed. Denny was awake, but bleary-eyed and confused. I stood out of the way while they asked him questions and he muttered yes and no answers, with the result that a nurse turned a knob on one of the tubes. They asked me to leave for part of whatever they had in store for him. I leaned against the wall in the hallway, flattening the small of my back to ease the ache, heart-sick about Denny's suffering. People in blue scrubs came and went, ID tags swinging around their necks. The hallway smelled of food and cleaning products. I was careful not to wonder what was going on inside Denny's room.

When I was allowed back in, he was asleep, his breathing rasping a little. The staff—doctors? nurses?—filed out. None of them said anything to me. They had been matter-of-fact. Maybe his survival was a little more likely.

I returned to the hostile recliner and listened to my stomach growl. If I left to find the cafeteria and lunch, Marcie might return to find Denny unattended. It was a good bet she would regard that as a major dereliction of duty. On the other hand, I couldn't sit here and starve forever. I was about to take my chances when she showed up. She looked better, but denied having napped. I gave her an update on the morning. "I'll be back tomorrow and I'll get Hap and Linda to spell you."

"That's not necessary." She was firm. "My neighbor will take care of the cats, so I'm fine here from now on."

I didn't like the sound of that. "Marcie, this is going to last a long time. Pace yourself. Let his friends help."

"Iris, I know what I'm doing. Please don't worry. I'll handle this." Her voice was the old Marcie's, calm and certain, but there was a look in her eyes that troubled me. I left her with Denny, wondering whether she had crossed some border between obligation and obsession.

Chapter Twenty-five

I'd done what there was to do for Denny and Marcie. What came next? The possibility of a big Rottweiler bleeding in a ditch decided me.

I found Cheyenne alone at Denny's house. Standing in his chaotic living room, I told her I was there to look for Strongbad. She looked uncomfortable. She said, "I shouldn't have said that about him. I actually like dogs. Maybe we'll get one after we settle into our own place."

What could I say? They kept their plans secret and bailed on me when I needed all the stability I could get. It felt as if another relationship was eroding underneath my feet. "I'm going to walk the road to the highway and look for him."

"You know, we never stayed any place this long before. We always moved on and left the hassles behind." She added, as though I might misunderstand, "But they'd all be glad to have us back."

Okay, Cheyenne, you and Pete had an enviable career in zoos and sanctuaries all over the world before you hit little Finley Memorial Zoo. Everywhere you worked, people appreciated you. Why are you telling me this now? Silence seemed like my best option.

Cheyenne ran fingers through her thick, frizzy hair. "And we're buying a house, so I guess that means we'll stay a lot longer. I don't want to, you know, shit in the nest. I guess I need to get better at dealing with stuff. With people."

We'd lived together for two and a half years and never had an intimate conversation. "You guys were fine as housemates. It couldn't go on forever."

"You were so good to us when we first got here. You're really loyal to people. Like now. To Denny and his dog. Even after he dumped your friend."

News gets around.

Cheyenne's round, tough face clenched up. "If I owe you an apology, this is it. I'm sorry if we...*I* didn't do it right. Leaving, I mean. If it's bad financially. We'll pay for another month for sure. More, if you can't find a housemate right away."

An apology. This was the first evidence she was capable of one. I shrugged. "The money is way far down on my list of concerns. I'll go for Calvin's job and the extra money might be enough. I can't worry about it until I can move home and Denny's okay and a thousand other things are better."

"Just so there's no hard feelings."

"Well, Robby really misses you. It would be great if you could make a little time for him when things settle down."

Her face relaxed. "That would be great. We'll never have a kid—Pete doesn't want to—and Robby's as close as we'll come."

Maybe they would still be around, and Robby wouldn't learn that people could disappear from his life without warning. I hoped so. "Let's see if we can find that dog."

Cheyenne looked as if she'd put down a backpack full of bricks, and I was happy to change the subject. We tried to figure out how the intruders had managed to kidnap Denny despite the excitable dog. None of the scenarios were pleasant. She suggested a paper flier and helped me design it on Denny's computer with a description of the dog and both our cell phone numbers. I printed off a couple dozen copies and we split the territory. She took one side of the road, I took the other.

I started with Denny's next door neighbor. The concrete deer in the garden, drift boat in the driveway, and American flag decal in the window implied that this house was owner-occupied and not a rental. An intense middle-aged woman with a lot of makeup answered my knock. I explained who I was. "Did you hear a big ruckus over there? Did you see a green van?"

She'd heard the dog bark in the middle of the night, "but he always does that" and she hadn't seen a green van. "The police asked me that. I seem to recall there was some kind of beige-y car there. The guy that lives there, he's kind of weird. Is he selling drugs?"

I assured her that no one was selling drugs. "Denny is a zoo keeper friend of mine and so are the two people staying there while he's in the hospital. Did you hear a fight?"

She hadn't heard a fight. She wanted to know a good deal more about these neighbors, but I managed to work in another question—whether she'd seen the dog running loose. She said she hadn't. I handed her a flyer. "Let us know if you see him."

She said she would and I retreated.

Cheyenne and I walked our sides of the unpaved road, dodging puddles and calling for Strongbad. No boisterous Rottweiler romped out to greet us. No bushes offered cover to a large wounded animal.

Watching Cheyenne two houses ahead of me, I recalled that Denny and Linda had both speculated about Pete and Cheyenne moving out. They must have known the couple was house-shopping and were probably sworn to secrecy. They'd tried to warn me anyway. Cheyenne had dragged Pete out on one pretext or another four or five times a week, then she'd returned jubilant one night. If I was oblivious to all that, why did I think I had a prayer of tracking down the Tiptons?

Two long blocks later, I wondered if I'd feel so betrayed if my friendship with Marcie was more secure. Was it possible I was over-reacting? Maybe Pete and Cheyenne were right to keep from upsetting me while they worked out their own future. They'd helped me for over two years. What was done was done, and Cheyenne had apologized. Let it go.

We worked the mile up to the main road, leaving fliers tucked into screen doors or under door mats. Back at Denny's house, I called Ken to ask for professional advice and left a message.

"I'll call you if the dog shows up," Cheyenne said. "Don't worry about his other animals."

"I'll stop by the humane society on my way home."

She waved from the porch as I left.

Once the Tipton disasters were resolved, all I had to do was rejigger my finances, find a house mate if necessary, cook every night, and adapt to the lack of adults to talk to at home.

Loneliness bushwhacked me.

Maybe Craig would call. Or Ken.

◇◇◇

The humane society resided in a nice building with pleasant staff and clean dog runs. I didn't find Strongbad, but there was the black Boxer mix sleeping in one run and the half-size Doberman in another. She came to the wire and I scratched her through the mesh. A few good meals had brightened her up. She wagged her tail and put a paw on the wire, telegraphing that she was a princess unfairly imprisoned, victim of a serious miscarriage of justice. The sign on her cage said, "Not released for adoption. Check with attendant."

I checked with a volunteer, a tall, thin woman who avoided eye contact. "Can you tell me what the plan is for the Tipton dogs?"

"Tipton dogs?"

"Ken Meyers from Animal Control brought in a bunch of dogs from a drug bust two weeks ago. The Doberman was one of them."

"Ken? I don't know that one. You're sure he's Animal Control?"

"Yeah."

"If you want to adopt the Doberman, ask the manager."

A third dog was the last thing I needed, but I did want to see her in a good home. The manager told me that they were trying to create a plan with Mrs. Tipton, but Wanda wasn't sure what she wanted to do about the dogs. "We'll give her another try, and then we'll have to release them for adoption. We've already held them longer than usual."

"If that Doberman female—she's maybe six months—is available to adopt, would you let me know?" Nothing seemed to shake my irrational allegiance to Liana. I was sure the Dobe was her dog, with scant evidence, and I wanted to do right by them both.

The manager said she would keep me informed. I told her about Strongbad, gave her the flier, and asked her to call if he was turned in. She suggested a couple of other places to notify and handed me a piece of paper with the websites. I thanked her for her help and left.

Ken hadn't said how long he'd been with Animal Control, and the volunteer hadn't seemed all that swift. Maybe he was new on the job. Still... it bothered me. I'd have to ask him.

◇◇◇

Robby was on hands and knees racing a toy car around Amanda's kitchen hooting like a crazy child with red paint flying in all directions. Amanda instructed me to make sure he stayed on the big sheet of butcher paper. "That's a race track on the paper. He dips the car wheels in paint and traces it. Tracing is a pre-writing skill."

Clearly my child would never learn to write. He ran his fire chief's car through the puddle of paint and over the kitchen floor ignoring the race track and all instructions. Finally I caught him and held him until he calmed down enough to listen. Washing the car sounded good to him, so he did that while I wiped down Amanda's kitchen. Then we went home and I changed his clothing from top to bottom.

When my parents showed up from work, I announced that the two of us were going out to dinner.

"Oh, no," said my mother, "It's way too early and I've got dinner all planned."

"The two of you get to eat it in peace. Robby and I need some time together. Dad, I'd appreciate it if you'd go with me to feed the macaws when we get back."

Old Wives' Tales was the logical place to go. It was set up for kids. Soon Robby and another two-year-old were helling around in the playroom being trains. The pre-schooler was far more interesting than Mom, so I sat on a low, carpeted bench and made phone calls.

First up: Deputy Gettler. At a few minutes before five o'clock, he answered. What kind of schedule was he on, anyway? "About those tortoises stolen from the zoo two nights ago." Was it really that recent?

"I'm listening."

"The Tiptons stole them because they're broke, and they're going to sell them as fast as they can. We saw the cardboard boxes at the farm that they were going to use to ship the torts, so they should have a customer list or a website or some way to reach buyers. eBay and craigslist are probably too public for them, although we should keep an eye on those anyway. They might remember some buyers and email them. You guys have their computer and that should have the contact information for all their potential customers."

That was a little disorganized, but I was distracted by Robby flinging his body at me, giggling hysterically.

Gettler said, "We're on it."

I propped Robby back onto his feet with one hand. "I just think this is an opportunity to track them. I really, really want them out of circulation."

"Don't we all. Thanks for calling."

Well, I tried. Neal was up next. He often worked late and, sure enough, he answered his office number. I hadn't forgiven him for implying that Denny might have been a willing tool of the Tiptons, but he was still my—our—boss, and I still had to deal. I gave him a version of same speech.

He said, "I'll have Jackie watch eBay and craigslist and the reptile sites. Where are you staying?"

"I've moved to a, a secure location."

He didn't say anything for a second. "Okay. Good. Let me know if you need any help with that."

What could he do? "Thanks. Gotta go."

Neal said, "Wait. How's Denny?"

About time he asked. "I can't tell. I saw him earlier today and he responded a little to the doctors, but he's mostly asleep. Marcie's with him twenty-four/seven."

"His girlfriend."

"Sort of. I may need to take some time off. I want to sit with Denny at the hospital so Marcie can get some sleep and then look for his dog again."

Neal said exactly what he should have: "Do what you need to do. Keep me in the loop." Then he spoiled it. "Be sure to clock in and out each time you come in."

"Will do." *That* was what mattered?

I called Pete and reminded him I'd feed the macaws. It was a long way for him to drive from Denny's. My parents' house was less than two miles away.

My child and I ate a leisurely dinner and revisited the playroom after, but the other boy had gone and Robby wasn't interested. He climbed into my lap facing me. He put a palm on each of my cheeks and stared into my eyes from three inches away. "Go home now. *My* home. See Pete. Ride my train."

I hugged him and kissed his curls. "Soon, honey. But not yet. We'll go to Grandma and Granddad's house tonight."

He shook his head. "*My* home." A reasonable request. Impossible.

It turns out a person can feel adoring, anguished, and murderous in the same instant. My hands ached to choke the life out of the Tiptons.

◇◇◇

When Robby was settled in bed, I came downstairs and picked up toys. Now what? Read a book, check email, call Linda…none of that would help my problems. I walked the dogs and returned just as full of frustration. I needed a fresh approach before I started punching the walls or snarling at innocent bystanders. Such as my parents.

I put on my grownup self and sat down at the dining room table next to the most impatient person I know. Papers were scattered over the table in some system only she understood.

She held a yellow highlighter in one hand and a cup of tea in the other.

"Mom, can I interrupt? Here's a chance to hand out advice." She frowned at me.

"No, really. I'm not being snippy. I don't know what to do, and I can't stand sitting around."

She leaned back and focused on me. "You want to go home, and you can't because the Tiptons might show up."

"You and Dad are more than hospitable. You're wonderful. But you deserve some peace and quiet, and I need to get back to being an adult in my own home. I can't sit around and wait for problems to solve themselves."

"We both like having you here. I think you should sit tight. You haven't given it very long."

"Could you *try* to put yourself in my shoes? You would never sit and wait." I could see her start to argue, then her mouth closed.

She sat a few seconds, tapping the tea cup with the highlighter. "Safety first, of course."

I didn't argue. She stared into space. I thought I could follow the train of thought: What can I suggest that won't lead to more trouble?

She pointed the pen toward me. "What is it the fishermen say? 'Be the fish.' Something like that. What's the other one? I heard it on a spy show. 'Walk back the cat.' Examine each step in the crime." She sighed. "Your dad and I, we lead a quiet life, except for you. I'm not much good at this."

"No, that's good. Thanks." It *was* good. Not a flurry of suggestions and warnings, not a pile of expectations. Just a reminder to stop and think. I'd rather she had waved her magic highlighter and solved all my problems, but this would do.

I got up to leave her to her work. Her eyes followed me, concerned. I found myself continuing down to the basement. My father wore his coat of many colors, a white lab coat speckled with decades of paint spots. He gave me a nod and focused on a banner he was making for a friend. His brush traced a thin red line around each elegant purple letter of Happy Birthday, a fancy script on pale yellow vinyl.

I sat on a stool and watched his sure, skilled hands at work. His real sign shop was several miles away. The basement shop was mostly for house projects, but now and then he knocked out a small sign at home. A window fan sucked painty air out into the night. A little of it lingered.

I sat and watched him work and tried to follow my mother's advice. Where to start? The middle seemed as good a place as any.

An unknown, secretive person had helped the Tiptons with bail. It apparently wasn't Pluvia. A friend of Jeff or Tom, perhaps. I tripped over that. Ken knew them from years ago, when he was a kid. No, he was too nice a guy to be entangled in the Tipton enterprises.

I considered a business associate, someone I didn't know, someone Jerome trusted enough to tell where to find the bail money.

Maybe someone who knew how to set up a meth lab and fence stolen animals.

Who arrived about three months ago.

Who kept a very low profile. No hint of anyone other than the four Tiptons and Liana living at the farm. No other vehicles. I recalled the beige car my neighbor and Denny's neighbor had both seen. Both reports were vague. I set them aside.

What had Wanda said? Jerome bringing her a daughter was good, but she didn't want another son. She said Jerome had ignored her wishes.

I was inventing a young man, then. Someone Jerome found, as he'd found Liana. A man who was at the farm now and then, but didn't live there. Who hadn't been there when the bust came down or he would have been arrested with the rest of them.

Jerome brought him into their lives, and Wanda hadn't liked it. What had Jeff and Tom thought of it? Didn't matter. They did whatever their father told them to. And Liana? She was more independent, according to Pluvia. She might side with Wanda or she might be keen on more profit-making ventures.

What did I actually know about Liana? Almost nothing. She might have helped the Tiptons with the logistics of bail, or she might have been dead already. If she had just sprung them, why would they shoot her? So maybe someone else had killed her. She was the best candidate for hiding the plastic bag. A glass with a dirty bit of paper inside it hiding...what? Given the mud surrounding the Tiptons, perhaps the smear was no surprise. But she was the neat one. I couldn't picture any of the men keeping house that carefully and Wanda was too debilitated. Dirty facial tissue didn't seem to be Liana's style.

Of course.

Denny's cut thumb when we were moving the macaw cage.

What she hid was the glass itself and the tissue itself, not anything inside.

It wasn't dirt on the tissue, and Jeff and Tom hadn't taken that bag from the van at the zoo parking lot. Someone else had.

Someone who had to keep it away from the police at any cost.

I'd walked the cat partway back. Pluvia really was the key. She and Wanda.

Chapter Twenty-six

As best I could tell, the small town of Battle Ground has three supermarkets: Albertson's, Fred Meyer, and Safeway. I hopped from parking lot to parking lot, scrutinizing aisles and check-out lines. On my third pass at Safeway, I found Pluvia studying tomato cans in the canned fruits and vegetables aisle. She looked unarmed and a little fuddled.

"Hey, there," I said. "How's the shopping going?"

Her brow furrowed as soon as she looked up. "You again. How'd you find me? Never mind, I don't care. I don't want any more of you."

"Too bad. You don't have your firearm, and you're going to have to deal. We've got things to talk about."

"The hell we do."

"Yup. The hell. It's got nothing to do with gold, either. What kind of tomatoes do you need?"

She glowered for a minute and gave it up. "There's too many kinds. I can't decide. Plum or not? Salt or not? Whole or diced? Why do they make everything so difficult?"

"You must have bought tomatoes before."

"I never do. But I took a notion to make a stew and I want tomatoes in it. I'm tired of soup and toast."

I picked up a can of diced tomatoes in juice. "Use this."

She looked at me and then the can with suspicion. "Why this one?"

"Just try it. Let's go get a cup of tea."

"Leave me alone or I'll call for help and have you arrested."

"Go right ahead. I know all the deputy sheriffs by first name. Your ride won't show up for hours. You've got plenty of time, and I'm not going away."

"You don't know anything about my ride."

But she let me herd her toward the deli section.

She sat at a round metal table with her back stiff and her jaw clenched. I sat across from her on the hard chair and started in. "I apologize for saying you helped the Tiptons with bail. I guessed and I was wrong."

She sat immobile, holding her paper cup of tea, her mouth grim.

I said, "Remember the smuggled tortoises in the smaller barn? You saw us packing them up to take to the zoo. They're worth thousands of dollars. Two nights ago, men who looked like Jeff and Tom kidnapped my friend, the zoo keeper who was with me on the farm, from his house. They forced him to break into the zoo and stole some of the tortoises."

"Is this another one of your guesses?" Pluvia's face stayed mulish and resentful.

"No, it's not. It's all over the papers. There was a scuffle, and they shot my friend. It's not clear he'll survive."

"Sweet Jesus." Pluvia slopped tea from her cup. She put her hands in her lap. "There must be some explanation."

"Pluvia, Tom and Jeff need to be in custody."

She looked away and was quiet for a moment. "I can't help. I don't have any way to reach them. Even if I did, I can't talk them into turning themselves in. Jerome filled them with crazy ideas about the government, and Jeff hates me. Why, I don't know."

"I know they won't turn themselves in. You need to tell me where they're hiding out."

Pluvia pushed her chair back and stood up. "I don't know anything about their bail or their money or where they are. Leave me alone." She looked distraught and determined.

I leaned back. "Okay, I believe you. We're going to do something else. I'm taking you to see Wanda."

That frightened her. "You can't kidnap me. There's no point anyway. She doesn't know where they are either." She looked around for an escape route.

I stood up. She was so short and small. So stubborn. "Pluvia, she's your friend. I'll take you to visit her, and then I'll bring you back here. It's safe."

She shook her head, jaw set again. "I'm not going to do it."

I closed my eyes and breathed in and out. In a tight voice, the best I could manage, I said, "We are going to talk to Wanda together. I'm in danger and so is my child. *They shot Denny.*" I was ready to grab her arm and shake her until she came to her senses. This could *not* be another dead end. I had nowhere else to turn. "Pluvia, buy your damned groceries. We are going to the hospital."

She did what I said because she was afraid of me. I'd bullied an old woman into my car. It took an effort not to apologize.

At Legacy Hospital, I led her to Wanda's room. Wanda lay on the bed asleep, which was a relief. It had occurred to me that she might have been discharged.

I stood aside while Pluvia shook her arm. "Wanda, wake up. I've come to visit."

Wanda's eyes opened and she struggled to sit up. She pushed a button to raise the head of the bed. "Pluvia! You are the last person on earth I expected."

Pluvia drew back a little. "What a thing to say! Why wouldn't I visit you?"

Wanda adjusted herself awake. She was wearing sweats again, gray ones, but she looked better, not so pale and lumpy. "I'm just surprised, that's all. Have you heard about my troubles?" She seemed to be close to normal speed as well. Now that she had a little energy, she didn't look so old. She must be about my mother's age, years younger than Pluvia.

I stayed out of it while they caught each other up, holding my questions until they were settled and could focus.

Wanda said she was scheduled for discharge the next day. "I guess I'll go home. Will you come with me? I can't face it all empty."

Pluvia promised. I wondered how they were going to get there.

Wanda finally noticed me. "What's she doing here?"

"She brought me," Pluvia said. "She found me at Safeway and brought me."

"Well, that was kind," Wanda said.

"She wants to find Jeff and Tom and see them back in prison. They've been causing a lot of trouble."

That dumped everything out on the table.

Wanda sank back in the bed. "I was hoping they'd go far away. They could settle in Canada and send for me later. That's what I was hoping."

Pluvia glanced at me. "They don't seem to be leaving."

Wanda sat up straight. "They are good boys, both of them. I don't believe all this nonsense I'm hearing about them. The truth will come out." Her voice trailed off at the end, drained of conviction. Pluvia patted her hand.

I stepped forward. "Jeff and Tom think the cops will shoot them, but the cops had the chance to do that while they were in jail, and they didn't. So they should drop that paranoid nonsense and face the music. This will be much worse for them if they don't surrender."

"I can't help you," Wanda said. "I don't know where they are."

"They aren't at your house. What about friends and family?"

"Oh, Jerome cut us off from everyone years ago. I can't imagine who would take them in. Except..." She stopped.

"Well, I haven't," said Pluvia. "I saw Liana the day all the trouble started, but she left that afternoon, and I never saw any of them after that. I've been watching."

"Did you see who drove the green van away?" I asked.

Pluvia shook her head. "I just saw that it was gone."

This was going nowhere. "Look. Jeff and Tom broke into the zoo to steal tortoises. My friend Denny was shot during the robbery. He's in a trauma center a few miles from here, and he may not survive."

"Jeff would never hurt anyone," Wanda protested.

Pluvia glared at her. "Tom—"

I cut her off. "Here's the question: is there someone else involved in this? Either Jeff or Tom is a killer or someone else is."

They looked at each other, then at me. I could see hope rise in their faces. Had I led them into a lie?

Pluvia waited for Wanda, who pursed her full lips and looked away. "I don't want my boys in prison. Either one of them. You have to understand. I can't talk to you."

Pluvia turned to me, "Wait outside."

I hesitated. What story might they cook up together? On the other hand, I was stymied. Not much choice. Pluvia closed the door behind me. I could hear their voices, but not words. Angry voices, rising and falling.

I expected Pluvia, but it was Wanda who opened the door and waved me in. "What, you thought I couldn't walk? I can walk fine."

I sat on the guest chair. Wanda and Pluvia sat on the bed. Wanda looked at Pluvia, then at me, and took a breath before launching what she'd decided to say. I listened for deception.

"I told you Jerome brought me a daughter, and I will miss her the rest of my days."

I nodded. "Liana. He found her working as a prostitute at a truck stop and rescued her. He brought her home."

Pluvia flinched, but not Wanda. "That's right. We saved her from an evil life. And no one ever put a hand on that girl. We treated her like our own."

"I see."

"You'd better. She was a good girl once she got the chance, and I don't want no slander around her."

I didn't nod.

"What? You don't believe me?"

"Did she ever go into town?"

"She never set foot off our property. She was scared half to death that someone from her old life would find her. I made Jerome buy what she needed—tampons and such. I gave him no choice in the matter. He didn't like it, but he did it. She never left except to walk with me to Pluvia's."

Wanda and Pluvia checked that I was cowed into belief before Wanda started up again.

"Now, I had two sons and no need of more, but Jerome seemed to feel that since Liana worked out so well, he could bring home another stray." Bitterness oozed from her voice. "That was Ethan. He was a young fellow, real smart. He was pleasant, but he only stayed with us a week or two. He got himself a place somewhere nearby, and he'd come visit. He must be the root of all this."

"That was three or four months ago, right?"

Wanda's brow furrowed. "Doesn't seem that long, but I've been foggy in my mind."

"Yes," said Pluvia, "She's right. Along about last October."

I figured she knew because she spied on the place regularly. "Why didn't he stay?"

Wanda said, "Liana took a dislike to him. We all ignored it, but she wouldn't let it go. Finally he had enough and moved out."

"Why didn't she like him?"

"I have no idea."

Pluvia leaned toward her. "Wanda, why are you doing that?"

Wanda's eyes filled with tears. "Leave me alone."

Pluvia said, "It's important."

"It makes Jerome look so bad." Her pale eyes threatened to spill over.

I couldn't suppress an urge to rescue her. "Let's see if I already know. Jerome and the boys had made a living growing marijuana for years, but Ethan had new ideas, new ways to make money. It was his idea to set up the meth lab. And he knew how."

Wanda sat on the bed with her swollen white hands limp in her lap.

Pluvia said, "Of course it was. Jerome could never figure out how to do such a thing."

Wanda ruffled a little. Perhaps she was the only one who got to criticize Jerome. She turned back to me. "Ethan talked Jerome into spending a lot of money on equipment. I didn't know what they were doing. I wasn't well." Was that the tiniest bit of whine in her voice?

"They also brought in smuggled parrots and tortoises to sell," I said.

"I don't think so." Wanda looked confused. "I never heard anything about that."

"Well, they did. Tell me about when Ethan moved out."

Wanda shrugged a thick shoulder. "He had bought himself a car and he just up and left. Liana was happy as could be."

"Triumphant, like she'd won, driven him out?"

"I guess you could say triumphant. She was pretty unhappy about his plans for making that evil drug in the barn. I spoke against it, too, but of course Jerome wouldn't listen to me. He said people deserved their misery for being weak. Usually he'd listen to Liana, but Ethan kept talking about the money, and how Jerome could donate it to his causes. Patriot causes. Jerome meant well. He wanted to send money to people he believed in."

Meant well. I let that go. "But Ethan came back now and then."

"Yes, he did. He usually didn't come up to the house. He'd meet Jerome in one of the barns."

"Was his car a beige sedan?"

Pluvia said, "Cream color."

"Would Jerome call him to make bail and get a ride back to the house?"

Wanda's face went sour. "He'd tell Ethan where his money was hidden before he'd tell me or our boys. Not his own family, oh no."

I said, "All of the money or some of it?"

Wanda said, "Just the one batch, I expect. I know he hid it in more than one spot. Jerome made sure the government would never find it. He cared more about that than anything else."

Otherwise Ethan and the brothers wouldn't be looking for it. Pluvia patted Wanda's hand.

My next question wouldn't help find Ethan, but I wanted to know. "Do you remember if Ethan ever cut himself, like in the kitchen or something?"

Pluvia and Wanda looked at me as if I'd lost my mind. Wanda frowned for a minute and said at last, "Yes, there was such a thing. I remember it because it was the one time Liana was nice to that man. It was just before he left. He nicked himself out in the barn doing something or other. His hand was still bleeding when they all came up to the house for some reason. Liana put a bandage on it."

I told them about the bag I'd found. "I think he'd used that glass, maybe for a drink of water. Inside it was a tissue that must have had blood from his cut hand."

The two women looked at me blankly.

"It was an ID kit. His fingerprints and maybe his DNA were on file somewhere for crimes he'd committed. I think Liana told him she had hidden it where he'd never find it, and she'd turn it over to the police if he didn't leave. I bet she was pretty upset when he helped get the meth lab into production anyway."

I could tell Pluvia got it.

Tears spilled down Wanda's soft cheeks. "Liana tried to protect us from a criminal. Jerome wouldn't listen."

I nudged the tissue box on her bed tray toward her. "Your farm was as safe and remote as any place could be. Ethan must have thought he'd landed in heaven."

"He killed my girl. Ethan killed her."

Sounded right to me. "So. Where is his place?"

And they didn't know. Either of them. No idea.

Chapter Twenty-seven

I dropped Pluvia off at the Battle Ground Safeway to connect with the friend who would take her back to her cabin. On the way, she practically burbled. "Wanda is almost her old self again. It's wonderful to have her back. Thank you *so much* for taking me."

I nodded politely. Panic was skittering across my brain on little sandpiper toes with depression and frustration trotting right behind. I'd pinned my last hopes on those two women.

Pluvia said, "She'll have a hard time at home, with everyone gone. I'll do what I can, but sorrows take their own time." She was quiet for a mile or so. "I wish we could help you find Jeff and Tom. I know they're in big trouble. I never thought Tom would act like that." She lapsed into silence, which suited me fine.

I had a name, but it was certainly false. I had a description that was largely useless—white, average height, dark hair, a thin mustache and a little beard patch, no special characteristics. I pictured a guy a few years older than Liana—closer to Jeff and Tom's age, probably a meth addict with bad teeth. Not the spider tortoise shopper at the reptile show, the descriptions were too far off. Maybe I'd seen him. Maybe he was one of the men with metal detectors roaming the farm.

I believed what the two women told me, and many details were now filled in. But the big question, the one that mattered, remained unanswered: where the hell *were* these guys?

Deep in hiding, that was where, holed up deep in the fir trees and big-leaf maples, hunkered down in some forgotten cabin that no one would ever find. They'd foray out at night, like feral cats, for food and mayhem and vanish at daybreak.

I called Gettler from the Safeway parking lot. Might as well tell him what I'd learned. Maybe he could pull something useful out of his official hat. "It's Iris. I talked to Pluvia, the neighbor."

"You didn't listen to me, did you?"

"I took her to the hospital to visit Wanda Tipton." I told him about the third man.

"Interesting. We haven't seen any evidence of an outsider. I'll drop by the hospital and talk to your friend if he's awake enough by now. He might give us some descriptions. I'll pay Wanda another visit, too."

Denny was too out of it to be useful, and I doubted Wanda would talk to the law. "Better you should run every fingerprint you found at the farm."

"Thanks. I'd never have thought of that."

Stung, I clapped my phone shut and pointed the Honda toward the Interstate and home. After a few miles, I realized Officer Gettler might be a little stressed himself.

Somehow I now had a regular hospital route. I took the exit to the Southwest Medical Center to see Denny and Marcie. Linda and Marion hovered outside the room. They wore civilian clothes, which in Marion's case was surprising—a long, colorful skirt. Linda was in predictable jeans and a sweatshirt.

Marcie, somehow unrumpled in a pink turtle-neck and tan pants, stepped out of the room to join us in the hallway. She assured us Denny was better, but I couldn't see any change. He was still limp, the machines still hummed, the tubes still dripped.

Linda said, "Marion and I can sit with him on our days off. Hap would, too, and Pete and Cheyenne. We can make a schedule."

Marcie smiled and shook her head. "Oh, that's not necessary. I'm fine here. Thanks for offering."

We stood around in the hallway, uncomfortable and worried, stymied.

"Marcie," I said, "you don't have to do this alone. Let his friends help."

"I have to be here." It was a statement of fact, not debatable. Marcie's eyes were hollow and brilliant and serene. "I have everything I need."

We took another peek at him and left. In the lobby, we shared a frustrated shrug and went our separate ways. Marcie would do everything humanly possible to take care of Denny, and there was nothing I could do to take care of Marcie. Better to focus on other problems. Like finding Strongbad.

Ken called while I was in the hospital parking lot on my way out. "Hey, sorry I didn't call sooner. Didn't notice the message. How's your friend? Have you found that dog?"

I told him what had happened to Denny and about my attempts to find Strongbad. "He's got a collar with some sort of ID tag, maybe a license. Denny never said anything about chipping him."

"Could be they just clouted him over the head to shut him up," he said without excitement. "He might have run off any direction. He might have tried to trail the car. You could search the route to the zoo."

"We did, but not all the way to the freeway. I'll go back and walk farther along the road."

"I'll meet you at Denny's house. What's the address? We can each take a side."

Driving to Denny's, I decided I would not regret sleeping with Craig. Even if I never saw him again, it had been worth it to feel like more than a harassed parent and dutiful employee, if only for a little while. Ken appealed, but Craig moved faster. I didn't owe either of them a thing. Everyone has baggage and a secret or two.

Ken was chatting with Cheyenne on Denny's front porch when I arrived and broke away with such an open, happy-to-see-me face that I almost stumbled. Surprised into shyness, I shook his hand and thanked him for helping out.

He and I started at the arterial where Cheyenne and I had stopped and worked toward the freeway. Few people were home and those weren't sociable. We left a flier at each house. The air was cool and damp. Instead of the usual gray ceiling with dull, even light, the sky was mottled and uneven. Daylight brightened and dimmed as the clouds shifted, dark bruises outlined in pale. The rain held off.

We quit at the freeway. "Worst case, he's injured and dying in the bushes somewhere," I said.

"Best case, he's holed up at someone's house eating leftover steak. Come on. I'll buy you a cup of coffee and a cookie. There's nothing more we can do."

We caravanned to a little café close by. The coffee was acceptable and a big chocolate cookie was the best part of this dismal day. Ken's fondness for pastries was hell on my waistline. I told him about seeing the Tiptons' dogs at the humane society.

"Nice place. They do a good job," he said.

I cocked a head at him. "But they don't know you. At least the volunteer didn't know your name."

"There's one woman there who cannot get it out of her head that my name is Benjamin, like her cousin the bus driver. Ben, Ken—way too close. I gave up telling her. What's next on your agenda?"

"No agenda. I'm stuck waiting. Waiting to hear if Denny's going to survive. Waiting to hear the Tiptons are in custody so I can go home. Waiting to hear about that damned dog that Denny never trained." The tortoises were probably being tossed around with other packages at the post office, on their way to some ignorant or ethics-free collector. I put my face in my hands. "I am so angry I want to throw up. I want to kill these people. I can't think of what to do to make this be *over*."

Ken said, "Sometimes waiting *is* what you do. Sometimes it's all you *can* do."

"Hasn't worked so far. If I wait, something bad happens. If I act, something worse happens."

I yielded to his bottomless calm and interested brown eyes. I ate the cookie and told him about my visit with Pluvia and Wanda and my failure to win over Gettler with my plan to trap Jeff and Tom. "I'm sure that someone else is using them as cats' paws. When those guys were leaving my house, Jeff said they'd better hurry up or they'd catch hell. I wondered who would be pissed off at them. It has to be whoever's taking Jerome's place in their lives."

He absorbed this. "I've wondered how those two managed to evade the law so long. Someone helping them makes sense."

My hands were on the table wrapped in an iron grip around my coffee mug. He put his hands on each side of mine, a mini-hug. "Slow down and let the solutions develop. Wait and watch for awhile. Less dangerous, for one thing."

I promised to consider that strategy. I felt better and it wasn't just caffeine and calories. He made me feel calmer and less frantic about the mess my life was in. I'd always been drawn to men who brought a challenge, a dash of risk, men who got my pulse pounding. Not men who slowed it down and made me feel safe. Calm and caution—would that evolve into "boring"? Might take awhile to find out.

I'd try following his advice, "wait and watch," only because, for the life of me, I couldn't think of a single thing to do.

Chapter Twenty-eight

Wednesday, aside from concern about Denny, Calvin seemed unusually cheerful as well as casual about the work. I didn't feel his eyes on me as I prepared the diets. He didn't seem at all worried about how many meal worms in this pan, whether the fruit was cut to the right size in that pan, what size the slivers of fish were. He acted as though I knew how to do it perfectly, and he could relax and putter around. It was unnerving.

At morning break, he disappeared. I called Marcie and learned that Denny was talking a little when he was awake. His meds had been changed, but I didn't follow the details. "I'll come after work."

Marcie said, "There's no point—he's asleep most of the time."

"Can I spell you or bring anything?"

"No, I'm fine, thanks."

This was her project, her realm, and I wasn't to be part of it. She was disregarding our friendship as well as all the years I'd known Denny. I didn't like it. She had to be near collapse from lack of sleep and stress. If she ended up sick or irrational, both of them would need someone to pick up the pieces.

Craig hadn't called and I didn't like that any better. I wanted to hear that we were okay. I wouldn't mind talking to Ken, while I was wishing.

Calvin returned and found me scrubbing the aviary feeding platforms. "Neal's got the job posted. You better get your application in." He shooed me out early for lunch.

Jackie, the department secretary, printed off the form for me. "Heading for the big time, huh? Don't forget us little people."

I snorted and was searching for a witty reply when she added, "Neal wants to see you."

"Here I am."

"He's Skypeing with the elephant insemination guy. He and Ian and Cheyenne. I think they're scheduling the next try at knocking up Nakri."

"I'll come back after lunch."

"No, he'll be at a meeting downtown. This thing will be over in ten minutes."

I sat and ate my sandwich until Ian and Cheyenne emerged. Ian pretended I wasn't there. Cheyenne gave me a cautious smile.

Neal saw me through the door. "Oakley. Let's talk."

I stepped into his office.

"Close the door."

I closed the door.

"Not to be trite, but there's good news and there's bad news."

The bad news had been really awful lately. I sat down. "Let's have it."

He massaged the bridge of his nose. "Did you plan to apply for the senior keeper position that just opened up?"

"Yup."

"I wanted to talk to you privately. Maybe this information is outdated." He pulled out a folder and rubbed his nose on the back of a hand.

"What information?"

"Your personnel file indicates you finished two years of college. Is that correct?"

"Yes. Is there a problem?"

"Senior keeper requires a degree. All our job descriptions were updated a year and a half ago. The requirement aligns the position with current standards in the industry."

"A college degree."

"A bachelor's degree in a related field."

I sat paralyzed with surprise and dismay. This could not be true. My next reaction was that my mother must never hear of this, followed by the realization that I was a dumb-ass moron loser. My eyes prickled.

Neal closed the folder. "If you pick up an A.A. degree and you're enrolled in a B.A. program, I might manage a temporary waiver. But you've got to get that bachelors to fill a senior keeper position."

"What about the fact that I have years of experience in that exact job, and I'm damned good at what I do? That doesn't count for squat?" Anger pushed the tears back.

He folded his hands on his desk. "I was pretty sure you hadn't read the requirements. I wanted to give you a chance to think it over."

Think? This was not a moment when thinking was an option. I stood up. "I can't deal with this now."

"Wait. You haven't had the good news yet."

I sat and tried to listen.

"A post office in Kelso found one of the tortoises. A clerk heard it moving around in a package. Postal Inspection Services notified all the post offices in southern Washington, and they found the other one, too. So they'll be back just as soon as the deputy who opened the boxes gets himself here."

"Good. Great." I was still sinking into a pool of dismay. I sat up straighter. Focus. Breathe. "That means that the Tiptons will stay broke, assuming they don't get paid until delivery. And now the police have the name and address of one or two of their customers."

"We'll have to see how that plays out. Apparently the clerk already bragged to the media, so it won't be any secret."

"Too bad."

"Might not make any difference."

I stood up again.

Neal turned toward his computer. "You think about my suggestion. I'll try to work with you on this." He scowled at me. "Also, I'd like to be informed immediately about anything that affects your safety, work-related or not."

"Sure," I mumbled and got out of there. What could he do about my safety? Let me move into the Penguinarium with Robby and two dogs?

I headed toward Birds, then remembered I was at Primates for the afternoon. That brought me by the lions, who were inside, and then to the young tigers. It was a cold, blustery day with fitful rain. They didn't care. They were *Amur* tigers, formerly known as Siberian tigers, adapted to climates far colder than this. They scoffed at our paltry winters. One of the sisters was in the pool slamming a floating Boomer ball around. The other paced the rim and yowled, sticking out a paw to bat at the big red ball whenever it was within reach.

The one in the pool—Katrina—lunged out, water sheeting off her sides, and chased Nadia down into the moat. Nadia raced back up and whirled around to grapple with her sibling, long tails flying. Young, healthy, beautiful. Full of life.

I'd never bothered to plan my career and now it turned out my job was a dead end. I liked my job, but "dead end" was depressing. And financially scary. Perspective trickled in. I'd trade a better job for a guarantee of Denny's survival in a heart-beat. I absorbed what I could of the tigers' vigor and trudged to Primates.

The mandrill troop looked good and gave my mood another tiny boost. The baby crept around on Violet's lap, little jerky movements. I waved to get his attention and he looked at me, big-eyed and alert. He was beyond adorable. I stalled for a few minutes. Sky ambled over and, to my surprise, Violet didn't flee. He made a casual pass at grooming her shoulder, nothing like Carmine's beauty-school-graduate expertise, and sniffed at his son. The baby froze as the big muzzle came close, but didn't freak out. Violet seemed unconcerned and perhaps a trifle smug. This baby business was working out for her. She had gone from Cinderella sleeping on the hearth to princess of the troop, a status she hadn't enjoyed since she was in estrus.

I found Kip at the cotton-top tamarins. "Kip, listen to this. Sky just groomed Violet so he could get close to the baby. You were right—he was never aggressing at Violet, he just wanted to see the baby." Sky would never be the monkey equivalent of my dad—that wasn't in the mandrill repertoire—but maybe he wouldn't terrorize his son in Jerome Tipton style.

Kip shrugged a no-big-deal shrug, but a hint of relief gave her away. "He hates it when the baby cries. He threatens everyone in sight and chases Violet. But now Violet lets the baby nurse so there's no crying, and everyone has settled down. I told you it would be fine."

Sure she did. "The baby looks great."

"Mr. Crandall asked a donor to name him. It's 'Mtoki.'"

"Which means?"

"It's a banana dish from the Cameroon. Supposed to be great stuff."

"I like the sound of it. Mandrills are from the Cameroon, right?"

Kip looked ever so slightly impressed. "Yes, they are. Mtoki is way better than 'Butchy'."

This was an ancient grudge from a Diana monkey that Mr. Crandall had named after a city councilman's nephew.

Calvin might have total confidence in my skills, but Kip didn't. I scrubbed cages and fixed diets under her careful eye until quitting time. Nonetheless, I found opportunities to list the reasons college was impossible.

I had a full-time job that left me physically tired.

I had a pre-schooler. Time I spent on school would come out of time with Robby.

I had to find roommates just to meet my bills. The only way to pay for tuition was loans and how was I going to pay those back?

And the big one—I wasn't that good at studying. I'd passed all my classes my freshman and sophomore year, but I gave Marcie's tutoring most of the credit.

It was impossible.

But other people with kids and jobs did it. How did they pull it off? No matter, it wouldn't work for me.

I'd been happy with my job until I found out I was stuck. I'd go back to being happy with it again.

◇◇◇

I was inspecting Comice pears at New Seasons grocery store in southeast Portland when my phone rang. Craig. Three days after I'd tossed caution to the wind. It felt like weeks. I stepped into the wine aisle where it was quieter.

"Hey," he said. "Haven't heard from you." His voice was neutral, cautious.

"I was thinking the same." I intended to match the neutral tone, but maybe that was too cold? Nope. I'd had a bad day, and he should have checked in with me before this.

"I wasn't sure you wanted to hear from me. You took off pretty fast."

I'd hurt his feelings by not staying for breakfast? My heart sank a little. "I told you—it was great, but I had to get back to my kid."

"How's your friend? The news said he was hurt pretty bad." Still neutral.

So this was a business call. Research. Now *my* feelings were hurt. "It looks like he'll live. He looks a little better every day."

"He's getting good care?"

"Bullet wounds are business as usual for the trauma center. They seem to know what they're doing."

"Good. You must be pretty upset anyway. Hey, could I see you again? Maybe tomorrow night?" His voice had warmed and shifted to personal.

That was better. "I'd like that. But I'm losing my mind right now with Denny and work and everything else. My life is in chaos. Can I call you tomorrow and let you know?"

"Yes, you can."

I didn't want to hang up. Three friendships were on the wane. I could use a new one. "Wait. Did you hear the two stolen tortoises were found?"

"That fast."

"Yeah, and they're still alive. A tiny piece of good news."

We both breathed for a minute. "Have you found out any-thing new?" Lame…I walked back to the fruit section. I needed to get home.

"Just what the news has. I'm really frustrated. Nothing's working out." He added, "Except for Saturday night."

"That did work out pretty well." I smiled at the apples, relieved. He wasn't staying mad. Maybe we had a future. I tucked the phone under my ear to free my hands and bagged up organic Fujis. Expensive, but my mother wanted organic.

"Atlantic turned me down, but I've pitched Harper's and they're nibbling. Some of the online sites pay fairly well, so I'm negotiating there."

"Um, I have a new theory." I told him about the third man while I selected carrots. I dropped one and had to put the phone down for a few seconds. "Say that again?"

"I said I like it. Your theory. I'm wondering how I can confirm it. Where are you?"

"Grocery shopping." I told him my plan to lure the whole pack of them out of hiding by telling them I knew where the gold was. "I tried to get Gettler, the deputy sheriff, to buy into it. He thinks I'm a lunatic." A woman with an infant in a front pack stepped away from me.

"He's entitled to his opinion." A pause. "For that to work, you'd need to be pretty convincing. Not that I think this is a good idea."

"I could be convincing." Milk. We needed one-percent and some half-and-half.

"Try me."

"Where would they put string cheese? It's not with the rest of the cheese. Oh, I forgot they have two sections. I misheard Jerome's last words. I finally figured out what he really meant and it points to where he hid his stash."

A pause. "They've failed with you once."

"I can make the case. And they're stumped. Otherwise, they wouldn't have tried for the tortoises. Did the Tipton van have a GPS gismo?" I'd forgotten lettuce. I headed back to the produce section.

"I can find out."

"I think Jerome buried his stash in the forest around the house or off the main road. Everything in those woods looks the same—fir trees, sword ferns, fallen logs. He'd either have to bury it by a landmark, which isn't all that reliable, or use the GPS. He could pick up the GPS coordinates of his hidey-hole from the device—I tested that with the one in the zoo's van—and write them down." Coffee. Peet's or another brand? They were out of Peet's French Roast. An experimental brand, then.

"We're looking for a string of numbers." Craig didn't sound excited.

I parked the cart at the self-serve bins. "Yup. That's why the barn was searched. And probably the house, after all the agencies left. But the Tiptons and their buddy didn't find it. Hold on, I have to bag up some granola."

"Did you really find a piece of paper with coordinates? You're not making this up?" Now he sounded interested.

"See? I convinced *you*. But I can't figure out how to make it work without risking my life. Or how to make it work, period. It's not like we're Facebook friends. I can't communicate with them." I tossed the granola into the cart.

"Let me think about it. Where'd you find the numbers?"

"Think away. I'm stumped." I was in the checkout line and distracted by loading groceries onto the belt. What I needed was a partner. Craig was smart and energetic. He could help me figure this out.

He said, "On second thought, Gettler was right. This is a terrible idea, for you, anyway. I'll find a way to tell them *I* found that piece of paper, and we'll take it from there. You don't have to be part of it. But you and I should meet first, when you aren't distracted."

"Um, you do remember that one of them shot Liana?" The teenage boy ahead of me gave me a concerned look. I smiled.

"I haven't forgotten. I'll take precautions."

"Like working with Gettler."

"Exactly. I think I can get him on board easier than a woman could. No offense."

Yes, offense…for about a second. This sounded great. But only for another second. "Hey, I didn't mean to set you up. You don't have to do this. It's truly risky." Now the clerk was looking at me.

"I can take care of myself."

Lame or not, he did seem as though he could do that. Hope flared that he would bust the Tiptons, get his article, and just possibly join me in the bedroom of my own home. How fine would that be?

He said, "As long as those boys are still in the wind, you need to be careful. There could be wild cards from some terrorist group that Jerome associated with. Listen, I did a feature on witness protection programs. I know how to keep you safe, so call me if anything happens. Promise?"

"Sure." I walked out of the store with heavy bags and a lighter step.

Chapter Twenty-nine

After dinner, my mother wanted us to watch *How to Train Your Dragon*. I walked the dogs first, keeping watch for Tiptons or home-grown terrorists jumping out at me. We got soaked and the dogs shook all over the kitchen. I didn't catch their feet in time to keep prints off the rug. I flurried around with a towel.

My father declined the cartoon feature in favor of finishing the dishes, so the three of us settled in front of the TV. Robby was glued to my lap, entranced. It was fun, but the scarier scenes inspired him to point at the screen and protest—"Him hurt on arm! Bad fire!"

"It's not real, honey," I said. "It's pretend. Nobody really got hurt." I could never tell if my commentary made any sense to him. How could it not be real if it was right in front of his eyes?

I liked the movie's concept—that understanding the dragons could turn enemies into allies and that yelling was not the optimal training technique. Still, it was upsetting Robby. I announced that it was bedtime and shut it off.

My mother said, "I'm so sorry. A friend said it was fine for little ones. I should have researched it more. I hope Robby can sleep."

"Mom, he'll survive. Don't beat yourself up." I repressed a guilty delight that the parenting boo-boo was not my fault and carried my child upstairs.

For his bedtime story, Robby wanted an old favorite, a Beatrix Potter book called *A Fierce Bad Rabbit*. He demonstrated with dramatic re-enactments using his stuffed bunny how the bad rabbit fought dragons, but it wasn't clear whether it actually won. I explained that his armadillo was really a species of good dragon that would protect him while he slept. Thankfully, he bought that and tucked it under his chin when he lay down.

My poor boy, exiled from his home, missing his friends Pete and Cheyenne, saddled with a mother who half the time was over-wrought by her troubles.

I stretched out alongside him and almost fell asleep myself. Damn. The macaws had to be fed.

I grumped about Neal as my father and I drove through slanting rain to my house yet again. Any curator worth the title could find a place to store those birds where someone else could look after them. I wasn't even getting overtime pay for this.

My father, tall in the passenger seat, wasn't interested in my resentments. "You've been out a lot lately. I'd be happier if you'd tell me what you're up to. Don't mean to pry into your personal life, but your safety is my business."

A lot of people seemed to feel that way. I couldn't complain. Where to start? I'd provided regular reports on Denny. I told him about the stolen tortoises being recovered, about my hospital visit with Pluvia and Wanda, and my conviction that someone else was helping the Tiptons. "And I seem to be dating two men."

We sat in the car in front of my house, reluctant to face the wet, as he absorbed all this.

He said, "Two. Complicated."

I opened the door.

"The job is okay?"

"No problems. My boss said to take the time I needed to look after Denny. Not that Marcie will let me near him." I shut the door again.

"Your housemates moved to Denny's, right? What makes them think they'll be any safer there?"

"Someone needs to look after Denny's animals." Which led to telling him that they were moving out permanently in a month.

Which somehow led to telling him about Calvin retiring.

"You going to try for the position? Your boss owes you after all this trouble with the Tiptons."

"'Fraid not. It requires a college degree."

I had to wait for his response.

"You're going to let that stop you?" He sounded curious rather than challenging.

"Well, it's impossible."

"We can help with the tuition."

"Thanks, but it's still impossible."

"Now why is that? You did all right for the two years you stayed."

"Dad. Listen. All I want to major in is biology, and I can't cut it. Calculus? Organic chemistry? No way. If all it meant was learning more about real animals, I'd be fine. But that's not how it goes. And I need a major that relates to my job, so it's not going to be Creative Knitting Studies or something. And I don't have the time anyway."

I got out of the car and shut the door. He did, too. He would have to tell my mother and I'd have to deal with that. How long could she hold off from "I told you so?" Then I would snap at her and we'd be stuck in the same house because of the Tiptons. Argh!

We collected real estate fliers and ads for gutter cleaning from the porch. I calmed down a little. My house felt cold and barren, lonely and a little spooky. The macaws yelled at us, which made it feel more like home. Maybe I'd miss them after they were gone. My father came down to the basement with me. I inspected the half-nude bird for feathers growing back and found a hint of regrowth.

The cage was due for a cleaning and I started in on it. The less-plucked bird, the one that had begun to warm up to me, flirted with my father instead. He, or maybe she, hung in front of him grasping the wire with feet and beak. I suggested rubbing his face at the base of the beak, with all due caution. My father tried it, the bird loved it, and I was relegated to char woman. The other bird let me scratch his forehead, but only out of politeness.

"You are the new Jerome Tipton," I told my father, who made a face. But he didn't quit petting the bird.

When I was done, he examined the cage and stopped at the basement door. "Look here. Is this the way it was?" It was barely closed, not enough for the latch to engage. The deadbolt wasn't turned.

Not good. Not good at all. I tensed up and glanced around. "I left it locked. Pete must have gone out and not closed it right."

"Or someone broke in."

No evidence of the signature Tipton pry bar. "It's a good deadbolt and nothing looks damaged." That reassured me not at all.

"Good deadbolts can be picked with a couple of bobby pins."

How did he happen to know that?

He shook his head at me. "There's a video online that shows how to do it. Let's take a look around upstairs."

I found a hammer in the kitchen junk drawer for him and grabbed a poker from the fireplace for myself. I rubbed my hand on the first step of the stairway to the second floor. The carpet felt a little damp, as if a wet shoe had passed that way recently. My father pushed past me and went up first.

My room smelled stale and seemed undisturbed. Pete and Cheyenne's room was shockingly bare. They really were gone, their stuff in storage or over at Denny's. The bathroom was tidier than usual without toothbrushes or hair products, just a towel or two.

"Iris. Here."

My father stood at the open door to Robby's room. I looked in and froze. Robby had a huge collection of stuffed animals courtesy of my zoo friends. I'd taken only a few of them with us. The rest were no longer heaped in the green plastic box where they lived. They were strewn around Robby's room like bombing victims. Soft-furred bellies gaped open, clouds of white polyester stuffing drifted on the floor and the bed. I picked up a slack, empty panda, stomach slashed open. Same with a musk ox, a bat, a polar bear. Eviscerated and tossed aside. My stomach twisted with nausea and my hands shook.

Why? I had nothing small and valuable to hide in the toys. Not robbery—malice. An outlet for anger and impatience.

My father said, "You can see the sidewalk and front yard from this window."

"We sat in the car for several minutes. Maybe he thought we were waiting for back-up."

"Ran downstairs and out the way he'd come. He didn't stop to jigger the deadbolt shut."

Bored and frustrated, he'd slashed them one by one while he watched, ready to move downstairs and lurk behind the front door to attack when I walked in.

I called Gettler and left a message, then the Portland police. After I told them this was connected to a previous break-in, they said they would send an officer out.

"Dad, the Tiptons wouldn't have the patience or skill to pick a lock—they'd break their shoulders busting in. It was someone else. This has to be Ethan. He's after the Tipton gold."

My father shook his head. "I think he's after you. You talked to Wanda Tipton and learned he really exists."

I shivered as this sank in. "He's been watching the house. He knew I'd be back to take care of the birds, and he could tell that no one was here." This was a guy who was determined to stay hidden. If I was right, he killed Liana to keep his prints and DNA safe from law enforcement. Yet he'd crept out from his hiding place to find me and lost his temper when he couldn't. How hard would it be to find out where I was staying? My skin crawled.

A police officer showed up while we were checking every cranny and window. When he had taken pictures and interviewed us, I asked him to escort us to my parents' house. "First, can you wait a few minutes?"

He said he could.

I couldn't leave Robby's room contaminated. I pulled two black plastic garbage bags from under the kitchen sink, and we went back upstairs. Little puffs of white polyester lay everywhere, almost too soft to feel between my fingers as I picked them up. Some of the stuffed animals had bare patches from Robby scooting them along the floor or rubbing their ears while he fell asleep. At first I put the ones that might be repairable into one bag, and the truly ruined ones in another. Soon I realized I could never bear to see any of them again and quit discriminating. I hauled the two bags out to the garbage can and set it on the curb for pickup. My father carried up the vacuum cleaner. A few swipes would have to do for now.

Nothing that simple would remove the sense of menace.

The police promised to keep an eye on my parents' house. That didn't matter. I knew Robby and I couldn't stay there any longer. I was sick with fear, and I couldn't think what to do.

When we returned, I galloped upstairs to confirm that Robby was safe. As a baby, he'd slept with his arms out, open to the world. Tonight, he was curled tight around his armadillo. I stayed a few minutes to watch him breathe.

By silent agreement, neither I nor my father mentioned the mutilated animals to my mother, just the basement break-in. I told them both, "This changes things. Robby and I can't stay here and neither can you. It's too dangerous."

My mother said, "Dear, you haven't checked whether Pete might have left the door open. I think you could be over-reacting. Jim, you were there. What do you think?"

My father said, "I think Iris and Robby are safe here. We're three adults, for pity's sake, and we can always call the police. I wouldn't panic."

I gave up. "I'm going upstairs. We'll talk in the morning."

I called the person I least wanted to ask for help.

◇◇◇

I eased out of the bedroom in the morning without waking Robby. My parents were having a peaceful breakfast reading *The Oregonian*. After a bracing swig of coffee, I handed each of them a piece of paper and made a speech. "Mom and Dad, we have an ugly situation here, and I need to be sure Robby is safe. These are tickets for a 3:15 Southwest flight this afternoon so you can visit your friend Cecile in Berkeley. Here's the one for Robby. I know you both have work commitments, but this is an emergency. You can take your laptops and work from Cecile's. You both do a lot online so that should help. I'll be moving to a safer place myself."

I do not understand why people cannot see logic when it's staring them in the face. I might as well have suggested we all put on clown noses and jump off Rocky Butte. Half an hour later, I'd described the mutilated stuffed animals, which upset my mother, but not enough to convince her that I was right. I was losing it, my reasonable voice frayed into shrill. "Look, do you not understand that a *murderer* is after me? Do you not get that he *will* track me here? What part of 'keeping Robby safe' is unclear to you?"

I'd stayed up half the night figuring this out and my credit card had taken severe damage, damage that would require years to heal. Now I had to scream at them to get this to happen?

Robby stumbled downstairs in his pjs, armadillo under one arm, wet diaper sagging on his rear. The discussion ceased. Robby climbed up on a chair and looked around. "Robby home today," he announced. "*My* home."

I nearly wept. "No, honey. Today you get to fly in an airplane. A real airplane, up in the sky." My intention was emotional blackmail directed at my parents, but it failed.

"No sky," Robby said. "Dragons. Fire. Go to *my* house."

Thwarted, I left the battlefield to deal with the diaper and help him into clothes.

Rejoining the conflict, I walked through it again while my mother scrambled an egg for Robby. "You guys can take a week's vacation at my expense. If Cecile can't put you up, I'll pay for a motel. You can go to museums and parks and stuff. It will be sunny and Robby will have a wonderful time. It's just for a week or so, because this can't go on much longer." That was nothing more than wishful thinking, but what else could I say? "I'm moving out, to a new place, where I'll be safe. Can I have the keys for the truck and the Camry? My Honda has that clouded leopard on the spare tire cover so it's too conspicuous."

I could count on the fingers of one hand the times I'd seen my father angry.

"You think you can shuffle us out of the way while you deal with this criminal? That we're going to run off and leave you to face it alone? What makes us so useless and you bullet-proof? Answer me that."

"Dear, you're scaring Robby," my mother whispered.

"Don't 'dear' me. I want an answer from her."

I had no recourse, no other option. I burst into tears. Robby burst into tears. "I can't leave Denny and Marcie," I sobbed, clinging to my child, "or I'd run, too. Marcie's going to collapse, and I have to be there for both of them. All I can do is try to keep my child safe, but you won't let me. I can't ask Mom to do this all alone. It needs both of you. I have a place to stay with the dogs, but I'm already pushing my luck and I can't ask for Dad to stay there, too. It's too much. I just need you to *go*. Please."

I won, but I was an empty husk, withered and exhausted, by the time they finally, finally started packing.

That afternoon, after dropping them off at the airport and crying my eyes out to see my child walking away from me, I set up timers to turn the lamps on and off, backed my mother's Camry out of the garage, loaded up the dogs and a suitcase, and moved in with Neal.

Chapter Thirty

Neal lived near the I-5 Bridge in an apartment building with a keypad at the entrance. As soon as we entered the lobby, we ran into a maintenance man, a short dark guy with bright eyes. Neal said, "Raymond, this is a friend of mine who'll be staying a few days."

Raymond didn't smirk or leer or look wise, which was a good thing because I'd have clocked him. Neal had my suitcase. I had a big bag of dog food, a tote bag of shampoo, toothpaste, et cetera, and two excited dogs winding their leashes around me. I was, without a doubt, at the end of my rope.

Neal shook hands with Raymond in a slightly peculiar way, and said, "The dogs are temporary. Let's not worry too much about them, okay?"

Raymond nodded with a fair amount of enthusiasm. "As long as they're temporary, Mr. Humboldt, I'm sure it will be okay."

Winnie and Range had never been in an elevator and weren't keen to try it. I hauled them in. They cowered and whined.

The apartment wasn't big, but it was classy. A wall of glass overlooked the Columbia River and the bridge. Cars and small boats went about their business as the late afternoon sky glowed with pink and gray. Living room furniture ran to steel and leather, with a bright modern rug under the coffee table. The bedroom Neal showed me was stark white except for two big color photographs on the wall above the bed: a giant anteater

walking a forest trail and two jaguar cubs attacking their tolerant mother. The pictures were high quality and reassured me
that Neal was from the same planet as his staff. The bed was
enormous and covered with a black comforter. A brown dog
hair drifted onto it. Winnie and Range, unleashed, roamed
the apartment sniffing vigorously, their toenails clicking on the
hardwood floors.

"Dogs aren't allowed?" I asked. "I saw you, uh, *tip* Raymond."

"They are, but you pay extra. Two big dogs visiting might
raise eyebrows. I have a neighbor who enjoys conflict."

"I'd like to reimburse you."

"No need. Do you want something to drink?"

"A double shot of tequila, if you don't mind."

"Coming up."

"I'm joking."

"You look like you need it." He disappeared into the kitchen.

I sat on the black leather sofa and wondered whether coming
here was final proof I'd lost my mind. I'd sought the last place
on earth anyone would look for me, and this was definitely it.
When I'd proposed couch-surfing for a few days and explained
why, Neal had said "yes." Now we were facing up to the reality—a
bizarre episode where my boss and I learned entirely too much
about one another. He came out and handed me a glass with a
good-sized shot of tequila. It tasted great.

He wandered around the room, staring out the window and
frowning.

"Is this your daughter?" I indicated the framed photo on
the end table. A dark-haired little girl with big blue eyes and a
shy smile. Aside from her eyes, she didn't look much like Neal.
Delicate features in a heart-shaped face instead of his square jaw
and round head. "How old is she?"

"Bailey. She's eleven now." He stopped pacing and stood with
his hands behind his back.

"Where does she live?"

He stiffened. "Florida. I see her twice a year. How's your
drink?"

I got the message. "It's great. Seeing those stuffed animals butchered freaked me out. Thanks for putting us up." I sipped at the tequila, which was calming my hunger pangs, warming me from the inside out.

"No problem. Stay here until the police locate those guys."

"I can use my dad's pickup, too. I'll keep switching cars when I go back and forth to the zoo so no one can track me."

Neal took a minute to digest this. "Let's see if I have this right. You think a murderer is looking for you, so you've gone to ground here. But you plan to work at the zoo as usual, a place that anyone can walk into."

The tequila was hitting pretty hard. My empty stomach, that was the problem. But it was lovely, relaxing, after a horrible day. "I wouldn't stiff you. You're short-staffed because Denny's on the sick list."

"Arnie knows the routine at Birds. I've got him and Pete to cover it when Calvin is off. Primates won't get extra help, but Kip will manage. You stay here."

I sat up straight. "Arnie? I wouldn't let Arnie feed a parakeet. I'll go in."

"The bears survive."

"Bears are tough. He cuts corners. I'll be fine at work. We've got security guards." That was weak—George, the main security guard, was about as dangerous as one of the tortoises. I just felt safe at the zoo.

Neal looked at me with narrowed eyes. I was used to his annoyance, orders, brainstorming, second thoughts. This I couldn't define. Was I coming up short?

He said, "We'll revisit this later."

I finished the tequila and decided not to worry about him being judgmental. Time to stop crying inside about sending Robby off. Focus on the relief of knowing my boy and my parents were safe. Would it be polite to suggest a refill?

Neal said, "I usually send out for dinner. Chinese okay?"

"Perfect." I wasn't hungry. Strange. I was always hungry. I felt fine. Maybe I should drink hard liquor more often. No,

I'd already had too much. In the future, stick to wine. More predictable.

Neal gave me a wary glance and walked to the kitchen. He looked really tense. Maybe he needed a drink, too. I heard him make the phone call to the restaurant and move around the kitchen.

I woke up when he buzzed someone into the building. I seemed to be curled up on the black leather sofa. Winnie lay on the colorful rug nearby. I didn't see Range anywhere. Robby? Oh, right. In California. I woke up again when Neal set a wonderful smelling big brown bag on the glass-topped coffee table. Range trotted up from wherever he'd been hanging out.

I roused myself and fed the dogs in his fancy glass bowls. Neal and I ate at the kitchen counter. The tequila wasn't sitting as well as it had at first, but food helped settle my stomach. Neal kept glancing at me. I couldn't read him at all, except that it wasn't cheerful acceptance. I'd put my foot in it somehow, but I didn't know what I'd done wrong.

"After I walk the dogs, would you go with me to feed the macaws?" I said as he cleared away the dinner debris. "I could call Pete, but he's a long way away."

"I'll do it. You'll stay here."

"But you don't know how. And it's safer to have two people, right?"

"I am starting to wonder about your survival instincts. You say you're scared, then you want to put yourself in the line of fire. Wrong mindset. Write down what you want me to do for those birds."

Humbled, I wrote instructions on the piece of paper he handed me. Neal disappeared into the bedroom and returned wearing a leather jacket. I checked for a bulge under the armpit and couldn't tell if he had a gun or not. Better not ask. He might think I thought he wasn't adequate to the task of protecting me.

Maybe the tequila was still affecting me and making this more confusing than it needed to be.

First we had to see to the dogs. We walked them in the dark at a little grass strip nearby. They were keen to check the smell-phone messages of strangers. While they sniffed, we debated how much they could learn from a strange dog's pee.

Idle chat, veiling the uneasiness.

When we returned, a couple in business suits rode the elevator up with us. She crouched a little to pet the dogs while her companion kept back, brushing imaginary dog hair off his black slacks.

Neal set up a movie, something about East Germany and a spy spying on an artist and his actress wife. After he left, I paused it and called Marcie. "How's Denny doing?"

"Thank heavens, he's better. They moved him out of ICU. We're on the seventh floor now. The discharge planner came by today to talk to him."

"Discharge? He was nearly dead yesterday. Are they crazy? Is this some insurance issue? He's *got* insurance."

Marcie said, "No, he really is better. He sits up and eats, and they made him stand by the bed for a minute. Tomorrow he's supposed to start walking."

"Walking. That's amazing. Now can you go home and get some rest?"

"Oh, I'm fine. I don't want to miss any information. He's still on pain meds and he doesn't remember everything."

"I'll stop by tomorrow if I can. Life is complicated right now."

"We'd love to see you."

We'd love to see you. That sounded un-Marcie-like, disconnected from real emotion. Disconnected from me. She was plenty connected to Denny. And she wasn't cutting herself any slack to rest up.

Next up was Gettler, who didn't answer. No point in leaving a message.

My folks reported they were fine at Cecile's, who was flustered by a two-year-old but managing. Robby decided the plane was a good dragon and safe, if boring. My father let him run up and down the aisle until the flight attendant intervened. Yes, the car seat and the stroller both came through fine. Tomorrow they would ride trolley cars and maybe go to the zoo.

I wandered around the apartment feeling bereft. When the heartache of missing Robby eased, I looked more closely. The neat shelves held books on military history, management theory and practice, zoology and animal management. I'd always wanted the modern *Wild Mammals in Captivity*, but my budget had never stretched that far. I pulled it off the shelf and thumbed through it. Why wasn't this in his office? I remembered that Neal's predecessor, Kevin Wallace, had a copy. Probably still in the office. I put it back. Tucked in at the end of a shelf were two books on parenting after divorce. One shelf held a small bronze sculpture of a maned wolf, an elegant South American canid that looks like a fox on stilts. That plus the pictures of South American animals in the bedroom aligned with what I knew of Neal's animal experience. I wondered how he felt about Finley Zoo's focus on Asian animals.

When he was hired, Mr. Crandall informed us that his background included the military, an MBA, corporate management, and running a small zoo in Brazil.

I'd seen evidence of all that. Neal kept up on zoo management and he'd studied management in general. He liked animal art, no surprise. He was scary neat. No pets. Well, he had a zoo—maybe he didn't need a dog or cat or lizard.

I could think of no explanation for an old wooden hand plane on another shelf, the kind used for woodworking.

I looked around the bedroom again, the dogs tight at my heels, anxious that I might abandon them in a strange place. A chunk of twisted metal sat on the dark wood dresser with a framed photograph behind it, a picture of six men in uniform. They kneeled, grinning for the camera, in front of a mud hut with a Coca Cola sign. I didn't know enough about the military to tell which branch of service. One of them looked like a young version of Neal. Was the metal fragment from an IED? A plane that crashed? An event they'd all survived or one that had killed some of them? It was from his military past and Neal looked at it every day. Not something I would be comfortable asking about.

No sign of a woman in the bedroom or bathroom. Maybe he was still recovering from the divorce. That made me think of not-quite-divorced Ken. I should ask about that next time I saw him. As for Craig, he seemed totally unattached. Wouldn't hurt to ask him anyway, come to think of it.

Neal was in my house, free to look around. What would he deduce about me?

I started up the movie. Neal returned before it was over, and I paused it.

"Everything was locked up. The birds look all right." He sat in an uncomfortable-looking leather director's chair. "I'll see if I can get a release from the feds right away and find some other place to hold them. Feeding them puts people at risk."

"A sanctuary would be peachy. Hap could give you a list." At last. "They're unbelievably noisy," I added to remind him that "managing the gap" was a pain in the rear. I shared Denny's medical update. "You get that Denny risked his life to stop the break-in?"

"I do. I was off-base to speculate in front of you at the hospital. I apologize to you and to him."

Good. "How can they discharge him?" I fretted. "He needs someone to look after him."

As soon as I said it, I knew how it was going to go.

Neal said, "If you need to take time off for that, let me know."

I just nodded.

He said, "The Amazon parrots are mostly sorted out. They'll go to a sanctuary in Mexico, but not for weeks. Doc Reynolds wants her quarantine rooms back, but she's out of luck for awhile."

I pulled away from thinking about Denny. "I wonder how many of them died before we got them."

"I'm surprised the Tiptons bothered. Most Mexican parrots aren't that valuable, and they aren't common in the illegal trade anymore. Mexico cracked down on it pretty good."

"Maybe the birds were a bonus for buying the tortoises. Maybe Jerome wanted them. He liked parrots."

Neal nodded. "The tortoises will be around for awhile, too. We'll ship five back to Madagascar. I'm negotiating to keep a few of the others, but reptile curators from two other zoos are hot for them and so is a breeding facility."

"So none of them are going back to the wild." I couldn't help feeling bitter.

"After they've been exposed to each other's diseases? You know we can't do that. People released pet desert tortoises in Arizona and infected the wild ones."

None of these animals would return to the life they were adapted for. "Is that the best we can do? People screwed them up, and now we can't fix it. Damn it, there ought to be a better way."

Neal stuck his legs out and crossed his ankles. A twitching foot contradicted the relaxed pose. "It's the optimal outcome given the limitations of the situation. Tell me who you think broke into your house yesterday."

I sighed and went along with changing the subject. "Three candidates: Tom, Jeff, or Mr. X. My money is on Mr. X." I explained the evidence for a third person associating with the Tiptons. "Somehow he knows I talked to Wanda and Pluvia and figured out he exists. I'm guessing it's a message to back off."

"You're not the threat. The cops are the threat. You don't know who he is or where he is."

"I have some guesses. He's probably wherever the Tiptons are, hiding out with them."

"Except he tracks who you talk to and watches your house?"

Maybe my assumptions were all dubious. Maybe I should lay all of them on the table. "I think he's young, maybe twenty, and probably a meth addict."

Neal recrossed his ankles. His fingers tapped on the leather straps that served as chair arms. "Addict or not, he set up a pretty sophisticated lab. He's eluded the police for weeks. He may be what kept those Tipton knuckleheads from getting caught. He sounds experienced."

I turned this idea over and around in my mind. Maybe Jerome hadn't picked up a young punk. Maybe somebody had picked Jerome. I slid off the sofa to the floor where Winnie lay and stroked her head, feeling the ridges on her skull and the soft fur around her ears. "This guy seems to be taking Jerome's place with the sons. He's bossing them around." I quoted Jeff's comment about catching hell. "Liana was a threat and he killed her the first chance he got."

"That girl? Could just as well be Jeff or Tom. Weren't they released before she died?"

I was sure about this one. "They made bail within the estimated time of death, but they liked her. They were upset she was dead. Here's how I think it went. She told Mr. X that she'd turn him in if anything happened to the Tiptons, and she had his blood and fingerprints in that baggie. She would be pissed off about the bust and hot to turn him in. He had to stop her and find the baggie before anyone else did." Winnie laid her head across my lap and I thought of the little Doberman. "I'm sure he found her and shot her, probably in the woods around the farm."

That led to a bad thought. If I'd gotten that wretched bag to a cop right away, Denny might not be in the hospital.

Neal shrugged. "For sure, at least one of these guys plays hardball."

"It's this third one. Remember how her body was staged? That wasn't to fool the cops, which only an idiot would try. It was to fool Jeff and Tom. Mr. X needed an explanation for why she was dead. He'd tell them that the cops shot her and were lying about it to protect themselves. That ties in with what their father taught them. And it does double-duty because it keeps the sons in hiding. No way will they turn themselves in after that. He doesn't want them talking to the law."

Neal didn't look convinced, but he wasn't giving me that "what is up with this crazy woman?" look. "That brings us back to why he broke into your house and threw a tantrum."

Behind Neal, the bridge was a bright line crossing darkness. Winnie rolled onto her back to help me scratch her belly. "Maybe he wanted to use me to take another run at the tortoises."

Neither one of us found that convincing. Too risky.

I said, "Maybe he's crazy and vengeful, and it was just a fit of rage."

He shook his head. "Maybe scaring you was strategic. What would he expect you to do?"

"Hide. Leave town. What good does that do him?"

We didn't know.

I got up and walked around. Winnie rose and followed me. I stood at the big window and watched the moving lights, red and white, the bridge and the water. Regrouping. "He's a criminal with a record. His prints or DNA or both are on file. He must be running from a warrant somewhere. He has enough clout to keep Tom and Jeff in line, although he might not have known they planned to visit me and ask about their father. He's experienced in the drug trade, maybe a beginner in the wildlife trade—he's not very good at it."

Neal said from his chair, "Everything he's tried has gone south. He's got another murder hanging on him with no drug profits and no animal profits. Why is he still here?"

"No buried treasure. That's why."

"If he thought you knew where the gold was, he wouldn't have left a mess at your house and scared you away. He'd want to try again later. He'd hope that you'd come back alone."

We sat in silence. The apartment was quiet, no sense of other people nearby. My excitement at a different, clearer picture of this guy faded as I realized that it didn't lead to anything I could do, only to more reason to be afraid. I said, "I think he shot Denny. He would be the one with a handgun."

Neal could have argued, but he didn't. He said, "Bottom line, your best move is to stay under cover and wait for him to stick his head out."

That sounded like Ken's advice. So far, it hadn't gotten me anywhere.

We watched the rest of the movie. When it finished, he got up and rubbed his nose. "I've got only one bathroom."

I said, "I don't plan to tell anyone I'm here. Ever. I think that would be best for both of us."

"I couldn't agree more. Having one of my staff sleep over…I think we can agree on discretion." He wasn't making eye contact.

My instincts had kicked in, late but on target. Offering me the tequila was a slip-up. This situation could cost him his job or at least a raft of awkwardness forevermore. "I actually like sleeping on sofas and I've already test-driven it. So no need to deprive you of your room."

He shook his head. "I'm guarding the perimeter." Was that a joke or not? "You get the bed." That was definitely an order.

I used about twenty percent of it and was disturbed only by two restless dogs.

Chapter Thirty-one

In the morning, after breakfast and walking the dogs on frosty paths, Neal and I discussed whether I was under house arrest or not. "I'll stay in the apartment," I promised, "unless something really urgent comes up." It was a delicate conversation that satisfied me more than him.

"Do not, repeat, do not, show your face at work." He gave me the door codes and departed.

I test-drove his soaking tub—many nozzles—and tried to be good. Television had nothing. None of his movies looked compelling. I called Linda, who was off work, to chat, but she didn't answer. Probably throwing pots at the ceramic studio she rented. Or else hanging with her new girlfriend. I missed Robby. I missed a lot of things.

Winnie and Range moved from rug to floor to kitchen tiles, unsettled. Winnie tried to scratch a soft spot on Neal's rug, which she knew was always forbidden. People walked down the hall talking, which set off hysterical barking despite my commands and hand waving. When they shut up enough to hear me, I scolded them at length, and they slunk away to flop down in yet another new place. That didn't stop them from barking again at trifles, including imaginary ones.

My poor unsettled dogs. "You have food and water and me," I told them. "You have to deal. It's all I've got."

Television news warned of an ice storm likely tonight. More likely just rain. Newscasters like to dramatize weather. I picked a movie at random and watched it until lunch time.

After leftover kung pao chicken and rice, I considered all the people I could call. If any of them had important information, they would call me. So I didn't. Neal subscribed to *Natural History* magazine. I read three issues.

When Range took a notion to go out and clawed a long scratch on Neal's door, I gave up. I pulled on a Ducks cap as a token disguise and left Neal a note saying I was moving the dogs and would pay for damages to his door. I dragged Winnie and Range into the elevator and found the Camry in the underground parking. I boosted the dogs into the back. A Camry station wagon is as anonymous as a car can get, it had been parked out of sight, and my stalker was unlikely to associate it with me or with this apartment building far from my house.

Sleet pelted the windshield, piling up along the edge of the wipers. The newscasters might have been on to something after all.

No one was home at Denny's. The gravel in front of his house was dusted with white. The breeze felt well below freezing. I had to yank on the gate to break the ice seal so that I could shut the dogs in the back yard. It was fenced well enough to hold Strongbad and therefore ought to hold my own milder-tempered dogs. I hoped Strongbad was somewhere warm and dry. Not dead.

The house key was on a little ledge above the front door where it always was. I refreshed the water bowl on the kitchen floor, set the bag of dog food on the kitchen counter, and left a note for Pete and Cheyenne. If Strongbad turned up, I emphasized, they were to call me right away. Putting him with my dogs guaranteed a fight. Range and Winnie bounded inside through Denny's home-made dog door, excited by Strongbad smells and a novel house and pleased to see I was still there.

Dumping dogs on people without notice is crummy, but I couldn't very well get Neal evicted or leave them in the Camry all day, nor could I risk going to my house or my parents' house.

I supplemented the note with a text message to Pete. I didn't want to talk to him and have to apologize and explain.

I looked around, at the mounted deer head, the comic books, the reptile tanks. Bessie Smith, Rick's iguana, was a lot bigger than when I'd had her. Beady eyes stared at me without moving. The place looked cleaner than I remembered it. Denny evolving or Pete tidying? Someday, Denny would be home again.

"This is your own fault, but I'm sorry anyway," I said to my dogs. "I'll come get you as soon as I can, honest." I got into the Camry feeling very much alone.

I drove to Southwest Medical Center, ice pellets pinging against the car, to find out what was going on with this plan to release Denny. The medical center was a public place with many eyes and a security force. Easily as safe as Neal's apartment, although the weather was a concern. I didn't want to be stranded at the hospital. I hadn't seen any chains in the Camry.

I pushed through the door to his new wing and stopped short. Denny stood in the hallway outside his room, his back to me, gripping a walker. I circled in front of him, tears crowding behind my eyes. "Denny! You're walking! This is wonderful. You had me so scared." I air-hugged him to avoid knocking him over. He looked like he'd crash from a finger-flick.

"Yeah. Ire. Good to see you." He nodded a couple of times, and I dropped from his attention. He focused far down the hallway, sliding his foot forward, slow and wobbly, a male attendant steadying him. He was up and moving, but he wasn't really back. Not yet. I had questions for him, but what little mental ability he had at the moment was consumed with putting one foot in front of the other. I'd wait until he was back in bed. I left him to it and walked into his room.

Marcie reclined in a vinyl covered chair, looking tired and content. "Hey, did you see him walking?"

I nodded. "Fantastic. What comes next?"

"He'll get released in two or three days. Isn't that great?"

Not as soon as I'd thought. Good. And he *was* better. No need to circle the herd around him, horns out, fighting off a premature discharge. "Where will he go? He seems pretty weak."

"Oh, my place. I'll look after him."

"You still have some vacation time?"

She shook her head. "No problem. My boss is happy to have me work from home. I've told everyone he's my fiancé and people are very accommodating."

"Fiancé?"

"I thought, what would Iris do? You'd say you were his fiancée. It really helped."

That took me a moment.

Denny would be back to his bed soon. I needed to say what I had to say. "Before he got shot, you two had broken up and you were a mess. Are you sure this is wise? Maybe Jack can take him."

For an instant, something moved in her eyes, something I'd never seen in her before. Something that looked a lot like rage. But she spoke with light certainty. "I'm way better at dealing with doctors than Jack is. We'll be fine."

"Marcie, let me say this once. Then I'll let it go. You're my best friend, and I want what's right for you. Okay?"

"Sure, Iris. Say whatever's on your mind."

I heard the warning in that and plowed on anyway. "I've tried to figure out why you were so destroyed when Denny broke up with you. I think you lost yourself in this relationship. You melded too far with him and compromised too much. Otherwise you wouldn't have been so wrecked when it ended. You need to still be you and not just you plus Denny. I don't know how to say it better, but I worry about how it will turn out in the long run, that if he leaves after this, you won't ever recover."

Marcie shook her head and flicked her fingers, dusting away my concerns with a smile. Her eyes held that brilliance again. "You want me to abandon him? I'll help him as long as he needs me and wants me. If it ends again, well, so be it. I won't be any worse off than I was before."

"That's not necessarily true."

"You don't understand. I'm a better me with him. The more time I get to be that person, the stronger I'll be."

It hadn't worked out that way before, but I knew defeat when I saw it. "I'll support you both anyway I can."

"Then you won't keep trying to break us up, right? I'm really tired of it." This time, there was no mistaking the rage.

◇◇◇

I stood in the lobby staring through the glass wall at weak daylight and slanting snow. Punched in the psychic gut. My long-time solid-and-sure friendship with Marcie was toast. She'd gone somewhere emotionally that frightened me, and she didn't want me there with her. What should I have done or not done to head this off? What would this do to Denny? It was simple on the surface—the ex takes care of the injured friend, people being adults. I knew deep in my heart that this was different. Was "pathological" too strong? Denny would be beholden to her forever—she dedicated herself to him when he needed her. Forever—he would understand she would be demolished if he left. What kind of relationship is based on obligation and obsession?

Nothing to do but wait it out and hope for the best.

Time to go hide at Neal's. Sit in his apartment and try once again to figure out what to do. Family, friendships, home—all disaster and disarray. I was on the run and useless to everyone in my life, even my dogs. I reached for my phone to ask Neal what I could pick up for dinner and felt a light hand on my shoulder. I turned, surprised.

"Iris. I didn't expect you here."

"Craig!" I lowered the phone. "I meant to say—"

"—that you're glad to see me." His smile hadn't the open enthusiasm I hoped for, but at least it was friendly.

"Um, yeah. That's it exactly. You must be here to interview Denny."

"That can wait. I'd rather talk to you any day. Hey, I know a steak house that's nearby and not too bad. We never did go over that draft."

There was the smile I'd hoped for.

I stalled. Neal would expect me soon and I'd lose all sorts of credibility if I didn't show up. "Are you sure? The last steakhouse I tried wanted twenty bucks for an appetizer."

"A meal with you is worth every penny of that, but this place is a little easier on the budget."

This was the chance to find out where he and I stood. Delaying awkward interactions with Neal also appealed. "We'll go Dutch. Give me a minute." I texted Neal that I was off to dinner with Craig and should be back in a couple of hours. As soon as I put the phone back in my pocket, it rang. Ken. I stopped and nodded an apology to Craig. "Hey, what's up?"

"I found Strongbad. Somebody clobbered the tar out of him, but he'll survive. Can you come get him?"

"You bet I can. That's terrific. Where are you?"

Ken gave me an address at least a mile away from Denny's house.

"I'll be there in ten, fifteen minutes."

Ken said, "I'll wait."

I clapped the phone shut. "This is great. Ken, the Animal Control guy, found Denny's dog. He's been missing, and I've been dreading telling Denny. What a relief. I need to take a rain check on dinner. I want to go get that dog." And what would I do with him? My dogs might be living in the Camry after all. No, if Neal went with me to my house, then I could—

"Let's think about this just a minute." Craig's handsome face was sober.

"Think about what?"

"How well do you know this Ken guy? You're about to go off and meet up with him by yourself in the dark. How about if I come along as back-up? You think some other person is involved in all this, and we don't know who it is."

I recoiled at the thought. "No, Ken's a good guy, trustworthy. No way." My second reaction took a few seconds. Ken knew the Tiptons from years ago. The animal shelter volunteer should have known who he was and didn't. A major in chemistry would be handy for setting up a meth lab.

Craig waited while I thought.

Ken fit the profile Neal and I had developed: smart and competent. Dismay settled in my heart as bits and pieces came together. "He saw me find the plastic bag and left the farm before Denny and I did. He could have beaten us to the zoo and waited for the chance to break into the van and get it back."

I'd told him at the reptile show that the tortoises were going to be shipped out. Maybe that triggered Denny's kidnapping and the break-in at the zoo's hospital. "I don't know. It's possible." More than possible.

"We're going to find out," Craig said, before I'd worked out whether Ken could dominate the Tipton boys. "Where are you parked? The garage?"

"Yeah." Craig was a little disabled, but he was no fool and he could dial 911. When we stepped out into the weather, I'd added in another factor. "Maybe it isn't Ken. He wouldn't have set up the tortoises that poorly at the Tiptons. He would find out how to do it right. It makes no sense to risk them dying from bad care. Somebody who didn't know anything did that."

"I'm still going with you."

Fine by me.

We took the sidewalk from the lobby toward the parking lot, hunched against wind-driven sleet stinging our faces. The path was crunchy with snow and it was piling up on twigs and rails. Craig said, "Just a sec," and paused to text something from his cell phone. I slowed down for him, going back and forth about Ken.

In the reflection from the parking lot's glass elevator, I could see Craig behind me, catching up in a few swift strides. We took the stairway together to the level where my car was parked. His shoes scuffed behind me. The mental vault swung open as the tumblers aligned. I turned back on the last step. "Darn. I forgot something. I'll be right back."

"What's the matter?" Craig, a step above me, put a hand on each of my shoulders.

You didn't limp, that's what's the matter. I punched him in the stomach, turned away from him toward the parked cars, and ran.

Straight into the outspread arms of Tom Tipton.

Jeff was there, too, he and Tom uncertain and hesitant, but determined to capture me. I twisted away and screamed, quickly muffled by someone's hand over my mouth. I almost tore free, but one of them kicked my feet out from under me. I caught myself with my hands. Someone pressed me flat, face down on the hard concrete. Car keys and phone in my pockets mashed into my flesh, smells of oil and tires. In a panic, I writhed, edging sideways to slide under a car. The hand over my mouth was relentless and I bit at it, catching tough flesh between my front teeth.

No one shouted at us, no one ran over to investigate.

We struggled on the concrete between the cars until my hands were wrenched behind my back. The hand on my face was yanked away, replaced by tape over my mouth. My hands and feet were bound. A hesitation and I was picked up by feet and shoulders and tossed into the back seat of a car, shoved down on the floor boards facing the underside of the passenger seat.

I struggled up, but a foot on my shoulder pushed me back. "Steady there, girl. Keep down." Craig's voice. The car started up. The lighting changed, darker. I hadn't seen the car enough to know, but I was sure it was beige. Craig was Ethan. The limp was faked.

No one said anything. The tape over my mouth set off another panic reaction, this time that my air supply was at risk. My heart was pounding and I could hear my breath whistling over the edge of the tape.

Craig said, "Sorry, Iris. This wasn't my first choice. You were supposed to come to me for protection with your kid, but you didn't. Extreme measures were necessary."

He had cut up the stuffed animals to frighten me into his arms, bringing Robby with me. Neal was right—it was strategy, not a tantrum. Run to him for protection with my child and two dogs? It had never crossed my mind.

From the front, Tom's voice, "We didn't hurt her, did we?"

"No, but God help me if I ever need you to tackle someone your own size." Craig took on an instructional tone. "Last time I hit someone over the head, he died. A risk, one I decided not to take in this case. That's why you guys are here. You didn't remember one single thing I told you, did you?"

The front seat was silent. Then Tom said, "Like that big dog died." His voice held a whisper of—what?—shame? resentment?

Craig said, "I told you, the dog didn't die. The damn dog is fine."

Nothing from the front seat.

"The tape over the mouth is a risk also." Another lesson. "A person can asphyxiate from choking or vomiting. You can guess how I learned that."

That did it. The panic I'd been repressing broke loose and I thrashed around, desperate to breathe freely. He sighed and reached over me to pull the tape off. "It goes back on if you start screaming."

I gasped for a few minutes, air going in and out. I willed self control, slow down, think. I felt his shoe resting on my hip.

Robby was in California. Robby was safe. I shuddered with relief.

I could imagine only one reason for this expedition. I'd convinced him I knew where the gold was hidden. He hadn't needed to hunt for me. He knew I'd show up at the trauma center to see Denny. And he knew that I'd tell him anything if he had Robby. He didn't have Robby. He'd try something else. I shifted a little, testing my wrists, feeling for some sharp projection to cut the tape or rope.

"Stop it." The foot nudged me. "This time, I'm in charge."

My cell phone rang. Craig reached into my pocket and pulled it out, an obscene touch, and tossed it out the window. His shoe rocked me a little. "Don't feel bad about being slow. I'm good at this. You saw me twice and didn't recognize me. Once at the Safeway when you were with that old biddy and then at the snake sale. Remember? You left the restaurant, and I called from the men's room to set up dinner."

I shook my head, then realized he probably couldn't see me in the dark. "No."

"I had you going pretty good about that Ken guy, didn't I?"

I lay jammed tight, breathing dirty socks and unwashed bodies. I had plenty of time to work it all out. Craig had changed his appearance and put on his reporter act at the farm so that he'd know if Liana's ID kit or the gold was found. Bold verging on reckless. He liked disguises. I found my voice. "How did you ever convince my boss that you're a reporter?"

"Easy. A friend's credentials. Well, more of an acquaintance. Not that hard to change the photo."

He'd delivered the bail and driven the Tiptons back to their home, where Jerome had flipped out when he thought we'd taken his birds. "It must have been a bad moment when Jerome died. You couldn't talk him out of his gold."

No response. I said, "You told Tom and Jeff you want the gold for his patriot groups, right? But you'll take it all." He'd brought up Jerome's favorite charities more than once.

"One more peep and the tape goes back on." His voice was matter-of-fact.

He'd seen me find the baggie and raced Denny and me to the zoo to retrieve it.

I'd told Ken some of the tortoises would be shipped back to Madagascar, but I'd told Craig, too. I hadn't made it clear that it would take weeks, so Craig had jumped on it and broken into the quarantine rooms. Denny was shot because I never saw through him.

The miles ticked off and I tried to step inside his brain, hoping for a tiny advantage. He was a career criminal, proud of his acting. He liked psychological levers—staging Liana's body for Jeff and Tom, cutting up the stuffed animals to drive me toward him. But everything he'd set up had failed.

It seemed likely that he'd succeed this time.

We traveled for a long time in silence. "Hey," I said. "This is really uncomfortable. Can I sit on the seat?"

Craig said, "Nope. Sorry." He didn't sound sorry.

Jeff said from the passenger seat, "Road's getting bad. You got chains?"

Craig said, "No."

The car slowed a little. I felt it slide loose on a curve and the rear end wag back and forth. Tom got it straightened out and went on a little slower. If he crashed, maybe I could get away. More likely, I'd freeze to death.

Finally we turned off the pavement and onto a gravel road, one that hadn't seen much maintenance. I listened for clues about where we were, with no success. After several jolting minutes, the car stopped. The front doors opened and cold air flooded in.

Craig got out. Jeff and Tom made an awkward business of hoisting me between them, slipping on ice patches.

"Take the tape off her legs. Make her walk," Craig snapped.

Tom used a pocket knife to cut my legs free. They each grabbed a forearm and walked me into a single-story house, indistinct in the dark. Craig followed us. The interior was as cold as the outdoors. The door closed behind us. One of them switched on a light, revealing a living room that featured kitsch and neglect. A row of plates along the top of the living room wall, plates with ships on them. Shelves full of elf figurines. Braided rug on the floor, edges unraveled. A sofa with a cotton cover in faded brown with white piping. I stood between Jeff and Tom while they waited for instructions.

"Drag a chair in here. This won't take long."

They both let go of me and went for the chair. Jeff walked to the little dining room. Tom stopped and turned back. He looked different. Hair cut short, shaved but with a little mustache, button-up shirt with narrow blue and white stripes, a clean parka. Jeff was also clean-shaven, pale-jawed with acne scars, cleaned up. Craig's efforts to disguise the brothers, I suspected. I'd have known them anywhere.

Tom started to say something to me and then didn't. He looked scared. Of what was about to happen? I mouthed, "Don't do this."

He looked beyond me, over my shoulder. I turned around to face Craig. He leaned against the door, relaxed and in control, arms crossed over his black jacket. "You were a lot of fun, Iris, so let's make this easy. Tell us where the gold is, and we can still be friends." His tone was amused, wry.

He's overdoing it, I thought.

It was bitter cold, no heat.

Jeff brought an armless wooden chair into the living room, left eye spasming. Without his beard, he looked less like Jerome and more like Wanda.

"Jeff, he killed Liana," I blurted. "He shot her and pretended the cops did."

Craig chuckled. "Oh, please. He's not going to believe you. He knows better."

Jeff glowered at me. I tried Tom again. "It's true. He shot Liana the night after the bust and moved the body to the blackberries. I'm the one that found her. There was no blood on the ground. He tricked you."

Jeff glared. Tom wouldn't meet my eye.

Craig pushed on my shoulders, down onto the chair, my arms still taped behind me. He stood in front of me and ran a hand along my jaw. I met his eyes and saw the arousal. He was having a good time with this. "Tell me," he said, low and whispery, intimate. "I don't want to hurt you. You and I, we're good together."

Even now, I felt a flicker of response, my body's betrayal. I took a deep breath. "All right. You win. I need to draw a map."

"No, I think you can just tell us." Craig smiled. I'd given in too easily.

"The hell I can," I snarled. "Look, if you want it, don't screw around. I can draw you a map. That's it, that's all I got. I want out of here. You can have the damned gold."

Craig considered. The smile vanished. He looked calculating, alert, capable. "Okay, we'll try that. Jeff, find paper and a pencil."

We waited while Jeff blundered around the house. A tiny corner of my brain wondered at his talent for turning threat into farce. Tom joined in and they both opened cupboards and pulled out drawers. Craig put his hands on his hips, looking disgusted. That pulled his jacket back and I saw the end of a handgun in a shoulder holster. He said, "Not one thing has gone right with this gig. These clowns couldn't cut butter with a hot knife."

Tom disappeared into a bedroom and emerged with a business-sized envelope. He carefully cut the edges with his pocket knife to open it into a flat sheet. Jeff carried a brown bag out of the kitchen like a trophy.

Craig pulled on my arm to stand me up. He used Tom's little knife to cut my wrists free. "Be a good girl," he whispered into my ear. I walked unsteadily to the little dining room table.

What was this place? I couldn't see into the kitchen. There must be a back door in there. Possibly locked and latched. Craig pulled a pen out of his shirt pocket and handed it to me. Jeff and Tom stopped looking for a pencil and stood awaiting further orders.

I sat down at the table. "Get me some coffee," I said, as an experiment. Jeff took a step and stopped, looking at Craig and winking. Tom scanned us all and, when Craig didn't say anything, went into the kitchen. I heard the faucet running.

I chose the paper bag and drew a line for the highway and added the Tipton driveway, in no rush. The men stood and waited. Half the distance from the farm to Amboy, along the highway, I sketched a snag and a rock. I added a highway mileage marker—32—and north of it, an X and a note—15 feet. "I think that's it," I said, suppressing the urge to add cars, houses, birds, anything to kill time.

Craig, behind me, put a hand on my shoulder. "So you've been there."

"No, I just saw a map of it. I found the map in that bag with the glass."

"And you remember it so well."

"I studied it. I have a good memory, especially when I'm scared."

"No GPS coordinates," Craig said.

"No, I made that up."

He turned to Tom and Jeff. "It's right off the highway. Do either of you know the spot?"

They both looked at the map and shook their heads.

Craig shot me in the thigh before I even saw the gun in his hand. I screamed from the noise, then the pain hit. He grabbed my jacket front in one hand, lifted me to my feet, and shoved me backwards into the living room and onto the chair.

The chair teetered and almost went over backwards. I flung out my arms for balance. When it steadied, I whimpered and clutched my leg with both hands, terrified of seeing arterial blood pumping, life taking the easy way out. Blood dripped down to the floor, starting a little pool, but no spurting and pulsing. My vision narrowed, a gray tunnel, and I knew I was close to fainting.

"Just a flesh wound," Craig said.

How trivial that sounded. I cowered, waiting for the next shot, dizzy.

"Where is it?" said Craig, iron voiced, jiggling the pistol in his hand.

He was going to kill me. Jeff and Tom, both larger males, were going to stand there and let him do it. I leaned forward to clear my head. "It's the macaws," I said. "They have it. It's at my house."

Craig fired at my other leg and missed, maybe on purpose. I screamed anyway.

"No, it's not the fucking birds." The cool was gone, replaced by rage and shouting. I recognized it as technique, but it was terrifying anyway. "I checked out their old cage in your basement," he ranted. "I checked out the place where they were in the house. They don't talk so they've got nothing to spill. It's not the god-damned birds. This is the time for your best answer or you won't have any of this to worry about."

"You can't *kill* her," said Tom in a small voice.

My teeth chattered. "He will," I said, stuttering, "like he killed Liana. Liana was right about him. Liana knew."

The gun pressed painfully into my collarbone, the spot where he'd first kissed me. "Say something useful or shut up."

I'd told him the truth, and he didn't believe it. I had nothing left. Blood oozed around my fingers where I gripped my leg. Tom made a little noise.

Craig ignored him. "Tell me now. This is *so* close to being over."

Behind him, Jeff said in a tight, gruff voice. "Liana was away when we was busted. She'd gone off in the woods. How could she of died then?"

"She was a *whore*. Why would anybody care?" Craig snarled.

Tom's voice was shrill and terrified. "Jeff, Liana was right. We can't do his bidding. This is the devil's work. He'll kill her like he shot that man."

Craig had overdone it, stepped too far into this vicious persona. He turned toward them, the gun in his hand. I opened my mouth, but nothing came out. He would shoot them both. I rose off the chair to push him, throw his aim off. But I was much too slow. With a wordless growl, Jeff reached for the gun with one hand and with the other embraced the smaller man in a bear hug. "She was to be my *wife*."

Craig slid down and made a quick motion that threw Jeff off balance, shoved the gun between them, and fired twice. He staggered as Jeff rocked back, still clutching him. Jeff let go and sagged to the floor on his back. Red flowed on his clean dress shirt. He moved one hand, helpless, and went limp. Craig whirled toward Tom and took aim as Tom backed away, hands held in front.

Teeth clenched and bared, I hit him in the head with the chair as hard as I could. The gun went off and Tom ran. Craig fell to hands and knees alongside Jeff's body, but kept the gun. Forcing my injured leg to bear my weight, I hit him again, a chair leg across his head and again across his back when he tried to get up. Each blow ran up my arms, jarring my shoulders and neck. I would have kept on hitting him, but a chair leg broke off, and I lost my balance. I went to my knees, the chair falling off to the side. I started to reach for it, then came to my senses and flailed around until I could flop on top of him and grab the pistol still in his hand. The gun went off again, and I nearly let go. As he struggled to get to his feet, I pulled on the gun to twist his wrist. He slipped on blood and went down again. His grip weakened, and the gun was mine. I scrambled up and away.

From the kitchen, a door banged. The kettle whistled.

Craig was on his feet as quick as a leopard, shaking his head to clear it. I backed up until I was braced against the front door. Were there any bullets left? Did it have a safety? I had never fired a gun. My hands were shaking, the muzzle wavering. The gun was heavy and still warm from Craig's hand, smeared with blood from my hands.

A bloody welt rose across Craig's cheek bone, a cut over his ear oozed. He was hurt—I could see it—dazed and in pain, but I watched his body gather and relax in a way that wasn't really relaxed. His head came up, and he pulled himself into focus. The terror escalated a notch as I recognized how truly outclassed I was. The gun seemed trivial, inadequate, and my hands shook so that I nearly dropped it.

He waited, facing me, giving us a little time. "Easy there, Iris. You don't want to kill me. I know you don't. You're not that kind of person. You're all about life, nurturing, not about killing."

I had to admire the control. His voice was almost perfect, soft and steady, nearly a whisper. Intimate. He took a slow step toward me, another, his eyes on mine, and reached for the gun. He did it well, the way you'd approach a frightened animal. Slow, relaxed, sure. His eyes, that voice, had me almost hypnotized. His open hand, reaching...

Then the rage ignited and my finger convulsed on the trigger. The gun jerked in my hand, always too loud. Craig staggered away and looked surprised.

I hadn't done very well. One hand clutched his upper arm and blood leaked through his fingers. "You threatened my son." I pulled the trigger again. This did the job, and he went down. "You son of a bitch."

Chapter Thirty-two

I swayed and shivered where I stood. I said to Craig's body, "You forgot the part about defending the cubs." I took a deep breath, no fainting allowed. "You shot Denny and Liana and abused those animals." It didn't work—the rage had burned out, leaving me with nothing but nausea.

I had to get out of here, wherever here was, and find help. The kettle shrilled in the kitchen. I hobbled to the stove and shut it off. I rinsed the blood off my hands and tied a dish towel around my leg. The back door was open, letting in an icy breeze. Tom was out there somewhere.

Tom had driven. Therefore he had the keys. How was I going to get out of here? I looked around for a phone. None. Craig had a cell phone. I'd have to touch his body to get it. If I called someone, what would I tell them? I didn't know where I was.

It was all too hard.

Two men turned into carrion, one by my hand. Hap wouldn't call me a sheep ever again. A leaking leg that began to blind me with pain. This was what Craig's dreams and schemes had brought about.

I sat down in the dining room and tried to think, then limped back to the kitchen and stuck my head out the door. The cold was a slap in the face, helpful. Trees and a shed were pale shapes in night air gone still. "Tom? *Tom!* He's dead. Get in here. I need help." And so did he. I made it back to the dining room and sat down again. The gun was on the table beside me. I moved it to the seat of the chair next to me, out of sight, where it was handy but wouldn't scare him.

Tom crept in a few minutes later and knelt next to Jeff. He looked at Craig and stood up.

I moved the gun to my lap. "Where is this place?" He looked at me empty-faced. I asked again. "Where are we?"

"My grandma's."

"She doesn't live here?"

After a pause, "They've been gone for years."

Jerome had steered his business partner to an abandoned place he knew well. "Tom, sit down." He did and I tried to pull myself together. "We need to make a plan." His eyes held no flicker of intelligence. "Tom, wake up. You are done running. We have things to figure out." No reaction. "Go into the kitchen. Make us some coffee. Right now."

That worked. He followed orders and came back with two mugs of instant coffee. He sat there staring at the mug until I told him to drink it. Then he gulped half. When he set the cup down, his face didn't look as absent. He said, "I guess I should go."

"Nope. No more running. You are going to help me, and I am going to help you."

He had enough wit to look puzzled. I drank some of the hot liquid. It tasted like pollution.

He said, "They're dead, aren't they? Jeff's dead. They're all dead now."

"Not your mother." The pain in my leg was unabated and blood had soaked through the dish towel. "Can you turn on the heat?"

He shook his head. "We're out of wood."

I was going to die of hypothermia. But not before I was done here. "Did Jeff go with your father to pick up those tortoises and parrots or was it you?"

He swallowed.

"Tom, you saved my life. You and your brother. I can help you. Tell me."

He looked at his hands on the table, his head bowed. "Me."

"Tell me about it."

He kept his head down and spoke in a mumble. "Jeff always went. This was my first time. We had the crop in the van."

"You delivered the weed and Craig...Ethan sent you to some new places to pick up the animals."

He nodded and his head came up. "He said it was our next step. When we were good at that, then guns. He knew how to get stuff. The meth stuff, too." A flash of resentment. "We was doing just fine until that got started. Liana knew. She said he was bad for us."

Step by slow step, I led him through what would happen and what his options were. It took maybe ten minutes, and I was shuddering with cold and reaction when we were done. Every time I looked at the bloody dishtowel I came near fainting. Time to get out of here. He'd have to drive me to the hospital. If he panicked, I still had the gun. Why didn't these things have an indicator showing how many bullets were left?

My heart nearly stopped when the front and back doors slammed open. Tom and I leaped up as men boiled in. I nearly shot one before I registered their uniforms, and possibly one of them nearly shot me. I dropped the gun as fast as I could, heart racing, and sank back into the chair, hands in the air. While they searched the house and handcuffed Tom, another wave of people entered, ignoring loud, insistent orders to keep out.

"*Ken*," I said, amazed and stupid.

"Hellfire! Are you all right?"

"Not really."

Pluvia inched in through the door and looked at me and then Tom, her face full of questions.

Wanda knelt on the floor and stroked Jeff's hair and cried.

Ken scanned the scene, looked at my leg, and picked me up. He carried me out to a pickup truck and tucked me into the passenger seat. When a deputy blocked him from turning the truck around, Ken said, "I'm taking her to the hospital. She's bleeding."

"Mr. Meyer, sir, you need to wait for the ambulance. The medical technicians can help her. They'll be here soon."

"Sir, you need to get out of the way. We're going to the ER *right now.*"

The deputy had the choice of moving or shooting him. The tires crunched in the gravel as Ken wrestled the truck toward the road.

I had enough presence of mind to note that low-key Ken seemed more than slightly agitated. I leaned against his shoulder the whole way, content to nod in and out of awareness.

◇◇◇

The little room in the urgent care ward was crowded. I had the bed and the really good pills. Ken perched on a stool alongside me, holding my hand. Actually, I held his hand. It was a good hand, strong and still. I didn't see any reason to let go. If I did, the shaking would start. My leg hurt and hurt, but I cared less and less as those pills kicked in. The world had slipped a little out of focus. The image of dead men lying in blood was fading, the feel of the gun bucking in my hand was fading. Later I would have to deal. Not yet. Not yet.

A neat bandage had replaced the dish towel. Gil Gettler wandered in and out with questions when the nurses weren't tormenting me.

"You found me," I said to Ken and gave him my best smile. "Uh, it *was* you who found me. Wasn't it?"

He said, "You didn't show up to get the dog. You didn't answer your phone. I went with the worst-case scenario. That meant the Tiptons had you. So I drove to their house."

"The farm? Wanda was there."

"And Mrs. Whitley. She was my sixth grade math teacher."

"Wanda Tipton was your math teacher?"

"No, the other one."

A man in scrubs pushed an empty gurney past my little room. In the next room over, a woman was saying, "He just *does* these things. I don't know why."

I tried to focus. "Pluvia? Those women told *me* they had no idea where Tom and Jeff were. But *you* show up and they decide to tell all? You must have been really hot at math."

"I *was* pretty good. But they'd been thinking about it. Mrs. Whitley—Pluvia—made Wanda tell me. Jerome Tipton's parents used to have a place about twenty miles farther north. He wouldn't pay the taxes on it. The county sold it years ago, but no one ever moved in. Wanda thought he might have told Ethan about it. So we all crammed into my truck. I called the sheriff and they followed. We never would have found the place without those two women."

I raised my head toward Gettler. "You'll check Ethan's— Craig's—fingerprints? I'm sure he's on the run from something."

"I sure do appreciate the suggestion," Gettler said. "That's a great idea."

"Sorry. Sorry."

Ken's free hand brushed my cheek.

"Gil—can I call you Gil?—about Tom…"

Officer Gettler looked at me narrowly and didn't answer.

"He saved my life, him and Jeff. Well, Jeff only sort-of. More Tom, really. And he knows where he and Jerome picked up the smuggled animals. He can turn—whatchacallit—state's evidence and then he won't have go to jail so much. Right?"

Gettler said, "Those could be factors."

I made a sad, puzzled face. "Is that the best you can do?"

He said, "That is the best anybody can do. You, lady, are stoned on pain pills."

I'd ask him again tomorrow. "Ken, my leg feels like Tasmanian devils are chewing on it. Can I go home?" My voice didn't sound much older than Robby's. Home, what a concept. "Oh. Strongbad. I need to pick him up."

Ken said, "I left him with a friend. He's fine."

"Where are *my* dogs? Oh. Right, Pete and Cheyenne have them." Good. "Ken? We have to get the Doberman and give her to Pluvia. Don't let me forget. She was Liana's."

"You can stop now. All this can wait until tomorrow."

"Neal. I have to tell Neal." I remembered most of his number and got it on the second try. Maybe the third. He was pretty worried and thought it was a rotten idea for me to go home. "They're all dead or in jail," I told him. "All of them." He wasn't having it. "I've got a friend with me. He's really strong. He picked me up. He'll take me home and stay." I raised my eyebrows at Ken. He nodded. Neal still protested. I giggled and handed the phone to Gettler.

Somehow I was in a wheel chair floating out of the hospital into the glistening night. The moon was a pale circle in the clouds. Every surface was frosted with ice over snow. A fairyland in white, where wishes could come true. "Ken, will you help me get my college degree? You're good at math. Please?"

He took me home.

Epilogue

It took months for the wildlife traffickers to be busted, but it finally happened, with Tom Tipton's help. A few people were out of the sordid business for a few years. I was glad of it, but I didn't exaggerate the impact.

Tom's lawyer told me that my testimony at his trial helped reduce his sentence.

Neal and Hap settled on a good sanctuary for the macaws. I had a few days notice before Ken and I drove them to the facility. At home alone, I petted them and fed them popcorn. When they were okay with the pliers I held, I pulled open the blue bands on their legs and took them off. Jerome wasn't a totally rotten father. He did think of his family when he knew he was dying. Not "look after Stridder" but "look *at* Stridder." He'd hidden the GPS coordinates where only he could get at them. I put the bands in a dresser drawer.

Pete and Cheyenne took Strongbad and Denny's reptiles when they moved into their new house.

Denny stayed at Marcie's. She was always too busy to get together with me. When Denny came back to work, he was quiet and distant. I missed him almost as much as I missed Marcie. One day at lunch, he fell into a ramble about American bank executives, their underground connection to the Russian mafia, and the implications for missions to Mars. My heart soared. Linda and I bumped fists under the table. Even Marion refrained from rolling her eyes.

When Linda kicked off Bowling for Rhinos, I decided it was time to seek my fortune. I bought a GPS unit and took the bird bands and a shovel on the road. I had better luck than the gold hunters that roamed the Tipton farm. Much better. After my trip, small, heavy packages traveled from several post offices. I sent one to Wanda Tipton and a dozen to conservation organizations.

That took care of half of what I'd dug up. I went to the Internet and found companies that would sell gold for cash and sold the rest. I set aside enough to pay off my credit card debt and buy a new cell phone. That was all. I'd pay off the house and save for Robby with my own clean money.

I didn't tell Ken about any of this. If I got caught, I didn't want him implicated.

I told Linda that an anonymous donor had picked up my name somewhere and was routing his Bowling for Rhinos contributions through me. She gave me the fish-eye, but let it lie. Laundering drug money through wildlife sanctuaries—very satisfying. I made three big donations, then I was out of the hidden treasure business and the Bowling for Rhinos campaign was off to a great start.

Ken stayed for a week while I healed up and the nightmares tapered off. One night after Robby was in bed, he told me he didn't want to overstay his welcome. "I'd better move out. You're okay now. I don't want to take advantage of you being hurt and upset…and assume…" He looked everywhere but at me. "I mean, we could see each other…if you want to."

He was right, of course. We'd skipped eleven of the twelve steps from Building a Healthy Long Term Relationship, or however many steps there are—I hadn't a clue. Robby and I would be all right without him, I knew that. My problems were the kind with solutions.

I said, "I suppose we could step back and start over, take it slower. If you want to."

"You bet I do," he said, finally meeting my eye.

Or we could do it my way.

I closed in on him and undid a few shirt buttons. I tugged on his t-shirt until I could run my hands under it and across the skin of his chest and back. "I know you don't like to rush," I murmured. "You leave whenever you want," and I kissed him with the best kiss I've got.

Author's Afterword

Endangered is a work of fiction, but the pet trade in illegal exotic animals is real. The parrots and tortoises in this mystery find a (relatively) happy ending. If only that were always true in the real world.

The United States is the world's largest importer of wildlife, with 90% of these animals intended for sale. The majority of this trade is perfectly legal. It generates billions of dollars in profits and provides interesting and delightful pets to many. But my focus here is on the downside. This trade sometimes entails breaking national as well as international laws that are intended to protect wildlife. Aside from exterminating local species through over-collecting, the pet trade in wild animals also spreads diseases among humans (especially salmonella poisoning) and among native animals when the pets escape or are released.

The majority of wild-caught pet animals die prematurely due to the stresses of captivity and poor care. Even captive-bred exotic animals can be unwise choices. After all, they evolved to succeed in a specific habitat that likely bears no resemblance to your living room or back yard.

If you feel you must have an exotic pet, please do the research. Talk to other people who have this kind of animal, use the internet, look for resource books. Don't rely on the person who will profit from the sale to be fully accurate about the amount of time the animal will require or the expense of caring for it.

Consider whether this animal will live for decades. When you can no longer care for it, who will? Do not expect a zoo to accept it. Do not expect to dump it on a rescue organization and walk away guilt-free when, for example, your child leaves home and you tire of the responsibility—these private facilities are over-full and desperate for money to feed their charges. And don't turn your pet loose—it will die or it will succeed all too well, as with Burmese pythons breeding in the Florida swamps.

If you decide to go ahead, please be as certain as possible that the animal was bred in captivity and not wild-caught. Be thorough in this, especially with reptiles and amphibians. Then do your best to set up a proper habitat and provide the right food and mental stimulation.

Do not kid yourself that you are contributing to conservation by providing a home for a rare animal. Contribute to conservation by discouraging the trade in wild animals, by showing your children the natural world, by moderating your own life style, and by supporting organizations that protect wild habitats from destruction by human activity.

The author's profits from *Endangered* will be donated to non-profit organizations dedicated to preserving natural habitats.

Bowling for Rhinos is not fictional. It has my support and deserves yours. Contact your local zoo or go to http://aazkbfr.org/

Further Reading/Sources

The Lizard King, Brian Christy, a fascinating account of a father and son family business suspected of smuggling reptiles and the federal agent who tried to take them down.

The Last Tortoise, Craig B. Stanford, an engrossing introduction to the natural history of tortoises and an out-spoken description of what is happening to them all over the globe.

Stolen World, Jennie Erin Smith, true stories of reckless, unrepentant animal smugglers and the feuds among them.

To receive a free catalog of Poisoned Pen Press titles, please contact us in one of the following ways:

Phone: 1-800-421-3976
Facsimile: 1-480-949-1707
Email: info@poisonedpenpress.com
Website: www.poisonedpenpress.com

Poisoned Pen Press
6962 E. First Ave. Ste 103
Scottsdale, AZ 85251